THE
FORTRESS
AT
ONE DALLAS
CENTER

THE FORTRESS AT ONE DALLAS CENTER

RON LAWRENCE

ISBN: 1-55547-210-9

Manufactured in the United States of America

Chapter One

Professor Russell O'Leary finished grading his last English paper and neatly stacked it with the others. He then straightened up the items on the top of his desk and returned his grade book to its place in the bookcase. Satisfied at last that all was in order, he removed a shiny black .38 caliber revolver from his desk drawer, placed the barrel in his mouth, and blew the back of his head off.

Three weeks earlier . . .

North Dallas—flash, glitter, power, the Dallas Cowboys, mile after mile of stylish restaurants and posh clubs, old money and the new rich. A late model Jaguar sedan pulling into a reserved parking space under an exclusive high rise condominium wasn't a sight to turn a head. Dark hair—a touch of premature gray—worn stylishly just over the ears, an expensive three piece suit with gold cuff links, and a black leather briefcase all gave the impression that the driver was a successful young attorney or business executive—or a man who lived well beyond his means.

His entire body convulsed as the first blow struck him from behind, just over the right kidney. As he fell to his knees beside the car, a vicious kick to the stomach from a sharp-toed boot was followed by another to the ribs.

There were two of them; there always were. The spokesman twisted him around as he lay face down so that he saw them at last. "You didn't show."

Blood trickled from his mouth as he tried to speak, almost choking, but his attacker didn't wait for a reply. "There's a story about what they did to a guy in Chicago. This was back when Al Capone was running things. They took this guy who owed 'em and broke his neck with a baseball bat. Then they tore out his tongue and gouged out his eyes and ears with an ice pick. They dumped him at the hospital two minutes later, so there was no chance the guy would die—and he sure couldn't tell anybody anything. He lived for several years kinda like the opposite of a vegetable. He could still think, but he was paralyzed and couldn't see, hear, or talk.

"You got any idea what it would be like to lie there, never able to tell anybody when you hurt or when you're hungry or thirsty? Just lying in a black void praying you could die? They say the guy probably went crazy after a while, but then how could you tell?

"This guy's name was Joey, and from then on, as a reminder to anybody who owed them any money, Capone's guys would just say, 'Joey was askin' aboutcha.' Get it? 'Joey was askin' aboutcha.' You want people to be saying, 'Frank was askin' aboutcha'?"

"No, listen, I—" The reply was cut off abruptly as the spokesman slammed Frank's head down against the concrete floor.

"Shut up and listen, loser. You're in so deep this time you've only got one way out. You're going to do something for us."

Frank managed a painful nod. "Sure, I've done you some favors before. Anything you want."

"There's a guy named D. J. Agnew. He got busted

in a drug deal and now the feds have him laid away somewhere. He's gonna spill his guts to a grand jury in three weeks."

"So?"

"So we want him hit."

"What! That's your business, not mine."

"You're an assistant D.A. You've got connections we don't."

"But not the kind of connections that can get people killed. Besides, once the FBI has a federal witness put away inside their protection program, nobody can even find him, much less try to kill him. There's no way in the world that anybody could ever get to this D. J. Agnew."

The spokesman stood and delivered a final jarring kick to the back of the head. "You got three weeks, loser."

He lay for a long time on the cold concrete floor, drifting in and out of a misty, pain-filled state bordering on unconsciousness. From his position on the floor, he could see back out through the garage entrance. Framed in a star filled Texas sky was Millard Tower, the lighted sphere which majestically rises fifty stories to dominate the Dallas skyline. As he focused on the sphere, balanced delicately upon its slender tower, it moved in a large arc, swaying slowly back and forth, becoming dim and then blindingly bright, finally fading away into the darkness.

"Excuse me, lieutenant. Frank Mosley just arrived."

Lieutenant Erwin, seated at his desk behind a formidable stack of paperwork, glanced up at the sergeant. "Good, has he talked to the lady?"

"No, not yet. I gave him the arrest report and he's waiting to talk to you."

"Where is he, downstairs?"

"Yes, sir."

"Okay, thanks."

Lieutenant Erwin rose quickly from his desk and hurried downstairs. He had no wish to keep an assistant D.A. waiting, and this was one case he was eager to follow up personally. He found Frank Mosley examining the arresting officers' report.

"Good morning, Frank."

Frank looked up from his reading. "Morning, Jeff. This arrest report doesn't sound like anything out of the ordinary. What's so special about it?"

"This one is special to me. We've been after this kid for a long time. He and a couple of his buddies have been preying on the elderly people who live in the projects. These people are afraid to go outside their own doors, though they're not much safer even when they're inside. If they don't open up when he says to, he just kicks the door in."

"Have you had him in on anything before this?"

"We've picked him up a dozen times, but it's never done us any good. Everybody's afraid to testify against him; and for good reason. The city has no funds for security at these projects, and the best we can do is to send an occasional patrol around. One old man finally got his fill and agreed to testify, but the day after the kid got out on bail, the old man went through the window of his third floor room. Of course, nobody heard or saw anything."

Frank scanned the report. "Angelo Martinez, age nineteen, five foot nine, one hundred forty-five pounds."

"The kid's deceiving. He doesn't look like much of a threat, but he's a pure psycho."

"What's the story on the old lady he assaulted?"

"She's a resident of the project; seventy-one, lives alone. She was walking back from the grocery store when he knocked her down and took her bag. Broke her arm when she hit the pavement. You know what she had in the bag?"

"What?"

"Cat food. She hasn't got a cat, Frank. She's living

on the stuff. That's all she has to eat, and then this little delinquent comes along and breaks her arm for it."

"And she's willing to press charges and then to testify against him?"

"Right. She's one heckuva gutsy lady. She knows what happened to the old man, but she's determined."

"Let's go see her."

Mrs. Bridges was a small stooped woman who couldn't have weighed over ninety-five pounds. The idea of her trying to defend herself against someone like Martinez was ludicrous.

"Good morning, Mrs. Bridges. How's your arm?" Frank asked.

"It's sore, but it'll be all right. It's my left one, thank goodness. I couldn't walk if I had my right one in a cast. I need it for my cane."

"Good, I'm glad it wasn't any worse than it was. I'm Frank Mosley. I'll be handling your case. Are you sure you're up to testifying against Angelo Martinez?"

"Yes I am," she stated firmly.

"All right then, in that case I'm going to have the police patrols stepped up in your area. And any time you need to go outside, you just call the police department and they'll send someone over to escort you personally. How does that sound?"

"Oh that won't be necessary."

"Why not? Aren't you aware of what happened to your neighbor who agreed to testify against Martinez?"

Mrs. Bridges smiled sweetly. "My husband looks after me, young man."

"Oh, I understood that you lived alone."

"I do. My husband died year before last, but he still looks after me. I'm not worried."

Frank exchanged glances with the lieutenant. "Well, we'll step up the patrols just in case. Thanks so much, Mrs. Bridges. I'll be talking to you again later."

As the two walked down the hall toward the detention room where Martinez was being held, the lieutenant fixed Frank with a quizzical stare. "You okay, Frank? You look like you're moving kind of stiff like."

"I've got some sore ribs. Ran into a wall while I was playing racquetball."

"That must have hurt."

"Yeah, it did."

A heavyset patrolman opened the door to the detention room and followed them inside. The lieutenant was right. Muscular but small, Angelo Martinez didn't look very dangerous. He looked disgustingly filthy more than anything else. His hair was greasy and unkempt, and he had one of those beards, if you could call it a beard, that consisted of little more than a few coarse stringy hairs. Frank's first reaction was to tell the kid to shave if he couldn't grow a decent beard.

But there was something else about Martinez; something about his eyes. He didn't have the sullen, defensive look that most strutting punks displayed when arrested. He fiercely met, rather than avoided Frank's critical gaze.

Frank had just one thing he wanted to find out. "I hear that you have a couple of buddies who hang around with you and make life miserable for these old people. I'll make a deal with you. You testify against them so that we can put them away, and we'll drop all the charges against you."

Martinez didn't hesitate even for a second, lunging across the table that separated them and spitting violently into Frank's face. Taken totally by surprise, Frank staggered backwards as the burly patrolman grabbed Martinez and kneed him in the groin, then slammed him back against the wall.

Frank walked quickly out of the room, leaving the lieutenant and the patrolman behind. As he wiped his face on his sleeve, he wore a grim smile of satisfaction. He had found out exactly what he wanted to know about Angelo Martinez.

*   *   *

The young woman entering the darkened apartment looked to be almost nine months pregnant. Because the light in the foyer was burned out, she closed the door behind her and felt her way cautiously toward the light switch in the living room. In the pitch black darkness she was unaware of the figure pressed against the living room wall. Just as she reached for the switch, she was startled to feel two hands reach from behind and grab her breasts. Her assailant then rubbed himself against her while holding her tightly.

"Come on, baby, how 'bout a little action?"

"You know what the doctor said, lover boy. You're in dry dock, or did you forget?" She reached out and flipped on the lights as she spoke.

Her husband gave her a final bump and then shifted his hands down to her full stomach. "Forget? How could I forget? How about some alternate satisfaction?"

She twisted around and gave him a deep kiss. "Well, maybe you'll get lucky later. It depends on what kind of dinner you fix me."

"In that case, how about caviar and champagne?"

She lowered herself onto the sofa with his help and raised her legs so he could help her slip off her shoes. "That would probably do it."

"What did the doctor have to say?" her husband asked as he headed back into the kitchen.

"He says we're going to have a baby."

"I'm paying $800 for that?"

"He says that I've got about three and a half weeks to go and that everything is okay from now on. We're past the danger stage, so if it comes a little early it won't matter."

Three years of marriage had produced one miscarriage and then a son who had died at the age of two weeks. As a result, both Russell and Kathy O'Leary desperately wanted and needed this child. The doctor had ordered them to stop intercourse early in the pregnancy due to the complications they had encountered in the previous pregnancies. Now that the time was almost upon them, they had at last begun to breathe a little easier.

Still, they had saved so they could afford one of the expensive newborn monitors that would give warning of the dreaded crib death that had taken their first child. They were sparing no expense to make sure that this baby made it.

"How was your day?" Kathy asked.

"The usual. I've got a ton of English exams to finish grading. I'm about as far behind as I normally am during finals."

"Oh, did I tell you that the girls are taking me to lunch at Millard Tower next week after the baby shower?"

"No, that sounds like fun."

"It should be. I'm really looking forward to it." Kathy picked up a baby magazine and had just begun thumbing through it when Russell announced that dinner was ready.

She looked up from her magazine suspiciously. "Wait a minute. How did you get that done so fast? Is this some sort of trick to get me into bed quicker?"

"No, it was almost finished when you walked in." Russell brought her a glass of white wine, helped her up from the couch, and escorted her to the table. A white tablecloth, candles, and roses greeted her as she entered the dining room.

"What in the world?"

He gently touched his glass to hers. "I love you."

After dinner they undressed and lay together on their sides for a long time, leisurely touching and caressing. When Kathy finally indicated her readiness, Russell kissed her once more, long and softly.

"I love you, too," Kathy whispered as she reached for him.

Chapter Two

About a quarter before midnight, Frank eased his Jaguar into a parking space at Chuck's Cold Beer Palace. The name of the bar was somewhat of a joke as the building gave one the distinct impression that it was on the verge of collapsing at any moment.

He didn't have to wait long. A couple of minutes later Angelo Martinez opened the door and got into the car. Frank cranked it back up and pulled out into the sparse traffic.

"Nice wheels," Angelo commented.

"Yeah. In another week I'll even be able to afford it. In another week you'll be able to afford one, too."

They drove for fifteen minutes with neither speaking again. There was no reason to do so, and neither felt any need to be artificially social.

Frank finally slowed and turned into the parking lot of an apartment complex. "We're looking for a blue Buick."

"What's so special about it?"

"It's not the car, it's who it belongs to." Frank paused and scanned another row of cars.

"Well? You gonna tell me whose car it is?"

"It belongs to a guy named Tom Agnew."

Angelo frowned suspiciously. "Tom Agnew. This

9

guy wouldn't be any relation to D. J. Agnew, would he?"

"It's his nephew."

"Why do you want his car?"

"We're going to make everybody think that Tom Agnew is running this show."

"That doesn't sound like such a good idea. I ain't saying that I'm scared of anybody, but it ain't good sense to be foolin' with somebody like D. J. Agnew."

"Don't worry—just keep thinking about that million dollars."

"We may never get to spend it if we go around tickin' off people like Agnew."

"Well I can promise you one thing. Agnew isn't going to bother us one bit after this is over. Wait a minute, there's the car," Frank said. "Can you get it going without a key?"

"Are you kidding? I can get in that thing quicker without a key than you can with one."

"Okay, you take that one and we'll drop mine down the street a little way."

Angelo hopped out and pulled a piece of wire out of his pocket. Then, true to his boast, he was inside the Buick about as quickly as he could have been with a key. Reaching under the dash, he soon had the engine started as well.

About five blocks away, Frank pulled into an empty space along the curb, got out and locked his car. He walked around to the driver's side of the Buick.

"Scoot over. I'll drive since I know where we're going."

Frank carefully pulled on a pair of leather driving gloves before touching even the door handle. He then got in behind the wheel. Twenty minutes later Frank came to a stop outside the entrance to his condo's parking garage. "I'll wait right here for you. There's a guy living in my building who's an assistant manager at the tower. He should have a key that'll open every door inside the place.

"I'll go call the guy and give him some story to get him down to his car. That'll be your chance to get the key. He's about thirty-five, average height and build, and drives a green Cutlass that should be parked in space 4E.

"Now this thing's got to look like a mugging or it won't work. You know, knock him around a little, and then make sure you take everything of any value—like his wallet, watch, and any rings."

"Well, I don't see no problems." Angelo's smile was disturbing because it conveyed an actual sense of pleasure over what was to be done. Frank felt a chill go down his back, but he managed to look normal.

He watched until Angelo disappeared into the garage and then drove two blocks to a phone booth. Frank pulled a piece of paper from his pocket and dialed the number written on it.

"Hello?"

"Mr. Pruet?"

"Yes."

"This is Dr. Kleebauer at Eastside General Hospital. We have a man here who was involved in an accident. He has no identification, but he keeps asking for you. I think he must be one of your employees. It sure would help us if you could identify him for us."

"I don't know who it could be, but I'll be glad to help if I can."

"Thank you, Mr. Pruet. You better hurry, though; he's in serious condition."

Frank hung up the phone well pleased with himself. That was too good to be true, he thought. That guy must really be a bozo to have bought that story.

Within a few minutes, Frank was once again parked down the street from the garage, his carefully chosen position affording a good view of the entrance without exposing him to anyone entering or leaving. He left the engine running and settled back into the seat to wait.

* * *

Once Angelo had reached the shadows, he pulled an old fashioned straight razor from his pocket and folded out the finely honed blade. From his vantage point beside the car and behind a concrete pillar, he could see the elevators about twenty yards from where he stood. His target would have to walk right by him to reach the green Cutlass.

About ten minutes passed before Angelo caught the sound of the elevator doors opening. As footsteps left the elevator and approached his position, he tensed his legs and waited. A man passed within three feet of him, heading for the Cutlass.

Angelo stepped out behind the man and took two quick steps after him. His soft-soled sneakers made no noise, so the man never knew he was there. Angelo raised his arm to slash at the back of the man's neck, but suddenly, he realized that the man wasn't going to the Cutlass. He was going to the car beside it.

Angelo ducked down beside another car and listened breathlessly. He hadn't been heard. The footsteps stopped, a door opened and closed, then the car pulled out of the garage.

Another five minutes passed before he again heard the sound of the elevator door and approaching footsteps. As this man passed, Angelo waited until he was sure he was going to the right car. He was. Angelo lunged across the eight feet of space that separated him from the man.

The man didn't actually hear anything. It was more that he sensed the danger or the presence behind him. He jerked around just as Angelo came at him, the razor already slashing in toward his face. The time left wasn't sufficient for the man to run or even to dodge. He had time only to throw his right hand up in front of his face.

The blade slashed down across the man's wrist, completely severing the tendons and nerves that control the movement of the thumb and first two fingers. Most people who slash their own wrists cut only the veins which lie just beneath the skin. But this was far different. Also severed were the main arteries which run much deeper.

Thus, in an instant, the man's right hand was rendered virtually useless, and life-sustaining blood spurted out forcefully, not to be easily stopped. As the man jerked back away from Angelo in blind fear and panic, he jerked his hand back as well, slinging blood in an arc as far as fifteen feet away.

Angelo slashed a second time with no hesitation, aiming again for the man's face, and primarily at his eyes. This time the man's left hand was throw up for protection and the last two fingers were almost completely severed, left hanging only by a thread of skin. But far more damaging was the fact that the tip of the blade traced a line across the man's forehead and over one eye, just penetrating deeply enough to slice open the eyeball.

With a cry of agony, the man stumbled back against the car and fell to the ground, which would prove to be his death sentence. If he had only run blindly back toward the garage entrance, he might have been able to escape with his life.

As the man lay on the ground trying to cover his face with what was left of his hands, Angelo slashed savagely, time and time again, so that the man's hands, arms, and face were quickly shredded. The man could do nothing but try to kick weakly—and ineffectively—as his strength spurted and flowed away.

Tiring of the one sided contest, Angelo grabbed the man's arm and pulled it away from his face.

"Be still!" Angelo commanded. "Move your arm."

Hoping desperately that Angelo would show him some mercy for cooperation, the man moved his arms away from his face. But more critically, they were also moved away from his throat. Angelo placed the blade against the man's throat and waited for just a second so that the man would be sure to feel it—and realize what it meant—then he pressed hard and pulled the blade across the windpipe.

Angelo stepped back and wiped the blade off on the man's pant leg as gurgling noises came from his throat. The man jerked a couple of times as his arms flailed about helplessly, then he lay still.

Angelo straightened up and looked around before moving quickly to the rear of the Cutlass. Frank's idea about faking a mugging was stupid. It left too many loose ends and too many chances for things to go wrong. This was quick, simple and efficient.

The man had dropped his car keys on the floor. Angelo stepped over him to pick them up and then moved back to the rear of the car. The first key he tried slipped in and easily opened the trunk lock. Angelo bent over and patted the man's pockets, removing his wallet, then gripped him by the collar and dragged him back to the rear of the car. He shifted his grip to the man's armpits and, with a grunt, heaved him up and into the trunk, then closed it.

Angelo took a final look around to be sure he hadn't been seen, then started briskly back toward the garage entrance. Once he was back in the car, Frank snapped on the headlights and pulled away from the curb at a normal rate of speed. "How did it go?"

"Like taking candy from a baby," Angelo replied as he jangled the keys in his hand.

"Let's see," said Frank, reaching for the keys.

He held them up and frowned. "It's not here. These are just car keys and a key to his apartment."

"You sure?"

"Yeah, are you sure this was all he had?"

"Yeah, I went through his pockets and that was it."

"Then the one we're after must still be in his apartment. Great, that means that we've got to go back again. This might get complicated. Is he out for a while?"

Angelo's reply was smug and sure. "Don't worry about him."

Frank didn't like what he heard. "What happened? Did something go wrong?"

"Let's just say that things didn't go exactly like you had 'em planned out."

Frank's next impulse was to angrily demand an explanation. But he suddenly realized that he didn't want to know. He didn't think he had the stomach for it.

"Anybody see you?" Frank finally asked.

"Naw."

Frank made a couple of turns and headed back toward the condominium. "I'll drop you off and wait in the same place. This guy's not married, so his apartment ought to be empty, but watch it."

Frank dropped Angelo at the entrance once again and pulled down the street. Three minutes later Angelo stepped out of the elevator directly across the hall from a door marked 4E. Just to be on the safe side, he pressed the doorbell and waited a few moments—glancing up and down the hallway—before inserting the key and slipping inside.

As he closed the door quietly behind him, he found himself standing in a small entryway which opened into a plush living area. The only light came from an adjoining bedroom. A quick inspection of the room revealed a collection of books and magazines but no keys.

As Angelo moved toward the bedroom, he suddenly became aware of the sound of running water. He pulled the razor, still sticky with blood, out of his pocket and peered cautiously through the doorway. A large mirror, mounted on the ceiling, reflected a round bed with a white fur bedspread. To his left was a door opening into a bathroom where the sound of running water originated. Still moving cautiously, he had almost reached the open bathroom door when a tall slim girl with long dark hair suddenly stepped out, almost bumping into him. Probably in her mid twenties, she was barefoot and clad only in a short bathrobe of thin, clingy material.

The girl gasped and simultaneously whirled around to flee back to the bathroom, but Angelo caught her by the arm and jerked her back. Before he could react, long perfectly manicured nails raked across his face leaving three deep furrows down his cheek. Shocked, he hesitated for an instant which gave the girl just enough time to jerk away and stumble back against the wall, just missing the doorway. As she drew a deep breath and opened her mouth to scream, Angelo violently smashed his fist into her soft stomach. The scream turned to an agonized grunt as she doubled over onto her knees.

Angelo stuck the razor back in his pocket and wiped his hand across his cheek. When he looked at his fingers, he found them to be bloody.

"You piece of—"

He grabbed a handful of hair, jerked her head up and back, and viciously struck her with the back of his bloody hand. The blow snapped her head to one side and sent her sprawling over onto her back.

"You think you're something real classy, don't you? Well I'm gonna show you what I do to snotty, stuck-up broads." So saying, he grabbed her by the hair again and threw her bruisingly against the bed so that she lay half on it and half off, on her stomach. Using a pair of hose, Angelo tied her hands tightly behind her and then gagged her.

"You think you're too good for me, don't you? In a couple of weeks I'm gonna own a whole stable full of classy broads better than the likes of you."

With a flash of panic, she heard the sound of Angelo unfastening his belt, then unzipping his pants. She screamed, again and again, but there was no one to hear; no one to care. It was just her and just him—for as long as he wanted it so.

Back in the car Frank had begun to worry. He didn't know exactly what time Angelo had gone back into the building, but he was certain that he had been gone at least thirty minutes, maybe more. He started the car for the second time to get a little heat. Why do my feet have to stay so darn cold, he wondered. Frank's heart missed a beat as the car door was suddenly jerked open. Angelo slid in and closed the door.

"You go to sleep or something?" Angelo asked.

"No, I was messing around with the heater and didn't see you come out. You almost scared me to death. Hey, what happened to your face?" he asked, seeing the deep gouges across Angelo's cheek.

"Maybe this guy wasn't married, but he had a real classy lookin' piece up there. Tight in all the right places—just the way I like 'em." Angelo grinned nastily. "How about you, Frankie? You like 'em tight, too?"

Frank ignored the question. "What happened? Did anybody see you or hear anything?"

"Don't worry. Nobody saw nothing and nobody heard nothing. Here's the keys," he said as he pulled another set of keys out of his pocket.

Frank accepted the keys and turned up the dash lights for a closer look. They were exactly like the ones he had already seen, but there was a fourth one with an official looking code number stamped on it.

"Oh yeah," Frank breathed. "This should be it."

"I looked around real good," Angelo remarked. "Those were the only other keys I could find."

"I'm sure that this is what we're after. This is the type of key that you can't get copied unless you have it done from the factory and have special authorization. What about your face, though? Do you think you need some stitches or something?"

Angelo touched his cheek gingerly. "Naw, it'll be all right. I can't believe that I let a broad do that, but she ain't gonna do it again—ever."

"You're positive that nobody could have seen or heard anything?"

"No way. There wasn't any noise and I didn't see anybody. The apartment is right across from the elevator, so I just walked out and went right in."

Frank slipped the keys into his coat pocket and began picking at his lower lip with his thumbnail, a nervous habit which resulted in a chronic chapped lip.

"The girl's dead," he said, more as a statement than a question.

"Ain't gonna get no deader."

"Okay," said Frank, still picking at his lip with his brow furrowed in deep thought. "How does the apartment look? Did you have to tear the place up to find the keys?"

"No, they were sitting right on top of the dresser. I didn't have to touch a thing."

"You know, this may work out okay. If anybody suspected that this key was missing, they would change the locks and have extra security guards swarming all over the tower so fast it would make your head spin. But this way, if anybody should come looking for this guy, they'll find the girl and think that he did it and then skipped out.

"Tell you what," Frank said turning to Angelo. "Go back upstairs and get a bunch of his clothes and a couple of suitcases so it'll look like he's left town real quick. Wipe off anything that you left prints on like the doorknobs. Then we'll dump his car somewhere. By the time they find him and figure out what happened, we'll be long gone. The only problem is, where'll we leave his car?"

"Why not put it at the airport?" suggested Angelo. "It could sit out there for weeks before anybody noticed it."

Frank looked at him with a pleased expression. "That's perfect. How did you think of that?"

"Cause I ain't as stupid as I look," replied Angelo with an equally pleased expression.

There was a lot of truth in what Angelo had said. Though his appearance and manner would lead one to believe otherwise, he was actually quite intelligent. He also had a very cool head and, except for his temper, didn't rattle easily.

Chapter Three

Awakened from a vivid dream about a blonde with gyrating hips, Tom Agnew angrily groped for the phone in the darkness.

"Hello," he groaned in an irritated voice.

"Is this Tom Agnew?" demanded the voice on the other end.

"Yeah, who is this?"

"Have you got a blue Buick?"

"Yeah, why?"

"Why? Because the thing's been sitting in my parking lot for four hours, and if you don't get it outa the way, I'm gonna have it towed!"

"Wait a minute. What do you mean that my car is in your parking lot? Where is it? Who is this?"

"This is the manager at the gas station across from the Cotton Bowl. Now I'm warning you, if this thing isn't moved in thirty minutes, I'm gonna have it towed."

"Hang on a minute. How do you know that it's my car?"

"Because it's got your name on the registration, that's how." The voice on the other end was at full volume by now. "Now you get this thing off my lot within thirty minutes or I'll get it off myself!" A loud click indicated that the phone had been slammed down by the irate caller.

Tom shook his head in disbelief. Still in the dark, he fumbled to hang up the receiver and then reached for the light. Sliding out of bed, he grabbed a pair of jeans, then stepped out onto the balcony of his second floor apartment to survey the parking lot below. He couldn't remember exactly where he had parked his car, but it didn't take long for him to realize that it was missing.

Returning to the apartment, he pounded on the door to his roommate's bedroom. "Hey, Ralph, wake up."

"What do you think you're doing?" groaned a sleepy voice from behind the door.

"Come on, get up. Somebody's swiped my car and I've gotta go get it."

"Huh?"

"Some gas station just called and said that my car is on their lot. I just looked outside and sure enough, the thing's gone."

The door quickly opened and Ralph stepped out zipping up his pants. "Where is it?"

"It's at some gas station across from the Cotton Bowl."

"Well let's get going. I've gotta get back and get some sleep before my chemistry test in the morning."

Twenty minutes later they stopped alongside what indeed was Tom's car parked on the corner of the service station lot. "It looks like somebody just took it for a joy ride," Ralph said.

"I bet you ten bucks my tape deck is gone," Tom said as he opened the unlocked door and cautiously peered in. The tape deck was still in place. He then glanced into the back seat to make sure that it was empty. He turned and waved. "It's okay, I'll follow you."

Ralph waited until he saw Tom's car start and the headlights come on before making a U turn and heading back toward their apartment. Tom quickly followed, but a yellow light brought him to a sudden stop. As he watched Ralph's tail lights disappear, he heard a horn begin to blow. Looking in his rear view mirror, he could see only one car stopped behind him—a Jaguar sedan. The driver was sounding his horn in a series of short blasts.

"Can't you see that the light's red?" Tom demanded, knowing full well that the other driver couldn't hear him.

Unexpectedly, he heard and felt muffled thudding noises coming from the rear of his car. Thinking that the driver behind must be bumping him, he jerked around in his seat for a better view. As he turned he was astonished to see the backrest of his back seat slam forward. The opening that was now exposed into the trunk was filled by a young man pointing a gun at him.

"Don't do nothing, college boy. If you move one inch, I'm gonna blow your head off."

Tom's initial shock and astonishment instantly turned to terror and panic. He remained frozen in fright as the intruder squeezed through the opening and into the back seat. The cross beams which normally would have blocked the opening into the trunk had been cut away.

After glancing around to satisfy himself that they weren't being watched, the gunman reached out and roughly grabbed Tom by the collar. "Turn around and keep still," he ordered. Then with a quick move he slid over into the front seat and plopped down beside the terrified young man.

"Look, I've, uh, I've got some money in my—" Tom was abruptly cut off by a stiff slap from the hand that had been on his collar.

"Keep your mouth shut."

The Jaguar that had been behind them now pulled around and started through the intersection where the light by now had turned green. "Follow the Jag," the intruder commanded with a wave of his gun.

"Come on, move it!" A painful jab from the gun accompanied the angry order.

After a few blocks Tom was finally able to settle himself down somewhat. "I think you may have me mixed up with my uncle, D. J. Agnew. I don't have anything to do with him or that side of the family."

"I tell you what, college boy. You keep your mouth shut and do what you're told and you won't get hurt. How's that sound?"

"Okay, don't worry. I won't give you any trouble."

Forty minutes later the Jaguar at last slowed and turned off the main highway onto a small unpaved road. They wound along for several more miles, beside a small river, before coming to a stop in front of an abandoned old farm house. The man who emerged from the Jaguar was in vivid contrast to the one with the gun. He was obviously in charge. He opened the trunk of the Jaguar and removed a coil of heavy rope.

"All right, out," the gunman ordered.

Tom opened his door and climbed out as his guard got out on the passenger side. Any thought of making a run for the woods was dispelled when he noticed that the second man, now standing by the front fender, was also holding a gun.

"Listen, this is all some sort of a mix-up," Tom explained to the new man.

"There's no mix-up. You won't be hurt, you're just going to spend the next few days in this old house. Let me see your wallet."

Tom handed it over, watching silently as Frank carefully went through it, the car's headlights providing illumination. He examined the credit cards and several other items but left the money untouched. One scrap of paper he found was a wadded up laundry receipt containing Tom Agnew's name and phone number. Frank stuffed the receipt into his coat pocket and handed the wallet back.

"Angelo, you take care of him. I'll move his car around back."

Fresh out of arguments, Tom followed his captor wordlessly up toward the farm house but paused just before they stepped up onto the porch. "Listen, you can't leave me out here for days with no food or water."

"Don't worry, if you're real lucky somebody may find you before you die," Angelo answered smugly.

"But you said that if I did what you said I wouldn't get hurt."

"I lied," Angelo replied with a sneering grin.

Instantly, Tom bolted back away toward the road. Frank had started the Buick and had just switched on the lights when out of the corner of his eye he caught the motion of Tom darting in front of him. With only a split second to react, Frank did so without thinking. He simultaneously jammed the gas pedal to the floor and jerked the shift lever into drive. The car leapt forward and smashed into the back of the Jaguar.

Tom had but an instant to realize that the car was coming at him. Reflexively trying to dive out of the way, he stumbled to his knees so that, as the two cars crashed together, the bumpers caught him squarely in the stomach. The force of the impact was so great that Frank was thrown against the steering wheel, splitting his upper lip. When he jerked his head back away from the wheel, he was looking straight out through the windshield at a sight that was so grotesque and sickening that it would be imprinted vividly into his memory for the rest of his life.

Tom's face, ghoulishly illuminated from the head-lights reflecting between the cars, was swollen and purple, the veins protruding to the point of bursting. His eyes bulged from their sockets as his mouth opened wide in a silent scream of agonized death, the tongue thick and protruding. His hands clawed futilely against the hood of the car, breaking the nails and ripping through the paint to bare metal.

Blood and vomit gushed violently from his mouth, splattering the windshield in front of Frank's face. Then with a final spasm, the upper part of his all but severed body fell backwards into the open trunk of the Jaguar.

Frank sat paralyzed by shock for a moment, then fumbled to get the door open as his insides churned violently. He fell out onto the ground retching and gasping for air, blindly half crawling and half staggering as he tried to escape what he had seen. Not even aware of what he was doing, he finally collapsed into a ditch, his insides still convulsing.

Angelo had witnessed the incident from a different angle and farther away than Frank so that the situation hadn't appeared nearly so shocking. Frank lay face down, shaking slightly, as Angelo bent over him. "Hey, man, you okay?"

No response. Angelo turned Frank over and pulled him up to a sitting position. Covered with vomit, dirt and blood, he still showed no response. Angelo shook him a little and finally gave him a bone-jarring slap.

"Frank! Look at me!"

Frank at last focused his eyes and mumbled something.

"Come on," Angelo grunted, hauling him to his feet and guiding him down toward the river's edge. When they reached the water, Angelo threw Frank to the ground and then shoved his head under the icy water. The effect was instantaneous. Frank came up gasping and wheezing, his mind finally clear.

"You okay now?"

Frank nodded, still feeling sick.

"Good, now you just stay here; I'll take care of this mess. I don't want you freakin' out again."

Angelo had to back the Buick up in order to get the body loose. Once he did so he was easily able to drag it down to the water and stuff some heavy rocks inside the clothing. One quick push and the body then sank from view.

Now for the cars. The Jaguar had a little blood in the trunk and on the bumper, but it was hardly noticeable. The Buick, however, was a different story. Angelo scraped up a double handful of dirt and tossed it onto the blood-covered hood. Satisfied with the effect, he continued until the mess covering the entire front end of the car was obscured by a layer of dirt. The impression one now had was that the car was merely well splattered with mud.

"Come on, Frank. Let's get outa here!" Angelo shouted.

Frank hadn't moved from where Angelo had left him. He dully raised his head at the call and then, after a long pause, rose weakly to his feet. He walked unsteadily toward the cars but halted just short of them.

"Come on, Frank. I've got it cleaned up. All you can see is some mud. Here, you drive yours and I'll take the Buick."

Frank still hesitated.

"Get in this car or I'm gonna kick your tail!"

Startled into motion at last, Frank moved past the Buick, unable even to look toward the front of the car. He passed Angelo wordlessly and deposited himself into the Jaguar.

"Now you follow me," Angelo directed. "We've got to find a do-it-yourself car wash and then leave this thing at the airport."

Frank blankly nodded in agreement as Angelo slammed the Jaguar's door and trunk. With the Jaguar in trail, Angelo followed the winding dirt road back around to a paved street and headed for the airport.

On the way home from the airport, Frank stopped in a twenty-four hour emergency clinic and thirty minutes later emerged with six stitches inside his mouth and five outside.

When he finally dragged into his apartment, it was after four o'clock. He threw off his clothes and crawled into bed, aching all over, but restful sleep never came as his dreams were filled with visions of Tom Agnew vomiting blood all over him.

Carl Benson peered cautiously through the peephole in his apartment door before opening it. "Good lord, what happened to you?" he asked as he caught sight of Frank's cut and swollen lower lip.

"I bumped into a car and cut my lip on the steering wheel," Frank answered truthfully. "It hurts when I try to talk or eat, but it's not anything that should cause us any problems."

Frank touched his lip gingerly as he spoke. "Angelo Martinez will be here in an hour. That should give us enough time to go over things once more before he gets here."

"Don't you think he might get upset when he realizes that he's not being included in all the planning?"

"Well, I don't plan to tell him that he's being left out. So far I've put him off by telling him that you and I have been working on the technical details. I trust Angelo implicitly as long as he needs us, but you never can tell what someone from his background might do for an extra million dollars or so."

Actually, Frank didn't care if Angelo knew all the details or not. He had carefully managed to take each man into his confidence against the other, so each thought that the other was an outsider they were including only because they needed an additional person. In this manner Frank had virtually eliminated the possibility of Carl and Angelo plotting together against him for his share of the money.

If either one of them were to make an individual move against Frank, the other would probably come to Frank's aid rather than standing idly by. In fact, if one of the men did harbor thoughts of gaining an extra share of the money, he most likely would attempt to enlist Frank's help to do so.

"Let me show you a few things on these floor plans," Carl said. "As you probably know, there are three levels at the top of the tower. The first is an observation deck with a gift shop and an FM radio station that broadcasts from a glass booth. The revolving restaurant is on the second level and then the revolving cocktail lounge is above that. In addition to the three elevators, the tower has a set of emergency stairs running down through the central core all the way from the top down to the ground. Last of all, in addition to the emergency stairs and the elevators, there is a big fancy spiral staircase that connects the restaurant and the cocktail lounge."

For the next hour the two men concentrated on the drawings that Carl had made after half a dozen trips to the top of the tower. A heavy knock at the door an hour later finally signaled Angelo's arrival. Frank opened the door and ushered him in as Carl rose to meet him.

"Carl, this is Angelo. Angelo, Carl."

Carl extended his hand, but Angelo stared at him coldly, leaving his arms crossed over his chest. Tall, thin, and slightly stooped, Carl's white hair made him appear almost frail.

"Ain't he too old?"

"Don't let the white hair fool you," Frank answered. "He got most of that from working with explosives for the last fifteen years. Now Angelo, Carl knows all about your problems. We have no secrets from one another. He's here for the same reason that you and I are. He needs a new start, and he can't do it without a lot of money."

"Yeah, what'd he do?" Angelo asked.

"He's been indicted for stealing explosives from the construction company he worked for. If you're convicted for assaulting the old lady, you'll get two or three years at the most. If Carl's convicted, he could get ten."

"Why'd he steal the stuff?"

"His wife's got cancer and his insurance ran out. He's got to have the money to keep up her treatments."

"So what does he know about explosives?"

"He knows everything we need him to know," Frank said.

"Yeah? Well if he's so smart, why did he get caught?"

Carl spoke at last, sharply and biting. "If you're so smart, why did you get caught?" The two stared coldly at each other for several long moments, a relationship, or at least an understanding finally established after the initial probing and testing. Angelo finally plopped down onto a nearby chair and leaned it back on two legs. "So now what?"

"Carl, do you have the grenades?" Frank asked.

Carl reached into a drawer and pulled out a very impressive looking hand grenade. He casually tossed it across the table to Frank.

"Are you sure this thing's defused?" Frank asked.

"Sure, don't worry about it."

"Okay, now I've seen plenty of these in the movies, but I never have fooled with one. How about you, Angelo?" Angelo shook his head no, eyeing the grenade nervously.

Frank looked it over and pulled the pin out. He then moved it around in his hands while trying to keep the clip from springing loose. Satisfied, he reinserted the pin and passed it to Angelo who somewhat hesitantly repeated Frank's motions and then tossed it back to Carl.

"You've got one defused grenade for each of us and then one live one as well, right?" Frank asked.

"That's correct."

"How can we tell the live one from the defused ones?" Angelo asked.

"I wrapped a piece of masking tape around the live one."

"That's good," Frank said. "We'll wave the defused ones around and scare everybody half to death. Nobody's going to mess with us if they think we're holding live grenades."

"What's the real one for?" Angelo asked.

"That's just in case we need to show that we really mean business. We can toss it out the window or down the stairwell."

Angelo nodded his approval. "That sounds pretty good."

Frank continued. "We looked at the shotguns the other day, so Angelo, the only other thing I want you to familiarize yourself with is this." Frank pointed to the .45 automatic pistol lying on the table.

"This thing is real and it's loaded. We've got one just like it for you. Do you know how to use it?"

Angelo smoothly popped the clip out of the handle and snapped the slide back, ejecting the shell from the chamber. He then reloaded it and passed it back to Frank.

"Good," Frank said. "Carl has a shoulder holster for you. That'll keep your hands free for your shotgun. Carl, since you've got everything down in your notebook, why don't you take us through our schedule? Angelo, if you have any comments as we go through it, let's hear them."

Angelo nodded as Carl opened a notebook and started a thorough run-through. Angelo interrupted on several occasions to make comments, a couple of which they incorporated into their plans. Their preparations finally finished, Angelo departed, leaving Frank to take care of a final detail.

"Are the suitcases all ready?" Frank asked.

"All set." Carl reached under a bed and pulled out three large suitcases.

Frank popped the latches on each one and inspected the contents. Each suitcase was just large enough to hold two fully packed parachutes.

"Perfect." Frank reached into his pocket and pulled out the crumpled up laundry slip that he had taken from Tom Agnew's wallet the night before. He carefully inserted it into a lining pocket inside the first suitcase and then closed the latches once again.

Half an hour later Frank entered Union Station, the elegantly restored turn of the century train station which is connected by underground walkway to the huge hotel and tower complex across the Amtrak rails. Frank opened a baggage storage locker and found that it would just hold one of the bulky suitcases. He took keys to three lockers, left all three suitcases, and then walked quickly away.

"Wake up!" A sharp elbow to the ribs followed the order.

Russell O'Leary sat straight up in bed. "Huh? What's going on?"

"I think I'm having labor pains. Get your watch, we'll time them."

"Yeah, okay." He fumbled for his watch and began to time contractions, but half an hour later they came to the conclusion that the pains were nothing more than false rumblings.

"Why don't you just keep the watch on your side of the bed and next time make sure that it's the real thing before you wake me up?"

"Forget it, Sleeping Beauty. If I've got to be up, then so do you. Besides, I can't time them by myself. I get mixed up because I'm concentrating so much on trying to concentrate on something else besides the pain."

"Oh, all right. If you're unable to tell time, then you can wake me up. But why don't you wait a little longer next time to see if they just go away by themselves? I've got to get up early and grade papers all day. I don't get to sleep late and then have an expensive lunch at Millard Tower."

Kathy snuggled up as close to her husband as she could get and looked up at him. "I'm sorry you were waked up in the middle of the night for nothing. Would you like a little reward for your help?" As she touched him, he smiled. She knew what he was thinking. He had once told her that when she touched him and loved him like that he always thought of the lyric from the country and western song *Behind Closed Doors* that says, "And then she makes me glad that I'm a man." Finding that Russell was ready for her, Kathy kept her eyes on his face, enjoying every indication of the pleasures of her touch.

Chapter Four

From the inside, as the doors closed and it began its ascent, the elevator didn't look much different from any other elevator. But after climbing two stories, gaining speed quickly, it suddenly seemed to shoot out into open space. Bright sunlight topped by a brilliant blue sky greeted the occupants of the glass elevator as it moved swiftly toward the top of Millard Tower, some fifty stories above.

"Oooh," Tina squealed as Dallas began to spread out magnificently before them. Charles Laughlin placed his arm comfortingly around her waist as she pressed back against him. "Oh Charles, it just gives me goose bumps all over."

She put her hands over her eyes momentarily, not daring to look as the elevator rose higher and higher, seeming to move faster and faster. Laughlin couldn't have been more pleased. As he had surmised, she was the type that got off on being impressed; she was eating up every second of it. She had almost come on the spot when he picked her up in his Mercedes the previous Saturday.

She was one of those types who have a silly, transparent little code of honor. They won't put out on the first date, but just show them a little flash and watch out on the second. That lets them pretend

(mainly to themselves) to be prim, proper, and totally virtuous when all along there is no doubt in
anyone's mind about the final outcome.

Tina was that type right down the line. She had
acted coy and innocent the week before—until he
had taken her back to his condo and had gotten her
bra off. Then she had been all over him. She couldn't
rub those huge things on his face enough, throwing
her head back with her mouth open wide, her lips
drawn back to reveal her teeth like some sort of wild
animal. Her breathing had been loud and gasping as
she jerked back and forth and bucked against him,
scratching and clawing at his back.

She hadn't put out that night, but without actually
saying so she had let it be understood that if she
were treated right on their next date she would
make it well worth his time. And Laughlin knew that
the wait would be well worth it. She would be one
heck of a ride. Tina was what you called a sure
thing.

Laughlin watched her as she opened her eyes again
and peered cautiously out the window, gripping the
hand rail tightly as she did so. He wondered what it
was like to go through life in another world; unaware of much that is going on around you. It was
fortunate that Tina had been given a great body,
because she certainly had been left out when it came
to common sense.

Laughlin glanced out of the corner of his eye at
their fellow passengers. The pregnant lady and her
two friends seemed to be enjoying the view, but the
tall slim white haired old fellow with the fat briefcase
seemed to be even more nervous about the sensa-
tional ride than Tina was. He gripped his briefcase
tightly and shifted his eyes rapidly from side to side,
looking everywhere but out the window as he nervously licked his lips.

Tina squealed again as the elevator suddenly shot
up into the bottom of the tower, her breasts jiggling

as they came to an abrupt stop at the restaurant level. "Oh Charles, could we go upstairs and have a drink before lunch? Could we please?"

Laughlin smiled obligingly. "If that's what you'd like to do, then we surely will." The way things were working out, Laughlin was glad he had rearranged his schedule to have the rest of the afternoon free. He waited until the nervous white haired man with the briefcase had exited the car and then pressed the button for the next floor. A few moments later the hostess greeted them as they entered the lounge.

"We have reservations for lunch, but we would like to have a drink up here first," Laughlin said. "Could you make sure that they keep our reservations open downstairs? The name is Laughlin."

The hostess made a quick note on the pad in front of her. "Yes sir, Mr. Laughlin, I'll take care of it. Right this way."

Tina gave a giggle of excitement, overwhelmed at the first class treatment. Laughlin couldn't help smiling as Tina eagerly followed the hostess. She was so easy. Her rear wriggling with every step, more than a few heads turned to follow the movement of the tall, eye-catching bleached blonde.

Laughlin smiled politely a few moments later as the pregnant lady and her two friends passed by and took the table behind them. He could hear them laughing and talking about the baby shower they had just come from. The pregnant one was holding her stomach, laughingly declaring that the elevator's sudden stop had definitely been noticed inside, setting off a fit of kicking.

Carl Benson had been the only one to leave the elevator when it stopped at the restaurant level. He now stood leaning over the sink in the men's room, deathly afraid he would vomit. He wanted to turn around and run, but he knew he wouldn't. He couldn't. He concentrated on breathing slowly and deeply for several minutes, then wiped his face with a cool wet paper towel and walked slowly back out to the hostess stand.

"Lunch, sir?"

The voice of the hostess startled him back from his thoughts. "Oh, uh, yes. I have a reservation for Johnson. I'll have someone else joining me in a little while."

"Fine, would you like to wait here or at your table?"

"I'd like to wait at the table if it's all right."

"Sure, Mr. Johnson. Right this way."

Carl followed the hostess halfway around the circular revolving restaurant which provided a magnificent panoramic view of the entire Dallas area. When they passed the table where Frank was already seated, Carl walked straight on by without slowing, purposely turning his head away. Had he been too obvious? Should he have glanced at Frank casually rather than making a point of staring away? Was it possible that someone had noticed his behavior?

"How's this?" asked the hostess as she stopped before an empty table.

"Fine, thank you." Carl took the chair closest to the window and carefully placed his briefcase on the window ledge so that it rested safely between him and the window. Only then did he relax his tight grip on the handle, his palm red and sweating.

It really didn't matter what happened to him anymore. The insurance had run out long before his wife had started the radiation treatments, and they were so far behind now that he didn't even bother to open the bills when they came. He should have taken the cancer policy that had been available through the company, but by the time he had gotten around to it, it had been too late.

When the unexpected offer had come for the explosives it had all seemed so easy. And the first time it was. Everything went exactly as it was supposed to. The company was so big and was involved in so many construction projects that he had been able to alter the records and cover the missing explosives so that no one ever knew that anything was missing. No one was hurt, and the company made so much money that they would never miss it.

He originally intended to do it only once. But as helpful as the money was, they needed so much more. The second time things didn't go quite right, and then he was not only in jail and facing huge legal expenses, but was out of work, too. He was good at his job and quite experienced, but there are few construction companies that handle explosives, and this was the sort of news that traveled fast. No one else would hire him after what he had done, and he had no other skills; that was all he knew how to do. When things seemed that they couldn't be any worse, suddenly they were.

But now, if things went like Frank said they would, everything would be okay. In fact, even if things didn't go like Frank said, it would be okay. The $150,000 life insurance policy he had taken out three days ago was enough to take care of his wife.

With the mess he'd made of things, she might be better off without him anyway. He wanted so badly to call her and explain that he was more sorry than he could ever say; that things would be much better soon—one way or the other.

"Would you care for something from the bar, sir?"

Startled that someone was addressing him again, Carl looked up at the waitress. "No, not right now thank you. I'm waiting for someone."

He would have liked a drink. Maybe it would settle him down and make him feel less nervous. But Frank had said not to. Carl put his hand out without even thinking about it, to touch his briefcase, and realized suddenly that it was gone. He jerked around and looked at the empty window ledge, then realized that the floor on which he was seated rotated but the window ledge did not. He jumped from his chair and wildly looked around.

There, on the window ledge next to the table behind him, laid his briefcase. "Excuse me, pardon me," he said as he bent over and around the woman sitting at the table and retrieved the case. Flushed, his heart beating rapidly, Carl sat back down and placed the case on the floor securely between his feet.

Frank had been seated only a few minutes when Carl had come in. So far everything was right on schedule. A few minutes later he did a double take when he realized that Angelo had just walked by. The dirty jeans and torn T shirt had been replaced by sharply creased slacks, an Izod sport shirt, and a navy blazer. The long greasy hair had been washed and blow dried. He could have just stepped out of an SMU fraternity house, except for the scraggly beard. Frank's detailed directions for Angelo's dress and appearance had included firm instructions to shave, but the few stringy hairs that could barely be called a beard still remained. As a result, Angelo still looked slightly out of place.

"Ready to order?"

Frank smiled comfortably at the waitress. "I'm waiting for someone, so I'll need just a few more minutes."

"Fine, I'll check back in a little while."

Frank looked at his watch for the nineteenth time. Just another five minutes.

If they had taken a table together, they wouldn't have had to worry about timing things so precisely. But while three nicely dressed men with briefcases eating lunch together wouldn't have attracted undue attention, after things were all over people might remember the three men who had suddenly disappeared just before the three masked men had appeared. There were enough people moving about the restaurant at any time that it wouldn't be obvious at all if they moved from three different places.

Frank gazed out the window at the incredible view but didn't see it. He wondered why the fates, the gods, or whatever had conspired to bring him to this. At first, betting had been something that he had done for sport; the evenings at Louisiana Downs, the weekends at Vegas. But gradually it became something more. It was no longer the travel and the entertainment which drew him so much as the gambling itself. Maybe it wouldn't have been so bad if he hadn't won at first. Then by the time he started to lose he couldn't quit.

He had hocked everything he owned, borrowed to the hilt, and still kept going deeper and deeper. The last football season had finished him. The Cowboys hadn't beaten the spread but twice all year, and he had bet them heavily every week. Eventually he had started betting ever increasing amounts in a desperate attempt to pay off the people who were beginning to push.

Being an assistant D.A. buys you a little time and it gets you a few extensions, but with the people that he had come to owe, that was all the position did. They didn't care who you were. Running was an option, but not an appealing one. He couldn't just leave town and start up somewhere else. He wasn't dealing with a small time local bookie. They'd come after him. And they'd find him.

If he were to change his name and assume an entirely new identity, they might not find him—at least as quickly—but that wasn't a viable option either. He couldn't practice law under an assumed name, and there was nothing else he could do that would allow him to maintain the lifestyle he had come to require. And in his case it wouldn't be just a few broken bones. No, they had meant what they said.

Frank picked up his briefcase and walked resolutely back toward the elevators, past the hostess stand to the men's room. Angelo was waiting inside; Carl joined them within a few seconds. Frank leaned over and washed his hands while they waited for the one other occupant of the washroom to finish and leave.

"I thought I told you to shave," Frank snapped when they were at last alone.

Angelo stared back coldly for several long moments. "I don't shave for nobody. I got in okay, didn't I?"

"Come on you two, let's go," Carl said. He had already placed his briefcase on the counter and popped the latches. Within seconds he had fitted several pieces together to form a twelve gauge sawed-off shotgun. A .45 automatic went into the empty shoulder holster beneath his suit jacket, and a hand grenade went into his pocket. He then removed a black ski mask and pulled it quickly over his head, adjusting it so he could see and breathe.

Frank and Angelo dropped their confrontation and followed Carl's lead. Within twenty seconds all three men were similarly attired. They had debated whether to use fully automatic weapons or sawed-off shotguns and had finally decided on the latter. For one thing, it was much harder to buy something on the order of a submachine gun. M-16s were relatively available with few or no questions asked, but they were much too long and unwieldy to be used comfortably within the confines of the circular restaurant.

Although a shotgun has far less range, it would be more than adequate for the distances they would find inside the tower. Since the restaurant and lounge levels were shaped like a doughnut, with seating areas around the outside and kitchens, bars, bathrooms, elevators, and stairs in the center, they wouldn't need a weapon with much range. With the shotgun sawed off, and the choke therefore removed from the end of the barrel, the buckshot they were using would spread out in a wide pattern rather than staying tightly together as it normally would.

Using a twelve gauge pump shotgun loaded with

00 buckshot, they could fire forty-five lead balls, each the size of a .32 caliber bullet, into a target within a few seconds. Any one of those lead balls would be capable of killing a man at the distances inside the tower. There were few fully automatic weapons that could match that. And lastly, while any gun will scare people, there is something especially horrible about a sawed-off shotgun when one is on the wrong end of it.

Frank glanced in the mirror, almost intimidated by the sight of himself. He had never realized how horribly threatening the effect of the ski mask and the sawed-off shotgun together would be.

"Ready? Everybody know what to do?" Frank asked. The two masked heads facing him nodded wordlessly.

"Okay, let's do it."

Colby Knight stepped out of the elevator into the suite of offices that served as the headquarters of Millard (pronounced with the emphasis on the "-lard") Hotels International. As he walked down the heavily carpeted hall, he had to pass by Bill Post's office. Post, smiling and talking smoothly into the phone, caught sight of Knight as he passed and raised a hand in greeting. Knight gave a curt nod without slowing or even caring if Post saw it or not. He walked on down the hall past his secretary and through the door that read: Colby Knight, Executive Vice President.

"Good afternoon, Mr. Knight," his secretary cooed as he stalked past.

"Yeah," he growled in reply.

He sat down heavily and glanced at the newspaper lying on his desk. His secretary entered a moment later with a cup of black coffee. "Thanks, Linda," he said, finally managing a civil tone of voice.

"Sure, Mr. Knight." She flounced out, her rear moving back and forth invitingly beneath her tight skirt. Knight didn't even notice. He leaned back hard in his chair. Damn, how he hated Bill Post's guts!

Knight had been a vice president with a large financial institution until two years ago. At that time he was hired away by Millard Hotels, ostensibly to be groomed for the top spot in the company. The present president and chairman of the board, Mr. Millard himself, was planning to retire within the year and retain only the title of chairman of the board. The title of president and chief executive officer would pass on to someone else. That someone else would actually control Millard Hotels; the chairman of the board would become merely a figurehead.

Due to the problems the company faced over the coming decade of financing the construction of several billion dollars worth of new hotels around the world, the board of directors strongly favored someone with a strong financial background to step into the position. The company had hired numerous middle level managers with financial backgrounds over the last several years, and Bill Post had joined the company with that group about three years before. His fortunes had risen dramatically until, three months ago, he had been given a vice presidency. He was now considered to be the old man's fair haired boy, thus putting him in an excellent position for a grab at the top spot when it came available.

It wasn't that Knight had failed to perform; he had done quite well. Nor was it that Post had performed outstandingly, though he also had done well. Knight hated Post because of what he was. He had ascended as fast as he had mainly because he was a back-stabbing little brown-noser. He was the type who makes a good first impression but whom people soon come to detest—except for his superiors.

Post had been with the company about a year longer than Knight, a fact which he never missed an opportunity to mention. He always managed to be in the office a few minutes before Knight came in. If

Knight started coming in a half hour earlier, than so did Post. When Knight returned to his regular arrival time, so did Post. Nor would Post leave the building until Knight had. If Mr. Millard was out of town, though, it was a different story.

The casual wave to Knight while he was brown-nosing someone over the phone was Post's infuriating way of emphasizing that he had gotten back from lunch first. Though Knight had never said anything against Post, he constantly heard of things that Post had managed to drop about him. The two had attended an out of town seminar together about six months before. They had been forced to spend a fair amount of time together at the meetings, and Knight had actually enjoyed Post's company. After returning, Knight mentioned to several people how much he had enjoyed being at the meeting with Post. A few days later someone revealed that Post had been spreading the word that Knight's expense account was considerably higher than his own for the same trip. Post had purposely understated his own expenses so it would appear that Knight had overstated his.

The final straw had come a month before when Knight had accidentally dropped a cigarette on the carpet in the lobby. Being in a hurry to get to a meeting, he just snuffed it out with his foot rather than taking the time to pick it up and throw it into a trash can. Post had pulled out a notebook and recorded and dated the incident. He mentioned to someone else in the room that the damage to the carpet would come out of "Mr. Knight's" pay at some point.

Since then, Knight had wanted to kick Post's teeth in every time he saw his chubby little sniveling face. But how do you fight someone like that? If he came right out and told Post what he thought of him, then Mr. Millard would be sure to find out and Knight would look bad. If Knight went to the old man and complained, it would appear that he was just crying over minor interoffice politics. That was why he hated Bill Post so. People like Post were rarely successful in the long run, but they could cause a tremendous amount of damage over the short haul.

Knight took a deep breath and tried to relax. He was a desperate man backed into a corner, watching what he had worked for all his life slowly being stolen from him. He picked up the paper and tried to read, but he couldn't get past the headlines. He swiveled around and looked out the picture window of his thirty-first floor office. It was a beautiful day outside. The clouds of the last couple of days had vanished taking all traces of haze and smog with them. Dallas lay like a picture before him, with the Dallas Millard Hotel and Millard Tower complex standing out on the far side of the city.

Chapter Five

Frank and his three companions had turned and taken but a step toward the bathroom door when, unexpectedly, a fat little man in a business suit suddenly shoved it open and walked right in. Almost immediately he stopped and stared, wide-eyed as the door swung closed behind him. Angelo, in the lead, never even slowed down. He snapped the butt of his shotgun around so that he struck the man a stunning blow on the side of the head, knocking him back against the wall and down to the floor.

"Get outa the way!"

Angelo then jerked open the door and stepped out. Frank started to voice an objection to his treatment of the poor man, who had not shown the slightest signs of giving them any trouble, but then he stopped. Why bother; that was why he had included Angelo to begin with.

Frank followed Angelo through the door, trailed closely by Carl. The doors to both elevators were closed, indicating that they probably were in transit to or from the ground level. Carl pressed the call button for each elevator and then took up a position between them, while Frank followed Angelo toward the hostess stand.

Angelo removed the grenade from his pocket and

pulled the pin, holding it in his left hand so that the clip was still securely in place. With most of the shotgun's barrel sawed-off, it was possible to handle the weapon quite well with just his right hand alone. Angelo raised his shotgun to waist level, Frank following suit. Their first objective was to clear the reception area, gaining control of the public address system, and then to secure the elevators.

Two couples were standing in line waiting to be seated, their backs turned to the elevators. The hostess, just greeting the first couple, was the first to see the masked men. When she froze, her greeting smile quickly fading from her face, her expression was so stark that the people standing before her turned around to see what she was looking at.

The expression on each of their faces was at first one of surprise and confusion, but when they realized that guns were actually being trained on them it quickly turned to fear. "Move," Angelo said in a loud firm voice. "Get over against the windows."

The group responded immediately, needed no urging to move farther away from the gun wielding men. The hostess started to go with them, but Frank stopped her. "Not you," he said, trying to sound as calm and in control as possible with his mouth so dry that his tongue almost felt swollen.

The hostess stood still, her face now a deathly shade of pale. "How do you turn on the public address system?" Frank asked.

"Just, just press the button on the microphone," she said in a hesitant, subdued voice.

"That overrides the music, right?"

"Right."

"And this won't be heard up in the lounge or down on the observation deck, right?"

"No, just on this floor."

Frank already knew the answers to his questions, but he wanted to verify the information. The last thing they needed at this point was a stupid mistake due to an oversight or incorrect information. "Okay, you get over by the windows with the others." The girl moved quickly, doing exactly as instructed. Frank stepped up to the hostess stand and pushed the button on the paging microphone, blowing on it first to satisfy himself that he was coming over the speakers well enough to be heard clearly.

"Ladies and gentlemen, let me have your attention. I don't want anyone to move until I finish telling you what to do. Just stay in your seats. We are armed with sawed-off shotguns and hand grenades and have taken control of the tower."

From Frank's position he could see about two dozen tables. The diners were looking around in concern, but no one had moved or said anything.

"The grenades we're carrying are live and have the pins removed. That means that if anyone tries anything or even bumps into one of us, the grenades will probably explode. So if we have any heroes out there, I suggest you forget it or you'll get a lot of people killed."

Frank switched on the microphone again. "That was the bad news, now for the good. You all will be allowed to leave the tower in just a few minutes. There's one catch, though. The elevators won't be running, so you'll have to walk down the stairs. If anyone objects strongly to walking down fifty flights of stairs, then we'll be glad to have you remain with us as a hostage. Now just sit tight for a few minutes. I'll let you know when you can leave your seats and move to the stairs."

When Frank had begun his announcement, Angelo had quickly moved out into the restaurant and turned to his left. Halfway around the tower he came to the entrance to the kitchen. As he pushed through the swinging doors, several kitchen workers and a couple of waiters suddenly stopped to stare, but he paid them no attention, and no one offered any resistance as he walked across the room to the third elevator. This one was used primarily as a service elevator, so it usually remained in one place while the other two constantly shuttled people up and down.

The elevator doors were standing wide open. Angelo simply stepped inside, pressed the stop button, and leaned back against the wall, his position comfortably secure and defensible.

Frank was more than satisfied at this point. They had, in effect, established a beachhead and had taken over communications. Frank knew that there were other telephones on the floor in addition to the one in front of him at the hostess stand and that someone was probably calling the police at that very moment, but that made no difference at this point. They weren't attempting to take over the tower without anyone finding out about it, and they would need to contact the police sooner or later so they could make their demands.

The tower would be so isolated once they had finished securing the elevators that even if patrolmen happened to be driving by at this moment, they were of no concern. It took a good ten minutes to walk down the stairs, and it would take much longer than that for anyone to get up them.

Although Frank was no longer concerned about the elevators or the emergency stairs, it was still possible that someone might come down the spiral staircase which connected the restaurant to the lounge above. But since the hostess stand was positioned directly across from the open spiral staircase, Frank was in a perfect position to confront anyone who used them. He therefore had no fear of surprise from that direction either.

The two elevators at the entrance to the restaurant, Carl's assignment, were the next concern. The worst part was the waiting. Carl had no way of knowing for sure when those doors would suddenly fly open. A couple of minutes later he did have at least a slight forewarning as a swoosh of air announced the arrival of the first car. The doors slid open revealing about a dozen people. The first couple was about to step out when they stopped abruptly, having caught sight of the fearsome figure in the doorway.

Carl pressed the elevator call button and held it to keep the doors from closing. He then stood off to one side so there was room to pass by him but so that the occupants of the car could still see him and the shotgun clearly. He was afraid his voice would crack. He had practiced his lines so many times that the words came out sounding like a kid in grade school giving his first speech. At least he said it loudly, and coupled with his appearance his orders therefore carried more than enough authority.

"Listen and do exactly what I tell you. Everybody out right now and no one will be hurt. But if there's anybody still in that elevator in five seconds, I'll blow you away."

Carl waited expectantly, but no one moved; partially out of fright and partially out of the hope that the doors would close again, freeing them of this fightening specter. Carl was suddenly enraged. That was what he needed. That felt good.

"Move or you're dead meat!" he shouted. That hadn't even been in the speech. It was a line he had once heard on a late movie.

Whatever the source of his inspiration, it was the spark that finally started the first people moving. As usual, the herd instinct took effect and the rest followed right along. The group moved on out of the elevator but stopped again when they caught sight of Frank blocking the entrance to the restaurant.

Carl pointed to the stairwell door. "There are the stairs. Take them all the way to the bottom and don't stop or try to come back up. We'll be placing explosives on the doors behind you and they'll blow if anyone opens the door again."

Actually, Frank and his group had no concerns that anyone would want to come back up the stairs into the tower once they had been released. But they intended to impress the fact upon everyone that the doors would be wired with explosives so that the message would be transmitted to the police loudly and clearly.

The group from the elevator needed no shouted threats this time, scurrying quickly through the doorway and down the stairs, the door swinging shut behind them with a loud bang. Once the area was clear, Frank pulled two chairs over from the waiting area next to the hostess stand. He and Carl then jammed them into the elevator doorway so that the doors would be kept from closing. They made sure that the chairs were wedged against each other tightly enough to keep the doors from simply pushing them out of the way or knocking them over.

They waited only a few seconds before the doors indeed tried to close automatically. They moved only a couple of inches before encountering the resistance of the chairs and opening again. Their backup system now securely in place, Carl leaned over the chairs and pressed the elevator's stop button. Now the doors stood completely still and wide open.

Frank had been somewhat concerned about Carl's state of mind and how that might affect his performance and dependability, though he had been sure not to admit his doubts to Carl, or to Angelo. "How are you doing?" Frank asked.

The adrenalin flowing at last due to action rather than passive fear and worry, Carl felt better than he had all day. "Great!"

Carl impatiently waited for the second elevator to arrive, eager to finish his task. When the doors finally opened, he repeated his actions with the same results, Frank helping to jam chairs between the doors again after the passengers had exited down the stairs.

"Ready to clear the floor?" Frank asked.

"You bet. Let's move them on out."

Frank walked back to the hostess stand and pressed the button on the public address microphone again. "All right, folks, let me have your attention again. We're ready for you to start moving to the stairs now, but I have one last caution to leave with you. After you enter the stairwell, we'll be placing explosives on the door behind you, so don't turn around and try to come back up. The explosives will be set to blow if anyone tries to open the door.

"Now everyone stand up, take your purses and coats or whatever, and don't worry about your dinner bills; they're on us. Move in single file around to the stairs next to the elevators where you came in. Make it quick now or we might change our minds."

Once again, the herd instinct ruled the actions of the crowd. As soon as the first person stood up and started to move, the rest followed. They filed silently by the masked men, none daring to look directly at them. Frank and Carl had both joined Angelo in removing the pins from their grenades and now held them so that they were in plain sight.

"I'm sorry, but I don't think I can make it down that many stairs." Frank looked around at the sound of the voice to find a young man in a wheelchair stopped before him. A girl stood by the young man's side.

"What about you?" Frank asked her.

The girl shook her head. "I won't leave him."

Frank stared at them for a minute. The girl obviously meant what she had said. It was an unexpected complication, but it wasn't necessarily a problem. In fact, with a little planning it could probably work to their advantage.

"Okay, don't worry. We'll send you down in the elevator a little later. Just wait over there out of the way."

In little more than four minutes, with Angelo herding from the rear, everyone had exited the restaurant level into the stairwell. It had taken less than nine minutes for Frank and his group to take complete control of the middle level of the tower along with all three elevators. Things so far had gone even better than they had hoped. Their plan, which they had been unable to rehearse accurately, had alloted thirteen minutes to the first stage.

Frank motioned to Angelo. "Come on, let's check it." The two moved out toward the windows and then circled the restaurant in opposite directions, making absolutely sure that no one had remained behind. The main restaurant area was clearly deserted. They then checked the manager's office and the kitchen and storage areas, opening all doors, peering into all closets.

When Frank and Angelo returned to the hostess stand a couple of minutes later, Carl was standing over two women who were seated on the bottom step of the spiral staircase. "They wandered down from the cocktail lounge."

"Okay, send them on down," Frank said. The lounge would be crowded, and they didn't need every last hostage. At this point they merely were concerned with getting all the people out of their way who weren't already in place upstairs.

Carl motioned for the women to follow him as he walked back toward the elevators. He then opened the door to the stairwell and politely held it open for them.

"Take the stairs all the way to the bottom, ladies. And don't try to come back up, because we'll be placing explosives on the doors behind you." The two women hurried through the stairwell door and went clattering down the stairs as directed.

Frank suddenly remembered the man in the bathroom. He walked over to the door and pushed it open just a crack with the muzzle of his gun. "Come on, out of the bathroom," he ordered loudly. He surprised himself with the threatening, totally commanding tone of his voice. He was getting good at this.

Frank stepped back as the pale quaking man slowly opened the door and peered out. "Down the stairs," Frank said, motioning the way with his gun. The man wasn't about to wait for Angelo to hit him again. He stepped quickly through the door and then was gone, the echo of his footsteps lasting only for a few seconds.

Frank inserted the pin back into his grenade and returned it to his pocket. Angelo did the same, but Carl kept his in his hand. When they reached the top of the spiral staircase, Angelo and Frank would be in the lead where they might need both hands free. Carl, in the rear, would provide the threat of the grenade.

"Ready?" Frank asked.

Carl nodded, but Angelo pointed his gun toward the girl and the young man in the wheelchair. "What's to keep them from taking one of the elevators?"

Frank frowned as he examined the couple once more. After all three floors had been secured, and thus the entire tower was under their control, it wouldn't be as important that they have control of the elevators at all times. In fact, Frank had plans for their later use. But at this point it was vital that they retain total control of the elevators.

Frank wished that the girl were in the wheelchair. He wouldn't have hesitated for a second to leave her behind and take the guy upstairs. She had meant it when she said she wouldn't leave him; she wasn't about to run out on the guy. But Frank had no idea about him. He knew that it was difficult at best to predict how someone will react under abnormal or adverse circumstances.

"We'll have to take them upstairs with us," Frank said. "I'll take the lead. Angelo, you take his right side, Carl, you take his left."

When they carried the man up the stairs, either Carl or Angelo would have to hold his gun in his left hand and both men were right handed. Frank wanted Angelo to be in the best position to use his weapon since he would be the most useful if a situation suddenly called for any shooting.

"As soon as we get upstairs, drop him," Frank said. He then pointed his gun at the girl. "You bring the chair. Once we're upstairs, you sit down on the floor with him and don't move. Do exactly what you're told and you won't be hurt. Like I said, we'll send you down in the elevator in a little while but not until we're ready. Let's go."

Tina's second drink had arrived. It was one of those ridiculous things with an umbrella sticking out of it. "Oooh, it's so pretty," she gushed.

Laughlin smiled, slowly sipping his gin and tonic. The way she had put away the first one, this wouldn't take as long as he had thought. They might not even make it back to his place. After a couple more of those things, she'd probably be ready for it in the car.

Laughlin smiled at the thought of her thrashing around and moaning in his Mercedes. Tina smiled back and giggled. "Oh Charles, thank you so much for bringing me up here. I've never been before, and I've just wanted to come more than you could ever dream. This is all so exciting, it's just out of this world."

"I'm glad you're enjoying it." Most of the types like her, who you could impress right out of their pants, made a show of being nonchalant about things. Tina at least was open and honest; no shallow facade. Laughlin's thoughts and those of the other people in the lounge were interrupted at that moment by a loud voice coming over the public address system.

"Ladies and gentlemen, please let me have your attention. We have taken control of the tower, are heavily armed, and are carrying live explosives. If anyone should bump into us, there's a good chance that the explosives will go off. Explosives have also been placed at each of the exits, so there is no way out of the tower." At this point a few gasps were heard about the lounge, but the people for the most part remained silent.

"We are going to demand a sum of money for your release. As soon as we get that money you all will be released unharmed. After a few hours at the most, you will all be leaving the tower safely and will have a great story to tell your family and friends. Make sure, however, that you realize the desperate position we're in. The penalty for this sort of activity is very stiff. If we have to kill one or all of you to keep from going to prison for twenty years, we won't hesitate to do so. Remember, if you do exactly as you're told you won't be harmed. Now everyone relax and stay in your seats. Because of all the explosives, it will be extremely dangerous for anyone to move around."

The speech had been carefully composed by Frank and Carl to accomplish several things. Their first priority was to calm the people down so that they wouldn't end up with a hysterical mob on their hands. Thus, they had been quite emphatic in their assurance that no one would be harmed if they cooperated. Secondly, they had to convince the people that they would be in great danger if they didn't cooperate. And lastly, they wanted to discourage any would-be heroes from trying anything.

It was similar to the message they had provided downstairs in the restaurant, but it was much more important that they make a significant impression on these people on the upper level. The people in the restaurant had been given no reason to cause any problems since they had been assured of being allowed to leave quickly.

While the people in the restaurant had been frightened, they had been given hope. And that was what Frank and his group would need to provide for their hostages throughout the ordeal. Otherwise, someone might try something irrational out of fear and desperation.

Frank surveyed the pie shaped section of the lounge that he could see from his vantage point at the hostess stand. The lounge was designed much as the restaurant below, with the central core of the tower being ringed by a double row of tables and booths separated by a waist high partition. Everything was nicely stabilized for the moment and things were going as smoothly as they could have hoped.

Now that the situation was settled, Carl took a moment to help the young man back into his wheel chair and then pushed him out into the lounge toward the windows. "Over there," he said. "Wait by the windows and we'll let you know when you can leave."

At the sound of Carl's voice, a woman seated at one of the first tables had suddenly turned and stared at him, her mouth slightly agape. As he started to move back toward the entry area, he caught her eye and froze.

"Carl?" she whispered in disbelief.

He hesitated another moment, unsure of himself, and then turned quickly away. Frank had been preoccupied and therefore had missed the momentary confrontation, but Angelo had taken in the entire thing as well as its significance.

"Frank, did you see that?" he hissed urgently. "That old bag over there made Carl. She recognized him."

"What? Are you sure?"

"Yeah I'm sure. She said his name."

Carl would have just as soon pretended that the incident had never happened, but Frank immediately confronted him as he joined them again. "Carl, what happened? Who is that?"

Carl looked down uncomfortably, shifting his weight from one foot to the other. "She's one of the secretaries at the construction company where I used to work. I've known her for six or seven years, so I guess she recognized my voice, and then she could tell it was me even with the mask on."

Angelo spoke coldly, no pretense at tact. "We'll have to kill her. If she I.D.'s him, he'll finger us in a second."

"No, no you can't do that," Carl exclaimed loudly, his eyes wide with despair.

Frank knew deep down that what Angelo had just said was totally correct. If Carl were picked up, they would offer him a little plea bargain deal, it wouldn't take much, and he would jump on it in an instant. Frank and Angelo would never have a chance. Something happening like this in a city the size of Dallas was a million to one shot, but it just had and Frank knew that they'd have to deal with it sooner or later. Though he wasn't about to admit any of that to Carl, or even to Angelo.

"No, we're not going to kill anybody," Frank said. "We'll figure something out later. We don't have time to worry about it now, anyway; we're still not finished here. Carl, get your briefcase and let's get going."

Carl nodded with relief and started down the spiral staircase for his briefcase which was still in the bathroom on the floor below. Angelo reached out and caught Frank's arm as he started to follow Carl down the stairs.

"You know, we haven't got to do the old lady. We could do him instead. Then it wouldn't matter if she put the cops onto him or not; wouldn't bother us any. In fact, if you think about it, it makes more sense to do him. We don't get any more money for doing her."

Frank didn't want to hear this, didn't want to think about it. He pulled away without another word and started down the stairs after Carl.

"We've got to do one of them," Angelo called after him.

That was what scared and what sickened him. Deep down, though he tried to block it off, he knew that Angelo was right.

Chapter Six

"Inspector, the commander of the tactical squad reports that snipers are in position on the hotel roof."

Inspector Robert Harris looked around in irritation at his aide, Doug Baus. "Well get them off! They're out in plain view up there. Why does he think we came sneaking in here with unmarked cars? We're trying to keep a low profile, and that idiot is acting like he's John Wayne."

Doug spoke hurriedly into a walkie-talkie. "Inspector Harris wants all the snipers off the roof immediately."

The reply sounded disappointed. "Okay, roger that."

Doug addressed his superior again. "Sir, the people who were released from the restaurant all give the same story. There are three men with sawed-off shotguns and hand grenades. They claimed that they would place explosives on the stairwell doors so that no one could get back in."

"In that case, let's get a dog right up there and check out the explosives. It may be nothing but a bluff, but I don't want anyone opening a door to find out."

"Okay, but it'll take a few minutes to get a dog team over."

"Well get them here as quickly as you can. In the meantime, send four men up to the top through the stairwell. Tell them not even to think about touching any of the doors. Just find out if they're all closed. If they are, I want them to see if they can hear anything on the other side."

"Yes sir, right away." As Doug hurried away, Harris called after him. "And tell them to get rid of their boots. The echoes inside that stairwell would give them away before they got halfway to the top."

Harris leaned his head back and gazed up at the sphere fifty stories above him as if he might actually be able to see something. He knew that he couldn't, but then it worked both ways. His group couldn't be seen at the base of the tower by anyone at the top. The underground passage from the train station to the tower had allowed them to make their way to the base of the tower unseen after driving to the train station in unmarked cars. The offices they had commandeered at the base of the tower would now serve as an excellent base of operations.

Robert Harris had several gray hairs and a worry line in his face for every hostage situation he had been involved in, and he had been involved in a lot of hostage situations. He had spent seven years as an aide in this very unit and was now in his ninth year as the head of it.

He had been in as many hostage situations as anybody, maybe even more, and he was the best. His superiors knew it, and that was why they pretty well left him alone to his own devices, choosing not to argue with success; the people who worked for him knew it and that was why they put up with his often quick temper and demanding, driving manner; and last of all, Robert Harris knew it. But it wasn't the type of knowledge that allowed one to become big headed and cocky. Because in Harris's line of work you didn't win them all. No matter how good you were, you were going to lose some. And that meant that you were going to get some people killed. Nice innocent people with wives and husbands and children and dogs who were usually just unfortunate enough to be in the wrong place at the wrong time.

Oh, everybody said that it wasn't your fault when you lost one, that the situation had been impossible and that nothing could have been done, but Harris never saw it that way. That was probably why his stomach felt as if it had an ulcer for every hostage he had ever lost.

Harris usually didn't have any preconceived feelings going into these sort of situations because they were always so unpredictable. But he had a feeling about this one, and it was bad. He had been involved in hostage situations just about everywhere you could think of; in cars, in airplanes, out in the open, in houses and apartments. If he had ever seen a fortress designed for the purpose of holding people hostage, this was it.

A sniper on the roof of the hotel was almost worthless. The man would be totally exposed, and the tower was so much taller than the hotel that it created a firing angle so great that not much of the area inside the tower could be covered.

As if that weren't enough of a problem, with the firing angle such as it was, Harris wasn't even sure that a bullet could be counted on to pass through the glass without ricocheting. Even if it were deflected only a fraction of an inch as it passed through, that could be the difference between hitting the target or one of the hostages.

He knew that at this point surprise was his best card, and he intended to play it for all it was worth. The longer he waited, the more such an advantage would erode, since the extortionists would expect them to be in position sooner or later.

Frank opened the stairwell door and listened care-

fully for several moments. The noisy clatter of high
heels on the metal and concrete steps far below was
still clear and distinct, and still moving away from
them.

"What do you think?" Carl asked.

"It sounds all right, let's go."

Carl followed, while Angelo remained in position
in the lounge to discourage any sudden rush for the
elevators or stairs. It took but a few seconds to move
down the stairs to the observation deck level. Frank
was just about to open the door and burst through,
but then he stopped for a moment.

Carl almost bumped into him. "What is it, what's
wrong?"

"Shh, listen."

They suddenly realized that something was different. The sound of footsteps on the stairs far below
them had abruptly stopped. And now, from far down
the stairwell, Frank thought he could faintly hear the
sound of voices. He couldn't make out any words,
but he was fairly certain that people were speaking.
The two women and the man, the last people they
had sent down the stairs, might have slowed down or
even stopped for a quick rest, but they wouldn't have
stopped to have an idle chat.

"They must have met someone coming up the
stairs," Carl said.

"Yeah, I think you're right. We may be having
company pretty soon, so we better make this fast."
Frank opened the door and walked quickly out onto
the first level of the tower. It took less than two
minutes to round up the few people on the observation deck and send them down the stairs after the
others.

The clerk at the souvenir shop eagerly joined the
rush to the exits along with everyone else. The only
problem, and that just for a moment, involved the
disc jockey in the glass broadcasting booth. The door
to the booth happened to be locked, but when Frank

pointed his shotgun directly at him, making it clear that a glass wall would do him no good, he too had abandoned his post and gladly headed down the stairs.

Although they had managed to clear the first level of people, there was no way to secure it with explosives as easily as they could the top two levels. The only sure way for Frank and Carl to get back upstairs was to go back out into the stairwell and then up. If they allowed an elevator to come down to the observation deck level, and the elevator call button had been pressed on the ground floor, the car might end up taking them down instead of back up.

As on each of the two floors above, there were two doors leading into the stairwell. Carl placed a small explosive charge on one and set it to go off if the door were opened. Now the trick was to arrange a similar charge on the door which they had to go through to get back into the stairwell and upstairs.

Carl kneeled down in the stairwell and closed the door almost all the way, just leaving a crack wide enough to get his hands back through. Then he carefully began setting the charge as best he could.

Frank couldn't help noticing a little sweat on Carl's forehead. "Be careful," Frank cautioned. "You're not too shakey for this, are you?"

"No, I'm all right."

"Is it going to work?"

"Yeah. If the door's thrown open, it'll blow. But if someone who knows what he's doing opens the door just a little and then works on the charge, he'll probably be able to defuse it and get the door open."

Actually, it didn't really matter. Even if the police were able to gain access to this first level, it would be of no benefit to them in reaching the upper levels. Frank just didn't want to give them an easy toehold. He felt that it would be much easier to keep the police at bay if they were forced to work out of the stairwell rather than out of the first level of the

tower. He didn't think it made sense to make things
any easier for the police than necessary.

Carl finished his work and gently closed the door.
"That's got it."

"Good, let's go."

Frank and Carl quickly climbed the stairs to the
second level, the now empty restaurant, and stepped
back inside. Carl set about placing charges on each
of the two stairwell doors on that level, while Frank
moved back up the spiral staircase to join Angelo on
the third level. A few minutes later Carl joined them
and finished setting the explosive charges inside the
stairwell doors there as well.

Frank was suddenly struck by a thought. Their
takeover was now complete, and they hadn't even
needed the passkey which had cost two very innocent people their lives at the hands of Angelo. Frank
patted his pocket. The kicker was that he hadn't
even remembered to bring it.

Jack Hilliard figured that there must have been
almost 200 people in the lounge. Surely there was
safety in numbers. There were far too many people
to frisk or search. Still, he shifted uncomfortably in
his chair. He normally wasn't aware of the gun under his jacket, but today it seemed to weigh fifty
pounds and must have created a bulge that they
couldn't possibly fail to notice.

He wouldn't even have worn the darn thing, but
all off duty police officers were required to wear
their service revolvers, and recently a patrolman had
been suspended for failing to do so, effectively ham-
mering the point home. The off duty patrolman had
been drinking beer in a neighborhood bar, minding
his own business, when a knife fight broke out and
three people were stabbed, one fatally. The assailant
got clean away without so much as a scratch on him.

So Hilliard had worn his gun today just like he was

supposed to, but he almost wished he hadn't. When confronted by three men armed with sawed-off shotguns and hand grenades, it didn't give him much solace.

Betty was watching him anxiously. She knew he was wearing it, and she knew he might have to use it. Apart from the ever present possibility of getting himself killed, she was another good reason not to be a hero. If he were to become involved—anymore than he already was, anyway—then who he was with along with his reasons for being there would become glaringly apparent.

With four kids and a mortgage, he couldn't afford to have leisurely lunches in expensive places such as this. But Betty liked such places and, after all, she was paying for it. At first he had been uncomfortable about her picking up the tab for the expensive meals and gifts, but he had quickly become accustomed to it and now accepted it as an integral part of their relationship. Once he had gotten his male macho feelings out of the way, he had actually been somewhat flattered to realize that he was being used as a sex object.

He reached across the table and covered her hand comfortingly with his. "Don't worry, love, everything's going to be all right. Just take it easy, sit back, and relax."

Though she managed an appreciative smile for him, Hilliard knew that she was well aware of what was going on. She knew that the situation was deadly serious and that he was merely trying to make her feel better. At fifty-three she was fifteen years older than he, widowed and lonely, with a vault full of money her husband had left her. Eleven months ago Hilliard had answered a late night call from her expensive north Dallas home about a possible prowler. The well tanned, well muscled ex-marine had taken a few extra minutes to comfort the frightened, quite attractive "older woman" and had stayed for two days.

Now she kept him in spending money and picked up the tab for a lively night life while he, in return, serviced her. Not that it was some unpleasant chore for which he had to be compensated. To the contrary, he would readily have done his duty for free.

She wasn't able to have an orgasm every time they made love, though he always tried to bring her to it, but when she did have one it often lasted for several minutes. She would be almost in a delirious, semi-conscious state during the period, virtually out of her mind with the intense pleasure that kept growing and building upon itself. He had never experienced anything like it. His wife just popped off quickly about any time she wished and then was finished. It was like comparing the sound of a cap pistol to rolling earth shaking thunder that seems to rumble on and on forever.

Although he wasn't able to satisfy her so every time he tried, he now could control it to some extent, though it was more like the limited control one has over a huge roaring fire. He had at last learned how best to guide and sustain her whenever she did reach such a level.

But the best part wasn't the money or the sex, it was the way she treated him. Each time she had an orgasm she openly and sincerely thanked him for giving her such pleasure. Not in a way that was profuse and overdone, but in a manner that made him feel ten feet tall. She was always thankful for his attention, never making demands as so often happens in such a relationship. Rather than begrudging him the time he spent with his family, she showed him how much she enjoyed it when he had the time to be with her. She truly appreciated him and the pleasure he brought her and she never let him forget it.

After almost a year he guessed maybe that they

even loved each other, though such thoughts were never discussed. It was part of their unspoken agreement that he couldn't leave four children and a faithful, if somewhat overweight, wife of fifteen years.

The odd hours and ever changing shifts which were forever a part of his job made a perfect cover for his alternate life. Today, for example, his wife thought he was working. It would all fall apart if it were known that he were here instead, and he wasn't so naive as to think that he could have a shoot-out with three armed men in a place such as this and then just walk away with no questions asked.

At this point, though, there was no reason to feel that he had to do anything. There had been no real crime committed, at least as far as anyone really being harmed at any rate. It could turn out that the ransom would be paid and the men would simply leave quietly. It didn't have to be his problem.

But then, to a certain extent all such thoughts were purely academic. He couldn't take on three men armed with shotguns, not to mention the hand grenades. If he were to shoot one of the men while he was holding a live grenade with the pin removed, at least several dozen people would be killed and injured in the confines of the lounge. Hilliard shifted uncomfortably in his seat once again. No, it didn't have to be his problem.

Two heavily armed patrolmen and a German shepard moved quietly up through the stairwell, finally joining four more men who were stopped on the stairs three flights below the first level of the tower. All four were in sock feet, including the dog. Socks had been slipped over his feet and held in place with rubber bands to keep his nails from clicking too loudly on the stairs.

The group moved up cautiously, automatic weapons held at the ready position. The officer handling the dog led him carefully up to the first door to the observation deck, keeping a tight leash on him lest he bump against it. The dog nosed against the crack of the door but for a second and then promptly laid down.

"Explosives," whispered the handler. The dog was trained to lay down immediately any time explosives were smelled. Otherwise, a dog that suddenly become excited and jumped around uncontrollably might cause the explosives he had just discovered to explode.

The dog was led to the next door on that level and then the four doors on the upper two levels with the same results each time. The group then moved about eight flights of stairs back down the tower before the leader of the group pulled out a walkie talkie.

"Inspector Harris, the dog has identified explosives at all six doors."

Forty-some stories below, Harris grimaced and pulled a fresh roll of antacid tablets from his pocket. He had hoped it was a bluff. He had known that it wasn't, but still he had hoped. So much for the advantage of being there and in position before the extortionists probably realized it.

Harris clicked the transmitter button on his radio twice to acknowledge receipt of the message. With the way noise echoed and carried in the stairwell, they couldn't risk transmitting anything back to the group inside.

"Do you want the snipers back on the hotel roof?" Doug asked.

"No, let's not do anything that might make them nervous; at least not yet. We might as well try calling upstairs now and see if we can get in touch with them."

Frank had been impatiently awaiting contact by the police. He already had answered the phone three times and told the people that they would be accepting no more reservations for lunch or dinner. When the phone rang this time it was the call he had been expecting.

"This is Inspector Harris with the FBI. Who am I speaking to, please?"

"I'm the one you want to talk to, but don't worry about names. They aren't important," Frank said.

Harris's voice was smooth and silky from years of experience with such situations. He had spent much of his career talking to dangerously unstable and unpredictable people under tense circumstances. "That's fine, but we may be talking for a little while, and it's somewhat awkward if I have to say 'hey you' every time I want to say something."

"Okay, then you can call me Tom."

"Good, Tom. Have you got a last name?"

"Tom's good enough. You don't need to know anything else."

"Okay, that's fine. Now Tom, I'm sure you realize that there are an awful lot of cops down here. So this is the deal. If you come on down right now, things are real simple because nobody's been hurt. I'm not going to kid you, Tom. There would be some charges brought against you, but they wouldn't amount to much. For the most part they'd be considered minor. On the other hand, if this goes a little further, maybe things get out of hand and someone gets hurt, then you're in way over your head."

"Save the bull, Harris."

Harris sighed. Sometimes that sort of approach worked, but when a group of people were involved, instead of an individual, and something had been planned in as much detail as this obviously had, then such a line almost never worked. Still, one never knew, so for the record he had to try it.

"Okay, Tom. We've got a bad situation here. What can we do to make it better before it gets any worse?"

"You can get us $3 million, all in one hundred dollar bills. If the serial numbers are in sequential order or if the bills are marked in any way, I'll set fire to the money and throw it off the top of the tower. When we get the money, we'll let the hostages go unharmed. We've attached explosives to all the doors, and we're carrying live hand grenades with the pins removed, so don't try to come up into the tower or you'll blow up a lot of innocent people."

"Well Tom, $3 million is a lot of money. I don't know that anyone can come up with that sort of money without taking an awful long time."

"Millard Hotels can; I read their latest financial statement. Now get the demand passed along to them so we can get this thing moving. The longer this takes, the more nervous we'll get, and the more likely we are to make a mistake with the explosives."

"Certainly no one wants that," Harris replied soothingly.

"Another thing. I'm going to send someone down in the elevator to pick up a package for me. If she brings it back, I'll let her and her boyfriend go. But if she doesn't come back up, I'll throw the guy down the elevator shaft. And she comes back up alone. If anybody comes up with her, we'll start shooting the instant the doors open. We'll have a bunch of hostages standing in front of the elevator doors as a shield, so forget about sending up any of your heroes."

"No problem, Tom. The last thing we want is to get anyone hurt, so I see nothing wrong with what you're asking. What is it that the girl is supposed to get for you?"

"Don't worry about it, she'll know what to get and where it is. She'll be down in a couple of minutes. One last warning, Harris. Once this thing is all over and we leave, we'll be taking a hostage or two with us just to be on the safe side. Of course they'll be released unharmed once we no longer need them, so just make sure that you don't do anything now which might jeopardize their safety later."

Frank laid down the phone on the table and looked around for the girl and the young man in the wheelchair. Because of the slow steady rotation of the floor, they had moved out of his sight. Frank had to walk around to the other side of the lounge to find them again.

"I've got a deal for you," he said to the girl. "You go down in the elevator and bring something back up for me and then I'll let you and your boyfriend both go. How does that sound?"

The couple looked at one another and then quickly nodded. The girl leaned down to kiss her fiance and then followed Frank back to the elevator.

"Do you know what this is?" Frank asked, holding his grenade up so she could plainly see it.

"Yes."

"Can you see that it hasn't got a pin in it?"

"Yes."

Frank then pointed to the stairwell door. "There are also explosives on all the doors leading to the stairs. Now you be sure to tell the FBI that if they try to storm the tower these things will go off and a lot of people will get killed." The girl nodded vigorously.

Frank reached into his pocket and produced three keys. "Here, these will open three baggage lockers across the street there at Union Station. Bring me the three suitcases that you find in the lockers. That's all you can bring. I don't want you to bring anything or anybody else back with you, no matter what the FBI says. Is that clear?"

"Yes it is," the girl replied, nodding even more vigorously.

Frank continued. "If you don't do exactly what I've told you, I'm going to toss your boyfriend down fifty flights of stairs in his wheelchair." With that final warning, Frank removed the chairs which blocked one of the elevator doorways and reached in to pull the stop button back out. The girl stepped inside, the doors closed, and the car silently began its long descent to the ground.

*   *   *

Harris watched closely as Doug finished inspecting the last parachute. "Inspector, as far as I can tell they haven't got anything hidden inside the chutes."

Harris shook his head slowly. "No, I think this is a case of what you see is what you get. Anything that was small enough to be hidden away inside the chutes could have been carried in with them initially. They've already got all the weapons and explosives they need, so I would imagine that this is just what it appears. The suitcases were too big to take in with them without attracting undue attention, so they left them in the baggage lockers at the train station. The weapons and explosives could have been hidden in briefcases easily enough, and most of the people up there this time of the day are businessmen with briefcases."

"It's interesting that there are three extortionists and six parachutes."

"That really doesn't surprise me. They said they will be taking a hostage or two with them when they finally leave. The extra parachutes could be meant for the hostages, or they could be designed to keep us from tampering with the chutes. We can't rig them so they won't open if there's a chance they might put a hostage in one. Though I don't know how much good they think it'll do them to jump off the top of the tower in a parachute."

"There's one thing slightly different about these parachutes," Doug said.

"What's that?"

"These aren't regular parachutes. They're paraplanes."

Harris raised his eyebrows slightly at this revelation. "You mean the type of parachutes that are almost like a hang glider? The type that will let you glide instead of just dropping straight down?"

"Right. You can't glide nearly as far in one of these as you can in a hang glider, but anyone jumping off the top of the tower in one of these could cover quite a bit of distance in a hurry."

"How far could they go?"

"I couldn't say for sure; I've never used one. They could probably make it to the top of a few of the buildings around here and there's a good chance that they could make it all the way across the other side of the interstate highway there. That could give them a good head start."

Harris shook his head again as he stared at the parachutes. "These characters sure are original. I have to say that for them at least."

"Maybe they're planning to wait until after dark before gliding off somewhere. That might make it almost impossible to see where they go."

"That's a good point. I hope we won't be here that long, but you never know on these deals. If it starts to get dark on us, we'll get some heavy searchlights in here. In the meantime, Doug, check with one of the local jump clubs and find out how far they could glide in one of these things. The top of the tower is 570 feet high, and I guess that you'd have to take into account that they would lose a certain amount of altitude before the thing opened fully and started gliding."

"Yes, sir, that makes sense. Even if they jumped on a static line, which they probably would, they'd have to lose some altitude."

"When you find out how far they could go, don't forget to take the wind into account and then set up the police patrols at least a quarter mile farther out than that. The last thing we want is to let them get past us. As long as we keep them hemmed in we should be in good shape."

While Doug headed for the nearet telephone, Harris walked back into the adjoining office where the extortionists' appointed messenger girl waited nervously. "Well, miss, are you still bound and determined to go back up there?"

"Yes, sir, I have to. I don't know if they'll really let

us go or not, but I do believe they may hurt my fiance if I don't do exactly what they said."

Harris was impressed. He had known experienced agents who didn't have near the courage she did. "Okay, the suitcases are ready for you. If they ask you if we looked inside them, tell them the truth. We did. The suitcases were unlocked, so if you say that we didn't look at them they'll know that you're lying. I don't want you to give them any reason, however slight, to be displeased with you."

Harris walked her to the elevator and set the suitcases in beside her. "Don't worry, you're going to be just fine," he called as the doors closed.

Chapter Seven

At Millard Hotels headquarters, the buzzer on Colby Knight's intercom sounded, interrupting his deepest darkest thoughts about Bill Post. He reached across his desk and pressed the talk button.

"Yes?"

"Mr. Knight, Mr. Millard's secretary is on the line. She says that someone from the FBI is trying to get in touch with Mr. Millard. They say that it's extremely urgent."

"Well I'm afraid that Mr. Millard is on a nonstop flight to Honolulu right now and won't be on the ground for another five or six hours."

"Yes, sir, that's what his secretary said, so she thought that maybe you should take the call."

"Okay, I'll see if I can help them." His curiosity piqued, Knight waited for the call to transfer to his line. What could the FBI want with Mr. Millard that was so urgent? After a few seconds his phone gave a short ring. He picked up instantly. "Hello, Colby Knight."

"Mr. Knight, this is Inspector Robert Harris with the FBI."

"Yes, inspector, what can I do for you?"

"Mr. Knight, I'm afraid that you have, well, I don't guess that you would call it a hijacking, but that might be the most descriptive term. Technically, it's an extortion attempt."

"An extortion attempt?"

"That's correct. Three heavily armed men with explosives have taken over the top of Millard Tower. We're estimating that they're holding almost 200 people hostage in the lounge. The thing seems to have been very well planned, and they appear to know exactly what they're doing. They're obviously well organized. Of course, that can be both good and bad."

"How in the world can it be good?"

"Well there's little chance that the extortionists will panic or go crazy and start killing people. You always have that possibility if the person involved is a mental case or a political fanatic of some sort. But it's bad because they won't easily be misled or talked into giving up."

"But why? What do they want?"

"They've demanded a ransom payment of $3 million for the hostages."

"Three million dollars?" Knight was astonished.

"That's right."

"What do we do?"

"I'll be handling everything on this end. What I'd like for you to do is make arrangements to get the ransom money just in case we need it. Of course, it isn't our policy to pay off people in situations such as this unless it's absolutely necessary to save lives when all else has failed."

"Sure, I'll get right on it."

"Fine, I appreciate your cooperation, Mr. Knight. I'll be back in touch shortly."

Knight hung up his phone and pressed his intercom. "Linda, we have an extortion attempt in progress at Millard Tower. Get Hal Johnson and Ben Perkins in here right away."

"Yes, sir!" came the startled reply.

About three minutes later Hal Johnson, the company comptroller, entered Knight's office followed closely by Ben Perkins, the head of the legal department. Both men wore concerned expressions, indicating that they had been given at least some idea of the seriousness of the problem.

As soon as they had seated themselves, Knight began. "I just got a call from the FBI. Three armed men—extortionists they're calling them—are holding 200 people hostage in Millard Tower. They've got bombs and they're demanding a $3 million ransom for the release of the hostages."

Both men widened their eyes in surprise at the amount of the ransom demand. Knight continued. "Hal, can we get that much money on short notice?"

The comptroller rubbed his jaw. "Gosh, if we had two or three days it wouldn't be much trouble at all. On short notice we could get most of it by jerking funds out of our payroll accounts, but that means that the payroll checks would start bouncing. That might be the best bet, though. We could either get an emergency loan from the bank to cover the difference or maybe request that no one cash their paychecks for a few days."

Knight looked immediately to Ben Perkins. "Ben, Mr. Millard is on a plane to Honolulu, and we can't talk to him for another six hours or so. Do I have the legal authority to approve a ransom payment in an emergency such as this?"

Perkins nodded his head without hesitation. "The president of the company has such authority, and with Mr. Millard out of touch, those same powers would pass directly to you, the executive vice president."

"Okay, that brings up one last question. If we hand over any money to these people, will our insurance cover it?"

Perkins shook his head this time. "I'm afraid not. We used to carry insurance that would cover this type of thing back in the sixties when it was fashionable to kidnap business executives and blow up buildings. But in recent years, with that sort of thing going out of style, it hasn't been worth the cost to keep such coverage."

Knight sighed. "I was afraid of that. Hal, don't actually get the cash, but go ahead and lay the groundwork for it, so we can lay our hands on it in a hurry if we need it. Ben, would you coordinate with Hal on the legal aspects of what we need to do?"

"I'll be glad to."

By now the news of the Millard takeover had spread like wildfire throughout the headquarters. Just as Johnson and Perkins were rising to leave, Bill Post charged through Knight's office door without bothering to knock. "I just heard—fill me in," he ordered Knight breathlessly.

Knight's insides tightened. The muscles in his jaw stood out as he gritted his teeth, his lips pressed tightly together. The audacity of that two-faced little bastard bursting in like that and giving orders.

Perkins, well aware of the interoffice politics involved, diplomatically steered Post back toward the door. "Really, Bill, none of us know much at this point. We're all just waiting for the police to take care of things." Post accepted this summary of the situation for the moment and allowed himself to be escorted out by Perkins, who tactfully closed the door behind them.

Knight sat back in his chair breathing heavily, his fists clenched. He could see it coming. Post would try to act as important as possible. His preceding actions were a good example of the manner in which he would conduct himself. Knight also knew that Post would be sneaking around behind him documenting everything he did. Post would then miss no opportunity to point out to others how Knight had bungled things.

For the past three months Knight had been virtually obsessed with Post. He felt as if he were close to a breaking point. But suddenly, through the hatred and the frustration, he realized something. If he were to handle this emergency situation so as to demonstrate his leadership abilities, Post would gain nothing. In fact, Post would lose. With the proper outcome to the crisis, Knight would be practically assured of the presidency. His mind raced with the realization of what he could do. How would he go about firing Post? Lord, it would be fantastic however he did it.

He had it! He would walk into Post's office and pull a notebook out of his pocket. He would then announce that Post had caused a cigarette burn in the lobby carpet and that the expense of replacing the carpet would be deducted from his last paycheck.

Knight's tight lipped expression spread into a thin smile, exposing his still clenched teeth. He slammed his right fist into the palm of his left hand. That two-faced little bastard is mine, he thought with grim satisfaction.

When the elevator finally returned to the top of the tower again, Frank, Carl, and Angelo all three were nervously aiming their weapons at the doors which opened to reveal only the girl and three suitcases. Frank quickly reached in and pushed the stop button again, and then pulled the three suitcases out one by one.

"Okay, go get your boyfriend," Frank said. He squatted down and opened the suitcases one at a time, lifting each lid just far enough to see that each still contained two parachutes. He then felt carefully around inside the lining pockets until he located Tom Agnew's laundry slip which he had placed inside. He could tell from the position of the paper that it had been removed and then replaced.

Frank stepped back to the hostess stand and picked up the telephone. "Hello, Harris, are you there?"

The voice that answered was not the one he expected. "This isn't Inspector Harris, but I'll get him. Wait just a minute."

There was an annoying delay of two or three minutes and then the voice on the other end was just as silky and reassuring as ever. "Hello, this is Inspector Harris. Did you get the suitcases all right?"

"Yeah, yeah that worked out real nice. You keep doing everything exactly like we say and stay calm and we'll stay calm up here. I'm sending the girl and her boyfriend back down in the elevator like I promised, but I want the elevator back up here right away. If you don't send it back immediately, I'll pry the doors open and drop a grenade down the shaft. I'm not about to take a chance on you using it against us, so it won't do you any good to hang onto it. Is that clear?"

"Okay, Tom. We'll send the elevator right back up. There's something else I'd like to suggest to you, though. Our communications aren't very good with this telephone. We can't get in touch with each other very quickly unless we're both tied to the phone all the time. Why don't I send a walkie-talkie up to you? It's got a paging buzzer on it, so that would allow us to have immediate, open communications with each other all the time."

"What's the range of the walkie-talkie? Will you have to be up inside the stairwell with the other receiver?"

"Oh no, these things have a long range. I'll be down here on the ground with the other set."

"Yeah, that'll be okay then. You can send it back up in the elevator, but the same rules still apply. You can't send anything or anybody else up or we'll start shooting."

"Fine, that's just the way we'll do it then," Harris agreed amicably.

By now the girl and her fiance had returned to the elevator and were waiting quietly. Frank stepped aside so they could enter the car. "Okay, you're both free to go; take off." The doors closed as the grateful couple left the top floor of the tower for the last time, and Frank and his group were forced to wait nervously once again for the return of the elevator.

Doug gently laid the walkie-talkie on the floor of the elevator, but he hesitated for a moment, continuing to hold the doors open. "Why don't we put a man either on top or beneath the elevator?"

Harris shook his head no. "I don't think so. With the live grenades they're waving around, sending one man up there could be worse than sending none. If they were to figure out what we had done and panic, it could get a lot of people killed real quick. No, we had better stick with what we've got for the time being at least."

Now it was Harris's turn to hesitate as he stared into the empty elevator, his brow furrowed. He finally started to speak again, slowly, as if thinking aloud. "If we had a steel plate a few inches wider than the opening into the elevator and about an inch shorter, we could slide it in and prop it up over the doorway from the inside. With firing slits cut in it, it would be like having an armored car up there."

Harris straightened up and began issuing orders in rapid fire order again. "Doug, get with ballistics or whoever might know and find out how thick a metal plate would have to be to withstand a close-up blast from a shotgun or a hand grenade. Then make it a little thicker than that. Have them cut four firing slits in it, two high and two low, for two men standing and two kneeling. Tell them to get it down here as quick as they can."

"Are we going in?" Doug asked.

"No, not right now, but if we eventually end up having to, this sort of approach might work out a lot better than anything else we could do. Remember,

the girl who carried the suitcases said that all three
of them were standing there waiting for the elevator
and they weren't using any of the hostages as a
shield. We might be able to take them all out at once,
right there in front of the elevators."

"What about the grenades?"

"That's the only problem. We still have to worry
about those things going off in that crowded lounge,
so we'll use the shield only if we're forced to go in at
some point."

When the elevator arrived back at the top of the
tower it was empty again, exactly as Frank had instructed, except for the walkie-talkie lying on the
floor. Frank first took the precaution of pressing the
stop button before picking up the radio. He examined it closely for a few seconds and then turned to
Carl, silently mouthing the word "screwdriver" as he
pointed to a screw on the back of the case. Carl
passed him a small screwdriver and watched as Frank
slowly and carefully removed the six screws which
held the back cover plate in position. He then gently
lifted the back off and peered into the radio's inner
workings.

Having found what he was seeking, Frank held
the walkie-talkie up for Carl's inspection. As Carl
leaned down for a closer look, Frank pointed out a
small electronic device taped inside the case. It obviously wasn't a normal part of the radio. Carl nodded. Frank then quietly reattached the back of the
case.

Satisfied at last, Frank turned on the radio's power
switch and pressed the transmit button. "Hey, Harris, this is Tom. Can you hear me down there?"

Harris's answer was prompt. "You're loud and clear,
Tom. How do you hear me?"

"Good." Frank turned toward Carl. "Hey, this thing
works great. I'm glad we got it."

Frank pressed the transmit button again. "Okay, Harris, we just let two people go to show what nice guys we are, but if we don't see some money before long, you're going to get some people hurt. Now I don't plan to sit here and yap with you all day, so if you don't have something important to tell me, just keep your mouth shut. If you don't like it that way, then I'll just toss this thing back down the stairs."

Harris clenched his teeth, his face reddening slightly, but he kept his composure as he replied. "Okay, Tom. We'll keep the talk to a minimum."

Frank nodded to Carl and then held the walkie-talkie out between them without pressing the transmit button. Carl spoke first.

"Ah, hey Tom. We've been thinking. I mean, we were wondering; what happens if they won't give us the money? We don't mind shooting a few people if we have to, but what if it just doesn't do us any good? Then we could go to jail for murder. Maybe we should be doing what the cops offered. If we give up now they won't really have too much on us. Like they said, that's a lot of money for anybody to come up with on short notice."

Frank spoke next, still not pressing the transmit button. "What are you talking about? We've got everything set up exactly like we want it. They can't get near us. If they touch a single one of those doors they'll blow the whole top off this place."

"I don't know, Tom. Maybe, your uncle should have been in on this with us. He's the real expert on this sort of thing. Maybe we shouldn't have gone ahead without him after he got himself busted in that drug deal."

"I'm telling you, we haven't got a thing to worry about. I wish my uncle was here, too, but he isn't. It's way too late to back out now, so I don't want to hear anything else about it."

"Okay, Tom. You're the boss. We'll go along with whatever you say. But if you decide we should give it up, then we're willing to go along with that too."

Frank smiled and silently gave Carl a thumbs up signal, their carefully scripted conversation concluded. Carl turned around and began to walk back to his position, but as he passed behind the hostess stand he accidentally bumped his arm against it, dropping his grenade on the floor.

Carl grumbled to himself as he bent down to retrieve it. He had to fiddle with the thing for several seconds before he could get the clip back into place. It was an annoyance instead of a problem since he had dropped it behind the hostess stand so that none of the hostages had been able to see what happened. If he had done something that stupid out where someone could have seen it, they might suddenly have had a serious problem on their hands.

Only a couple of people had noticed Carl's actions, and they didn't really think anything about it or attach any special significance to it. But Jack Hilliard had noticed it, and it wasn't what he saw that got his attention so much as what he heard.

After six years as a marine drill instructor, it was a sound that Hilliard would have recognized in his sleep. The clip had popped off the dropped grenade. And the man's actions after he dropped it were telling indeed. He hadn't been frightened, he had been irritated. Hilliard understood then what he had been aware of all along without actually realizing. All three men were simply too relaxed, too nonchalant about carrying live grenades around. The grenades were fakes. They were just for show.

Maybe even the explosives on the doors were fake. At any rate, things were now far different from what they originally had seemed. If one or more of the men were taken down now, it would make no difference that the grenades might be dropped. Hilliard was no longer facing three men with explosives, it was just three men with shotguns. That in itself was a formidable match for one man and a .38 special, but then, no harm had been done to anyone so far. It still didn't have to be his problem.

Colby Knight's secretary buzzed his intercom. "Mr. Knight, Inspector Harris with the FBI is on the line again."

"Oh yes, I'll take it."

"Hello, inspector. How are things going over there?"

"Not very well at this point, I'm afraid. We managed to plant a listening device inside the tower, and we've been able to identify one of the extortionists. I hope we'll be able to find a relative who would be willing to come down and talk to him."

"That certainly sounds promising."

"Yes it is, but on the other hand, based on what we've overheard on our listening device, we believe that the extortionists are ready and willing to start killing the hostages if they don't get exactly what they want. For that reason, we'll need you to get the ransom money together just in case."

"But why even fool with the ransom?" Knight asked. "Why don't you just rush them? Get it over quickly."

"We've considered that possibility ourselves, but we now have a pretty good description of what's going on inside the tower from a couple of hostages who were just released a few minutes ago. The extortionists are carrying live grenades and sawed-off shotguns and they've placed explosives on all the doors. That means they could kill an awful lot of people before we could get anywhere near them. Taking the tower by force would be a desperation last ditch move in this case. It looks like we'll need the ransom money standing by just in case. Do you foresee any problems in getting it?"

Knight leaned comfortably back in his chair and propped his feet up on one of his desk drawers with the air of a man with complete confidence in himself. "Well at this point any discussion of a ransom payment is irrelevant."

Harris was puzzled. "I don't understand. Are you saying that you can't get the money?"

"No, I'm saying that we aren't going to give them any money."

"Wait just a minute, Mr. Knight. I guess I didn't make myself completely clear. We're not going to give them your money except as a last resort to keep them from killing the hostages. And even then they would have very little chance of getting away with it. We've got an excellent track record when it comes to recovering money that's been paid in these sort of situations."

Knight replied calmly and with great patience, as one would explain something to a child. "Inspector Harris, as you know, these sort of things tend to run in cycles. If these terrorists or extortionists or whatever you wish to call them get away with this, then a whole rash of nuts will try exactly the same thing. If not here, then elsewhere. If these sort of people knew in advance that they would get absolutely nothing, then they would probably never even consider such a stunt. In the past large companies, and the airlines are the best example, have just given in and handed over the money, thus making the problem even worse.

"Millard Hotels will not be blackmailed into negotiating with common criminals. We won't give them one red cent. Period. I don't care what they do or threaten to do. Now, I realize that the company's official stand on this matter might make these people feel trapped—as if they have no way out. I am therefore willing to offer them $5,000 out of my own pocket and will give them the use of our private company jet to take them anywhere in the world they wish to go. This isn't meant to be bribe money, and it isn't a case of the company giving in. I feel a deep personal concern for the safety of each one of those hostages, and my hope is that the $5,000 will give these criminals some incentive to let them go unharmed. Without any money at all, they might not feel that escape would be possible, and they therefore would have no reason to let the hostages go."

Harris was amazed. "Mr. Knight, you don't understand the situation down here. This is not some sort of a game we're playing. These people are fully prepared to start killing the hostages, so we must have the money, or at least part of it, as a last reort."

Knight leaned forward and pounded the top of his desk with his fist. "Millard Hotels does not deal with criminals! You tell them that. The next time some nut decides to pull something like this, you'd better believe that it won't be on us."

Knight calmly placed the telephone receiver back on the hook and leaned back comfortably in his chair once again. Not only would he be a company hero, he would be a hero throughout the entire hotel industry. He would be known as the man who singlehandedly stopped the hostage/extortion threat once and for all. When it was finally realized that large companies would no longer pay a ransom no matter what was threatened, the problem would practically go away by itself. He and Millard Hotels would be sure to make national headlines, business would increase, and he would be given a nice fat bonus in addition to the company presidency.

If things went as well as he hoped, he could even envision his picture on the cover of *Business Week* or *Fortune*. What kind of a picture would be best? One of those dignified shots of a high-ranking *Fortune* 500 executive in his office looking important? No, a shot of him standing on the roof of the Dallas Millard Hotel with Millard Tower looming behind him would be more impressive. The cover title would read something like "Colby Knight Takes Control." This undoubtedly would bring numerous job offers from other companies, both in and out of the hotel industry.

Knight's daydream was interrupted at that point by Bill Post barging into his office unannounced without knocking. "Just wanted to let you know; since the gathering together of the ransom money falls into the responsibility of my department, I'll handle the rest of the matter from now on."

Knight looked at Post. Normally, a ploy like this would have raised Knight's blood pressure dramatically, but this was a totally different situation. He basked in the knowledge that he was in control and could do with Post as he pleased. He owned Bill Post.

Knight rose calmly to his feet and leaned across his desk, resting both hands on its surface. "There are two reasons why you will be handling nothing in this matter. Number one, I am legally in charge as long as Mr. Millard is out of touch. And secondly, but just as important, this situation doesn't call for a pudgy little back-stabber who hasn't got any balls."

Post's mouth dropped open and then closed as his face turned a deep crimson. With a look which on a child would plainly have said "I'm telling," Post turned and scurried back to his office to document what had just happened.

It had been only a small expression of Knight's innermost feelings, but it had been extremely gratifying. It was the release he had needed desperately for months. Knight smiled as he propped his feet up and visualized the cover of *Business Week* once again.

Chapter Eight

When Harris realized that Knight had just hung up on him, he slammed down the phone so hard it rang, his stomach burning angrily. How do you reason with someone who's so self-righteous, who has all the answers, who gets to sit up in an isolated office somewhere and make decisions about other people's lives; someone who doesn't have to see and sleep with the results of those lofty, unrealistic decisions about life and death and what's better in the long run. Harris knew that he himself would have to live with the 200 people who might end up dead over this thing.

"Excuse me, inspector," Doug said.

"What is it?" Harris snapped.

"It checks out. Tom Agnew has an uncle, a D. J. Agnew, who was recently arrested in a drug operation."

"Good, any idea where is he?"

"Well, yes and no. He's the key witness in this federal drug case, so he's now hidden away in our witness protection program."

"That's Bob King's outfit. Get him on the phone."

Doug signaled Harris to the telephone a couple of minutes later. "Hello, Bob? Robert Harris here. How are you doing, old buddy?"

"No complaints, Robert. What can I do for you?"

"I hear you've got a guy named D. J. Agnew under wraps."

"Yes, what about him?"

"Well we've got a bad situation down here at Millard Tower. Three heavily armed men with explosives are holding almost 200 people hostage. They've made a $3 million ransom demand. We've found out that the leader of the group is a college student at SMU named Tom Agnew. He's D. J. Agnew's nephew. We've managed to plant a bug up in the tower and from what we've heard it sounds as if Tom Agnew would listen seriously to anything his uncle had to say. We need your boy to come down here and talk to him."

"Come on, Harris. You know we can't do that. We could let Agnew talk to his nephew over the phone, but we can't bring him down there."

"It won't be as effective over the phone. In fact, from what I can tell already, it isn't going to work unless it's face to face. This guy wouldn't believe that it's his uncle. He'd just say that we put somebody up to it."

"Aren't there any other relatives who could talk to him?"

Harris rubbed his temple where it was beginning to throb. "No, only a stepbrother who lives somewhere out on the west coast, but from what we've been able to find out, they've never gotten along very well. Tom Agnew's parents are both dead."

"No wife or girl friend?" King asked.

"None that we've been able to find. You'll just have to bring Agnew down here to try it in person."

"Sorry, Harris. You know we can't do that."

Harris's voice was still amiable and diplomatic, as it had been in dealing with the extortionists and with Colby Knight. "Come on, Bob, you don't have anything to worry about. Do you have any idea how many cops we have down here?"

"That doesn't matter. It's against all our procedures. We can't move him."

The civility and the diplomacy was beginning to fade fast from Harris's voice. "Listen, Agnew is the only shot we've got in this deal. Now if you don't get him down here, and fast, a lot of these people may end up dead. We don't have time to play around."

The voice at the other end of the line was polite but firm. "I'm sorry, I'd like to help you but I can't."

"Listen up, pal. There are a hundred newsmen waiting outside. If I haven't got D. J. Agnew in the flesh within sixty minutes, I'm going to tell them that you are personally responsible; that you are keeping him for selfish, idiotic, bureaucratic reasons; that if anybody in that tower is harmed, it's all your fault, your personal responsibility. I know how to set you up for the fall if any of those people get hurt, and I'll sure do it.

"You better make sure that your hair's combed and you look real pretty, because you're going to be a celebrity. You're going to have television cameras in your face wanting to know why you won't help those poor people up there. About three million people are going to see your smiling face on the evening news."

Harris paused only long enough to get his breath. "In fact, you'll probably be seen by more than three million people, because if this thing drags out much longer, you're going to have national exposure. You're going to be on the national news. Maybe we'll have about a hundred people dead by then. And I guarantee that I'm going to hang the entire responsibility for their safety on your tail. You've got sixty minutes."

Harris slammed down the phone without waiting for a reply. "Do you think he'll do it?" Doug asked cautiously.

"He'll be here in fifty-nine minutes," Harris declared. "He's a brown-nosing bureaucrat whose number one priority is worrying about how he looks and how it will affect his illustrious career. He's on the phone right now to someone above him. He won't take it on himself to bring Agnew down here. He'll get someone else to give the okay, and then he's covered his lily-white rear end from both directions."

Harris finished off the last of his antacid tablets with a grimace, patting his coat pockets for more. They didn't seem to do much good after a while, and all the waiting didn't help matters.

"Hey, Agnew." The prison guard's call was loud but certainly not disrespectful. When you work around hundreds of men who could slip a knife into you practically at will, you quickly learn whom you push around and whom you do not. The inside guards didn't even carry weapons, as they could too easily be taken away and used against their owners.

Paul Agnew looked up from a book. "Yeah?"

"Warden wants to see you and your brother on the double."

"Yeah, what's up?"

"Whadaya mean what's up? If I was the warden's closest confidant, would I be down here mixin' it up with the low life?"

"Oh, sorry Baker. I forgot for a minute that you're merely a scummy little pervert."

"Yeah, yeah. Come on, hurry it up. The warden sounded like it was really important. Where's your brother?"

"He's in the can. You wanna run in and watch? He oughta be wipin' about now—your favorite part." Baker didn't bother to answer, afraid he had run his mouth a little too much as it was.

A few minutes later D. J. Agnew sauntered casually down the corridor. No one would have known that the two were brothers. Paul was the younger. At forty-three he had graying hair and still had a trim figure, while D. J., on the other hand, was forty pounds overweight, with bushy red hair and a ruddy complexion to go with it.

No one would have ever put a protected federal witness in a prison, so that's why Bob King had done it—because no one would ever think to look there. D. J.'s brother was already there serving time, so they had simply stuck them into solitary together, and only a few people knew they were even there.

Paul looked up from his book as D. J. entered. "Hey, D. J., the scumball here says the warden wants to see us."

"Yeah, well he knows where we are. If he wants to see us, he can shag his tail down here."

"Aw come on, guys," Baker whined. "The warden sounded like it was something really important. He's gonna be mad if you won't come up."

"Well just great!" Paul declared as he slammed his book closed. "The only way we're gonna get rid of the stench is to go see what he wants."

The two brothers started down the hall with the subdued guard tagging along behind. They passed through the three checkpoints separating the warden's office from the prison population and entered the warden's outer office which housed several secretaries.

"The Agnews here to see the warden as ordered," Baker announced to one of the secretaries. The girl gave Baker a disgusted look and pressed the interphone button. "The Agnews are here, Mr. Casey."

"Send them right in."

Paul led the way into the inner office trailed by D.J. and Baker. The warden looked up from his desk. "Thank you, Baker, that's all for now."

Baker looked crestfallen. "Yes, sir," he said as he backed out of the room and disappointedly closed the door. There were two men in the room with the warden that looked like feds, and he was dying to know what they wanted with the Agnews. The men certainly weren't ordinary visitors or they wouldn't have been going through the warden.

Back inside the office, Bob King, one of the feds, gestured to a pair of chairs. D. J. and Paul sat down. King didn't look very happy. In fact, he looked somewhat red and flushed, as though he were quite angry.

"Problems?" D. J. asked.

"Yes and no," King answered. "You have a nephew named Tom Agnew?" It was more a statement than a question.

D. J. nodded. "Yeah, what about him?"

"Well, at this minute he's holding about two hundred people hostage at the top of Millard Tower."

D. J. and Paul exchanged skeptical looks. "You gotta be kidding or crazy or both." Paul nodded in agreement with D. J.'s statement.

"We're not kidding or crazy. This guy says that his name is Tom. He won't tell us his last name, but he had us bring him a suitcase from a baggage locker; the case belongs to Tom Agnew. We bugged the tower and heard Tom mention his uncle."

Paul and D. J. listened in amazement. They couldn't believe what they were hearing, but they had no reason to believe that the FBI had fabricated the story. Paul spoke again. "So you figure we're behind it, huh?"

"No, we know you're not involved from what we've overheard inside the tower. But D. J., we want you to come to the tower and talk to your nephew. He's got two other men with him who'll do whatever he says. He's the key. If you talk him into giving up, they all give up."

Paul frowned. "Why in the world should D. J. go up there? We ain't had nothing to do with the kid since his old man died. He's always been a little spacey, and it sounds like he's finally flipped out."

Bob King persisted. "Again, from what we've heard him say, we believe that he would listen to D. J."

"Yeah, well I still don't see why I should fool with you or him," D. J. snapped.

King leaned forward. "Your brother here comes up for parole in five months. He may or may not get it. If you come out and talk to the boy, whether it does any good or not, the agency will go to bat for Paul with the parole board. If you don't help us, though, the agency will make sure that the board hears about that, too. Now let's say that somebody gets hurt in this takeover. Even though Paul wasn't involved in it, they would probably treat him as if he were. Especially when we point out how he advised you not to help out."

D. J. narrowed his eyes. "You gonna put that in writing? That Paul gets out early?"

"We can't guarantee anything, but we will put it in writing that we'll inform the parole board of his unselfish assistance in trying to avert a potential tragedy."

D. J. glanced at Paul as he spoke. "Well, I'd wanna run it by our lawyer first." Paul nodded his agreement.

"Okay, but it has to be quick. We don't have much time."

D. J. leaned across the warden's desk and grabbed the phone, dialing a number from memory. "Yeah, this is D. J. Agnew. I gotta talk to Chuck right now . . . I don't care who he's in a meeting with, honey. If you don't tell him that I'm on the phone, you're gonna be sittin' on your can out in the street." He paused for a few seconds. "Hey, Chuck, D. J." He quickly repeated the happenings of the last few minutes, then listened intently.

"Three stipulations," he said, pointing the receiver at King. "You give us what you said in writing before we go, everybody signs it including the warden as a witness, and it's notarized. Then you give us a copy that we hand deliver to our lawyer who's gonna meet us at the tower. Second, in the statement you say that it was our idea to go talk to the kid. You just came to us to find out if we thought that it might be him. Last, I get to talk to the press at the tower—before and after I talk to the kid."

King looked quite uncomfortable, but he knew he had no other choice. "Okay, you've got it."

"Okay, Chuck, we'll meet you there." D. J. hung up the phone, then turned to Paul and slapped him on the shoulder. "Come on, I can't be seen like this. I've gotta get into something a little more respectable." So saying, they rose and banged out of the office, almost stepping on Baker who was seated just outside the door.

"Come on, hurry up," D. J. ordered as the two headed through the outer office toward the door. Baker jumped up and hesitated for a moment, looking questioningly into the warden's office. Since the warden and the two men were ignoring him completely, he finally turned and hurried to catch up with the Agnews who were already well down the hall.

Harris was wrong about Bob King delivering Agnew within fifty-nine minutes. He had him there in fifty-five.

King strode into the room accompanied by two uniformed police officers and four plainclothes men. He tried to look angry, thus putting the best face on what he perceived to be an embarrassing situation. "I hope you're satisfied," King snapped.

"Where is he?" Harris asked.

King pointed at one of the uniformed officers who had entered the room with him. "That's him."

Harris smiled for the first time that morning. "That's pretty good. Hide a tree in the forest."

King stood very close to Harris, his face reddening further. "Get this and get it straight. From right here on, he's yours. If anything happens to him, it's your rear, not mine."

Harris ignored King and picked up the walkie-talkie that linked him to the tower. The voice was silky smooth and accommodating once again. "Hello, Tom, this is Inspector Harris."

"Good to hear from you again, Harris. Things have been kinda quiet down there. Have you got the money?"

"No, no word on it yet. Like I told you, it takes time to get that much cash together, even for a large company. I called about something else, Tom. I've got somebody down here who would like to talk to you."

"I don't need to talk to anybody else."

"It's your uncle. He's very concerned about you."

Everyone in the room waited silently to hear what kind of response this sudden revelation would bring. After a long pause the radio crackled again. "You can cut the cheap tricks right now. You don't know who I am. Everybody's got uncles."

Harris responded in his usual calm and deliberate manner. "Tom, your uncle D. J. Agnew is here to talk to you. He would like to help if he can. Here, I'll let him talk to you now."

The response was immediate and incensed this time. "Hold it, Harris! I'm not talking to anybody but you. I told you before, if you try to start anything with this radio, I'll throw the thing right down the stairs. How did you find out who I am?"

"Tom, all we did was look inside your suitcase and find your name on a piece of paper. We're not trying to pull anything. We checked with your friends and family and found out that your uncle wanted to come out and talk to you. Let me put him on now."

"Forget it. I'm not talking to anybody. How do I know that you've really got my uncle down there, anyway?"

"I'll tell you what. I'll put him on and you can ask him a few questions to make sure that it's really him."

"Do you think I'm that stupid? You probably have a computer down there with everything about me and my family already in it."

"If you don't trust me, then why don't I just send

him up in the elevator? There's no way we could pull something that way. Come on, he wants to talk to you. I've gone along with everything you've wanted so far. Now it's your turn. Send the elevator down for your uncle; he'll come up all alone"

"Okay, Harris, you can send him up. You can send him up with the money. When you've got it, you send him up with it."

Harris rubbed his stomach, one his ulcers biting at him again. He pressed the transmitter button and then released it for a moment to rethink his answer once more. Finally he pressed the button and started talking. "Tom, the only problem with that suggestion is that we don't know how much longer it'll take to get the money together. If your uncle could come on up now, then when the money gets here he could come back down and get it for you."

Harris waited breathlessly for an answer. There was a long pause before anything else was said. "If my uncle's really there, I would like to see him. But if this is a trick . . ."

"No tricks, Tom," Harris hastily assured him. "He'll come up all by himself and you'll see him with your own two eyes. There's no way I could trick you about that."

"Okay, I'll send the elevator down. But I want his hands up and no coat on when those doors open. If not, he's a dead man."

"Okay, Tom, I'll tell him."

Harris laid down the walkie-talkie and turned to Agnew. "How well do you get along with your nephew?"

"I haven't seen him in a while, but we've never had any problems. He's maybe a little spacey, but he's always been a pretty straight kid. It's hard for me to believe that he's mixed up in anything like this."

"That's why we want you to talk to him. If he's just mixed up, then we've got a good chance of getting everybody down, him included, without anybody getting hurt. You better change clothes, though. You don't want to come popping out of that elevator looking like a cop."

D. J. quickly peeled off the outer layer of clothing and once again looked like a normal civilian. It was then that the commotion at the door was heard.

"You've got to let me in, I'm telling you. I've got a right to see my client, D. J. Agnew."

"What's going on over there?" Harris asked.

Bob King smiled. He knew that Harris wasn't going to enjoy this part, and that meant that King would.

Chuck Martin, the Agnews' sleazy looking lawyer, pushed his way into the room. D. J. shouted and waved at him. "Hey Chuck, this is some operation they got here. We could learn some things from these guys."

Martin nodded and then turned to face Harris, who appeared to be in charge. "I believe you have a document for me?"

"Who are you and what are you talking about?" Harris growled.

King handed Martin a folded piece of paper. "Here you go—signed, sealed, and delivered."

Martin opened the paper and scanned it thoroughly before placing it securely in his briefcase. "That seems to be in order. Now we'll speak to the press."

Harris's stomach knotted on him even more. "I don't know who you are or what you think you're doing, but you're not talking to anybody." Harris looked around at Doug. "Get him outa here!"

King grinned again. "This is Mr. Agnew's lawyer. We've agreed that they can speak to the press before Mr. Agnew goes up to the tower."

Harris didn't answer as he stared at King; his face just got red and the veins started standing out. King smiled at him, enjoying every second of it.

Doug tried to defuse the situation. "Inspector, maybe we could bring in a few of the reporters to

speak with him in here. That would be the best way
to handle it."

The lawyer shook his head. "Uh-uh, no way. We
talk to the whole bunch of them—out there—or no
deal. We've got it in writing that we can do it that
way."

"Get this circus over with," Harris snarled to Doug.

Doug quickly called to two other agents. "Wayne,
Jim, grab your coats. We need an escort."

The two agents joined them as they moved out of
the room and toward the unsecured area where the
press was gathered. As soon as they stepped into
view, a mob of reporters descended on them with
microphones and television lights. A flurry of questions hit them from all sides. D. J. Agnew had become quite a media figure since being hidden away
for the trial, so he was immediately recognized by
many of the reporters who had at least seen pictures
of him.

The lawyer played the crowd like a piano. "Please,
no questions," he shouted as he attempted to make
way for his clients. The agents weren't about to di-
vulge any information, and Agnew followed the lead
of his lawyer. When the crowd around them seemed
to have swollen to its greatest size, the lawyer finally
halted the procession.

"Wait a minute, please," he shouted, dramatically
waving his arms. "The FBI has told us not to comment, but I do feel that the press has a right to be
informed when the lives of so many people are at
stake."

The reporters quieted down considerably as they
strained to hear what was being said. The lawyer
continued the melodrama.

"The FBI, working on information provided by
my clients, D. J. and Paul Agnew, has reason to
believe that one of the extortionists is a nephew of
my clients."

At this revelation another flurry of questions filled

the air. The lawyer once again waved his arms dramatically. "Please, please. Mr. Agnew has volunteered to go to the tower in an attempt to talk the extortionists into releasing the hostages and giving themselves up. I'm afraid that the FBI has instructed us to say nothing more concerning the matter. Thank you."

The lawyer then began edging the group back toward the elevators as the reporters once again began to shout at the top of their lungs. Amid much pushing and shoving, the group finally managed to squeeze back through a door, leaving a crowd of frustrated reporters on the other side.

As soon as the door was closed securely, the reporters scattered in all directions looking for telephones. The information they had just received, though skimpy, contained the most surprising and dramatic twist they could have hoped for.

Chapter Nine

Linda stuck her head around the corner into Knight's office. "Mr. Knight, quick, they've got it on television."

Knight wheeled around and slid open a door in his bookcase to reveal a small television. "What channel is it?" he asked as he waited for the set to warm up and produce a picture.

"It's on almost all of them, but Channel 11 has the best shot of it from their helicopter."

Knight flipped the selector to eleven as the picture came into view. The screen showed an excellent view of the tower. The announcer was droning on about the latest developments concerning the attempt by D. J. Agnew to speak to the extortionists. The picture had been shot from the helicopter but now switched back to a view from the ground, which showed the helicopter hovering above the tower.

Knight scowled as he watched the helicopter. The announcer was going on boringly about how Newsship 11 (the helicopter) was on the scene as usual. Using a helicopter to cover the news was fine as far as Knight was concerned, but this station ran it into the ground. Every time you turned on the channel you had to see their stupid helicopter. If they ran a story about the underground sewers, they would have a shot of the helicopter covering the action. In fact, they had almost as much footage of the helicopter as of the news stories themselves. Having had his fill of Newsship 11, Knight angrily selected another channel.

Meanwhile, sets were being turned on all over Millard headquarters as the news spread that the airplane was on television. Most of the viewers, as Knight had done, tried to avoid having to watch Newsship 11.

Frank stepped into the bathroom and stuck the walkie-talkie down into his briefcase. He stuffed some paper towels down around it to muffle it further, and then walked back out to the elevators. He carefully checked his shotgun again, licked his lips anxiously, and wiped his sweaty palms on his pants. He didn't want to kill anybody. The other night with Tom Agnew had been a horrible unforeseen accident. He had just planned to tie him up and leave him for a couple of days. It would have worked, too, if Angelo hadn't started trying to scare the guy.

Nobody was supposed to get hurt on this thing. Not killed, not hurt. Except for this D. J. Agnew guy. He was the reason they were here. Frank knew that he had no choice. If he didn't kill D. J. Agnew, he'd be dead within the week himself unless he ran, and he had already concluded that such a move wouldn't work.

He had checked out the file on D. J. Agnew. Bad character; into drugs and all which went with it; suspect in half a dozen murders. The guy had a record that went back some fifteen years. They almost needed a separate filing cabinet just for him. This wasn't any innocent, upstanding member of the community. The man probably would receive the death penalty if all the truth were ever to come out in court. But even so, Frank didn't want to kill anybody, not even someone like Agnew. He just didn't have any choice.

Carl and Angelo didn't know about this part, why they were really here. The money was just extra. They thought they had set Tom Agnew up just to throw the cops off on the wrong track, to muddy the waters as much as possible. He would tell Carl and Angelo later that it had been a setup, that the guy had pulled a gun when the elevator doors had opened.

He signaled Carl to join him. "They're going to send this D. J. Agnew guy, the uncle, up in the elevator."

"But why? Why did you tell them they could do that? Even with the ski masks he'll figure out right off that his nephew isn't really up here."

"Don't worry, it'll be okay. The cops were starting to get real pushy, so I gave in to buy us a little more time. You and Angelo stay around the corner out of sight, and when the elevator doors open I'll tell Agnew to go back down because Tom has changed his mind about seeing him. Then I'll call the cops and tell them that they can send the uncle back up with the money when it comes. See how that'll work? That'll give them even more incentive to get us the money."

Carl hesitantly nodded in agreement. "Okay, I guess that sounds all right. I'll let Angelo know what we're doing."

"Thanks."

"Oh, one other thing," Carl said.

"Yeah?"

"Did you know that there's a helicopter over us?"

"What? Where?"

"We just spotted him a few minutes ago. He's trying to stay right over us, but a couple of times we've just caught a glimpse of him out the window."

Frank's face flushed red. He hurried across the room to the window and looked up. He didn't have to wait long to see the helicopter float into view, then move back out of sight directly above them. He walked back to the bathroom and retrieved the walkie-talkie. "Harris!"

The voice coming over Harris's walkie talkie was filled with anger. Harris was surprised at the sudden change in mood. "Yes, Tom, what's the problem?"

"You know as well as I do what's the problem. If that helicopter isn't gone in thirty seconds, I'm going to start throwing people down the stairs. In fact, I'm going to kick one out every thirty seconds until it's gone."

Harris hadn't even been aware of the helicopter. "Wait just a minute, Tom. That's not ours; it must belong to one of the television stations. I didn't even realize it was there."

"So get rid of it."

"Okay, I will. But since it's not one of ours, it may take some time to get in touch with it. You've got to give us just a few minutes, please."

"Okay, you've got two minutes and then I start kicking people out. I'm looking at a ninety year old lady here who's gonna be the first one." Frank didn't really see a ninety year old lady, but he thought it sounded pretty good.

Harris hurried into the next room where a communications center had been set up. Harris shouted to the police officer who was manning the radios. "There's a television chopper hovering over the tower. Get them out of there!"

The communications officer immediately began trying various frequencies. Newsship 11 was monitoring the police frequencies, as usual, so the officer was quickly able to raise them. "Will the helicopter hovering above Millard Tower please identify yourself."

The transmission from the helicopter was scratchy but readable. The pilot used the craft's "show" title rather than its proper call sign. "This is Newsship 11."

"You are hovering over a restricted police area without clearance. Clear the area immediately."

"Roger, we'll be finished here in just a minute."

Harris's stomach again churned as his ulcer gnawed at his insides. He reached over across the communication officer's shoulder and grabbed the microphone out of his hand.

"This is the FBI," he shouted into the microphone. "You're going to get some of those hostages killed in another minute. If you don't get out of there immediately, I'll give orders to open fire on you. Now move it!"

The pilot's reply sounded, on the whole, a bit disinterested. "Yeah, almost finished."

Almost in a fury, Harris grabbed a nearby telephone. "This is Harris. Bounce a couple of bullets off that chopper's landing skids."

Ten seconds later, two eager sharpshooters did just that. The pilot jumped as he both felt and heard the bullets hit.

Harris snarled into the microphone again. "Have I got your attention yet? Put it down right now on the pad beside the tower."

The pilot's voice was no longer so cocky and sure. "Ah, we're clearing the area back toward the airport now."

"Forget it, pal. Put it down where I told you right now or I'll blow your tail out of the sky."

Television viewers watching channel eleven were treated to the standard fare of the helicopter leaving the scene and then landing. The viewers were not shown, however, the picture of several FBI agents converging on the last flight of Newsship 11.

Back inside the tower, Frank had finally spotted the helicopter moving away. Satisfied, and believing Harris's story, he was sure that they wouldn't have to worry about any more airplanes or helicopters coming near them. Frank stuck the walkie-talkie back inside his briefcase in the bathroom.

*   *   *

Harris gave some last minute instructions as Agnew stepped into the elevator. "Make sure you tell him that it's better at this stage to give up, since nobody's been hurt. They'll get minimum charges and light sentences if any at all."

"Yeah, gotcha," Agnew said.

"But above all, keep them calm. Don't do anything to stir them up or make them mad."

"Okay."

Agnew pushed the button and the doors closed. Harris paced anxiously as he watched the lights which showed the elevator's progress. Harris then stopped his pacing and frowned. After less than fifteen seconds at the top of the tower, the elevator had started back down. With the way they had been keeping such tight control of the elevators, it didn't make any sense that they would let it get away from them like that.

No one said a word when the elevator doors opened. They assumed it was D. J. Agnew, but then no one could really tell. From a distance of three feet, a twelve gauge shotgun with 00 buckshot is probably the most deadly weapon ever devised. What had been the head was now a pulpy yellowish mass streaked with blood, part of which was on the back of the elevator wall and the rest of which oozed down over his shoulders and chest as he sat in the back corner.

The doors stood open for a full fifteen seconds. They finally closed again and the elevator once more moved back toward the top of the tower.

Frank keyed the walkie-talkie. "Harris, you there?"

"Yes I'm here. Have you gone crazy? You just killed your uncle."

"We didn't fall for your little setup. I said no tricks, but you didn't listen; your hero tried to pull a

gun. Don't worry about the hostages, we haven't
hurt any of them. We started to make an example of
a few, but we decided that your boy was enough. He
won't be doing you much good now."

Frank's purpose at this point was simply to do
enough talking and throw up enough of a smoke
screen to prevent a SWAT team from blasting their
way through the doors. He had to establish an atmo-
sphere that once again made that option undesirable.

"What do you mean?" Harris demanded. "We sent
your uncle up. Didn't you see that it was him?"

"I didn't have to see him," Frank replied. "He
pulled a gun on one of my buddies, so we didn't ask
any questions."

Harris by now didn't have the slightest idea what
was going on. Had D. J. Agnew really been carrying
a concealed weapon? Was he an impostor? If so,
where was the real D. J. Agnew? Was this part of an
elaborate escape plan? He didn't know if he should
order the SWAT team into action or not. It seemed
that the hostages were in no immediate danger, re-
gardless of the bizarre turn of events.

"I'm sending the elevator back down, Harris. Get
rid of him."

"Okay, Tom," Harris answered wearily. Nothing
was going right. The events seemed to be constantly
one move ahead of him. If nothing else, maybe this
would convince Colby Knight that the extortionists
meant business and that he therefore would have to
come up with the money.

Harris looked up as a shadow fell across him. Bob
King's expression indicated that he almost seemed to
savor the situation. He spoke softly, so as to add
emphasis to his words. "You're finished—pal."

Harris remained silent as King led his group from
the room. Harris sat unmoving for several minutes,
then wearily rose and walked down the hall toward
the rest room. He pushed through the door and
stopped when he caught his reflection in the mirror.

He looked older and even more tired than he felt, if that were possible. There would be internal FBI investigations. There would be congressional investigations. The press would dig up dirt and point the finger. He was just as trapped as those people at the top of the tower. Only two more years to retirement. Two lousy years!

He just couldn't take it anymore. He had tried, he truly had, but he just couldn't. His hand trembled as he reached inside his coat. He had just brushed against his service revolver when the door opened and a couple of uniformed patrolmen entered the rest room. Harris quickly bent over the sink and made a pretense of washing his hands. He then wiped the sweat from his face and walked back out of the rest room.

"Inspector Harris here, Mr. Knight. The situation at the tower has gotten much worse since I last talked to you. I told you that we had identified one of the extortionists and that we thought we might get a relative to come down and talk to him. Well, we found an uncle and sent him up, but they killed him."

"The guy killed his own uncle?"

"Yes. Something went wrong somewhere; we're still not exactly sure what happened."

The realization suddenly hit Knight that the plan to talk the extortionists into giving themselves up had failed totally, and that his own plan therefore would work. In fact, his plan now had an even better chance of succeeding. Now that someone had been killed, the extortionists would be desperate to escape; with or without the money. No one could say that it was Knight's fault that the man had been killed. That was the responsibility of the FBI. Knight would now come forward with his brilliant plan to end the standoff.

Harris interrupted his thoughts. "Mr. Knight, a man was just murdered. We don't know why, but it does prove one thing; the extortionists won't be bluffed into leaving without the money. They won't hesitate to kill more people if they don't get everything they want. We must have the ransom money."

"You need the money to cover your tails," Knight snapped. "You've blown it, and now you want me to buy your way out of it. No way; forget it. You tell those animals what I've said before you get somebody else killed."

Harris gritted his teeth but managed to retain his composure. "Mr. Knight, I've been in on a lot of hostage situations, and I can tell after a while what these sort of people will or will not do. If you don't come up with at least part of the money, these people will start killing the hostages. We don't have any choice."

"If you want to hand over the ransom so badly, why don't you come up with it yourself? The FBI has plenty of money."

"We can't get that kind of cash without getting approval from the Justice Department. It would take us a couple of days to get even a hundred thousand or so. If I could easily come up with it I would, but I can't. We can't do it without your help."

"Have you told the extortionists that we won't pay the ransom?"

"No we haven't. The last thing I want is to tell them something like that. It could be all it would take to set them off."

"Well that's the real problem here. You go ahead and tell them exactly what I'm offering. I'll take full responsibility."

Harris rolled his eyes toward the heavens. What a laugh! Knight would take full responsibility. He could just see himself at the review board saying, "But Colby Knight said that he would take full responsibility."

Harris tried once again. "Look, just give us part of the money. Make it a million. We can probably make do with that."

"Forget it. I'll give them my personal $5,000 and use of the company jet. I'll even make it $10,000 and use of the company jet, but that's all. Now the sooner you tell them that, the sooner this will all be over and done with."

Knight hung up the phone, beginning to lose patience with Harris. What did he have to do in order to get through to the man? Knight's door opened and his secretary, Linda, stepped in.

"Things aren't going very well, are they?"

"No, not exactly, but I think, or at least I hope they'll be getting better before long."

"I'm sure they will. However you decide to handle it, I'm sure that it'll be best for the company and for those poor people."

"Thank you, Linda. I appreciate that."

Linda smiled in return. "I just wanted to let you know that I'll be away from my desk for just a couple of minutes, but I'll be right back."

"Okay, thanks."

Linda left and closed the door. Her few small words of comfort had indeed been welcome. He hadn't stopped to realize just how much he had come to depend on her. She had gradually, over the last few months, become much more than just a secretary to him. Not that there was any physical relationship between them, but she was the one person he could talk to and confide in. Since his struggle with Bill Post had evolved, he had needed someone there to listen, and she had filled the need for him better and more completely than he could have hoped for.

Linda picked up a few papers from her desk and walked down the hall to Bill Post's secretary. "Hi,

Deb. I've got some more papers that I need Mr. Post to sign. Is he free?"

Post's secretary pressed her intercom button. "Mr. Post, Mr. Knight's secretary has something for your signature."

"Yeah, okay, just make it quick."

Linda smiled at Deb and entered Post's office, closing the door behind her. Post looked up impatiently.

"Yeah, what is it?"

"He just got another phone call from the FBI. He won't pay the ransom, but he's offered $10,000 and use of the company jet if they'll give up."

"What is he, crazy?"

"He thinks he's going to stop anyone from ever trying anything like this again."

Post laughed dryly. "I thought he was smarter than that. Maybe I gave him too much credit." Post paused for a moment, thinking before speaking again. "Well, is that it?"

"For right now."

"Okay, get back there and don't miss anything."

"Ah, could you come by tonight? I could cook."

"I've got too much to do," Post said brusquely.

Linda added a slight whine to her voice. "But it's been over a week and I—"

Linda wasn't able to finish her sentence as Post jumped from his chair and grabbed her roughly around the throat with one hand. He then knocked her back against the wall, causing her head to hit it with a painful thud. While he wasn't choking her, his grip on her throat was strong enough to make her gasp for each breath.

"Don't talk back to me," Post snarled through fiercely gritted teeth. "Don't you ever talk back to me again."

"I'm sorry, I didn't mean—"

"I'm not here for you. You're here for me—when I decide I want it."

Their relationship was based on simplicity. He enjoyed hurting her, and she let him. While he made her feel degraded and worthless and she often hated herself for it, after all else was said and done, she liked it.

Post loosened his grip on her neck slightly and smiled nastily. "You know, one word from me to your boss, and you're outa here. All I'd have to say is that you came in trying to give me information and that I wouldn't take it. Who are they going to believe, you or me?"

Post moved his hand around to the back of her head and grabbed a handful of her hair. He then bent her head back painfully and bit her hard on her ear, licking and slobbering at it.

"You know that Knight's held you back. You're more than just a secretary. I've told you before, and I mean it. When I move into the president's office, you're coming with me. And not as a secretary, but as my executive assistant."

Post released his grip on her hair and pinched her hard on the rear. "Now go on, get back in there."

Chapter Ten

"This Colby Knight character is crazy," Harris declared to Doug. "Isn't there anyone else up there who we could deal with? Surely they can't all be as unreasonable as he is."

"No sir, I've already checked around. Some of the other executives up there seem to be willing to compromise, or at least to listen, but Knight just won't go along with them."

It seemed like no time before Harris's walkie-talkie crackled with the sound of another call from the tower. "Harris, where's the money? We've given you more than enough time."

"The money still isn't ready, Tom. Like I said, it's going to take some time."

"Oh yeah? Well in that case I've got a little extra incentive for you. Some of the hostages are hurt; a couple pretty badly. When the shots went off a while ago they spooked and trampled each other. You send up the money and I'll let you have all the injured people."

Actually, other than some screams and near heart attacks in response to the shots, everyone was in fine shape. With nowhere to run, everyone had stayed exactly where they were.

Harris paused for a moment before replying. "It

sounds as if some of those people might need medical attention right away, Tom. Why don't you send the injured people on down. Then when the money gets here I'll trade it for the rest of the hostages."

"No! You get no more people until I see some money."

Was that an opening? It was worth trying. "I'll tell you what, Tom. They've got some of the money together, but they don't have it all. I'll ask them to send out what they've got so far and I'll trade that for the injured people."

"All right, we'll go along with that. Give me a call when you get the money."

Perhaps he had a toehold at last. Harris was immediately on the phone to Millard headquarters once again. "Mr. Knight, this is Inspector Harris once more. We need the $10,000 you've offered right away. I'll send a helicopter for it."

"Great! Now we're getting somewhere. It'll take me about ten minutes."

Knight hung up and buzzed his secretary. "Linda, would you please call downstairs to the bank and tell them that I'm on my way down? Tell them to withdraw $10,000 in cash from my personal account and have it ready for me."

Knight strode quickly down the hall past Bill Post's office and out to the elevators. He then rode to the ground floor and crossed the lobby to the bank. The bank manager jumped to his feet as Knight entered his office.

"Here's the money you requested, Mr. Knight. Ten thousand dollars exactly, right?"

"Right."

The manager handed him a medium sized bank bag with a zipper lock. "Here's the key to the bag. I know you're in a hurry, so I'll send up the withdrawal slip later for your signature."

Knight accepted the bag. "Thanks a lot. I can't tell you what a help this is."

"Of course, Mr. Knight. I'm just glad we could be of service. Good luck."

The last comment went unheard as Knight hurried back around the corner toward the elevators. Things had gone so smoothly that he beat the helicopter to the roof by several minutes. When it finally swirled into sight and landed, Knight ran across the roof to the pad, handed the bag in to the pilot, and the helicopter then lifted off again without the huge blades ever having slowed. Knight watched it head back across town in the direction of the tower and then returned anticlimactically to his office to await news of the outcome.

Harris was pacing the floor when the helicopter sat down in the parking lot across the street from the tower. Doug immediately rushed to meet it while Harris contacted the tower once more. "Tom, the helicopter just landed with the money."

"All right. Send it up and then I'll send the people down."

A few minutes later Frank eagerly picked up a bank bag from the floor of the elevator. When he unzipped it he was ecstatic; the bag was completely filled with money.

Frank laid his gun on the hostess stand so he could get both hands into counting the money. He quickly became aware, however, that there wasn't nearly as much money in the bag as there had appeared to be initially. There were a lot of bills, but most were tens. He had specifically told them to send hundreds.

Frank shouted into the walkie-talkie. "What kind of stunt are you trying to pull, Harris? How much money did you send us?"

Alert to any complications or objections when the exact amount of the money was discovered, Harris answered promptly. "I don't know, Tom. They didn't tell me how much they had. They just said they would send some of it on out while they were getting the rest of it together."

"That's bull! This is a stall and I know it. Well this is what I think of your penny ante stunt." Frank grabbed the bag of money and waved Angelo and Carl back to their positions. He then stepped into the elevator and angrily pushed the button for the observation deck. Thirty seconds later he was leaning far out over the railing. He realized that he was in plain view of any snipers, but he guessed correctly that they wouldn't risk a shot with two more men still upstairs with explosives.

Frank zipped open the top of the bag and dumped it upside down with a shake. Thousands of dollars suddenly burst forth from the tower and began fluttering down toward the ground, looking at first like a green snowstorm.

There were probably about four or five hundred people who had gathered at various places around the police barricades which blocked the streets for two blocks in all directions around the tower. As hundreds of bills fluttered downward, the wind swirling them around and scattering them further, it quickly became apparent to the onlookers on the ground that money was falling from the tower; a lot of money. First one person and then several more shouted that money was falling from the top. Then a couple here and two or three there ducked under or ran around the lightly manned police barricades and ran down toward the tower.

That was all it took for the dam to break. The next moment all the passersby and curious onlookers were scrambling and racing toward the falling money, shoving and pushing one another. And then they were all over the mall area beneath and around the tower, jumping into the reflecting pool and the fountain, fighting and shouting, as they grabbed at the bills.

The police officers who had manned the barricades had been able to stop only a few of the people. Now they scurried down the hill after the crowd, trying, with little success, to herd the people back behind the barricades. It was only a couple of minutes before all the money was grabbed up, but for that brief period of time there was total chaos as people kicked and screamed and fought with one another. At last, when there was no more money to be chased, the people began to move back away from the tower in response to the police officers' angry orders.

Harris's guts had knotted as he watched the money explode out from the tower. His only bluff had just blown up in his face. He listened wordlessly as the angry voice shouted a warning over the walkie-talkie.

"You see that, Harris? That's what I think of your tricks. These injured people can lie here and die for all I care. You don't get anybody else until we get all the money. No more partial deals and no more stalling. You've got thirty minutes."

Now that Frank was faced with the problem of getting safely back upstairs, he began to regret the brashness of his actions. Since the elevator had descended to the observation deck, it was possible that when he pressed the button for the lounge the car would continue down to the bottom of the tower before returning to the top. All he could do was try it and keep his hand on the stop button. If the car began to drop, he would have to hit the stop button and then try to pry the doors apart so he could climb back out onto the observation deck.

Frank held his breath as he pushed the button. Apparently the button had not been pushed at the bottom of the tower, because the elevator immediately moved back up to the lounge. Carl and Angelo were waiting anxiously when he stepped out.

"It was nothing but a stall. They only sent us $10,000, so I threw it off the observation deck and told them that they've only got thirty minutes to come up with the whole three million. We should be getting some response before long, so keep on your toes." Carl and Angelo nodded and then moved back to their positions, leaving Frank to his thoughts as he paced back and forth in front of the elevators.

"I'm going to the john, be back in a minute," Harris muttered. He walked back down the hall and pushed his way through the bathroom door as before, but this time he locked it behind him. He wanted no more interruptions. Having accepted what he had to do, he reached under his jacket again, brushing his hand past his revolver, and removed the flask from his inside pocket. As quickly as he could, he removed the cap and turned the container up three times in quick succession.

At first he had been able to handle it, but things kept getting worse with every hostage he lost. He could close his eyes and see every one of their faces. He kept what was eating at him all bottled up inside and then it spilled out at home, though he never meant it to, never wanted it to. Now that his wife, his third, had left him, home was nothing to go to but a cheap apartment in an old part of town. Meals were lonely affairs in a greasy spoon down the block. He now took it out on a bottle every night—and increasingly on his subordinates.

Harris's hands shook as he tried to screw the cap back onto the flask. His only hope was to stall as long as he possibly could; until he finally had to tell the extortionists that there would be no money no matter what they did. If they then started to kill the hostages, he would have no choice but to attempt an all out assault.

He still wasn't sure what had touched off the shooting. Maybe Agnew had been given a gun by someone. But what had he planned to do with it? Apparently, one of the extortionists other than Tom had seen the alleged gun and had done the shooting. Tom seemed to be totally convinced that the man wasn't his uncle. Harris's first thought of the dead man being an impostor was no longer valid, as Agnew's body had been quickly identified. He shook his head. Whatever the explanation, he would have plenty to answer for once all this was over.

Colby Knight, too, had watched the money come fluttering down from the top of the tower along with the resulting chaos below. It had been on live television, all three major stations now having crews on the spot. He had stared uncomprehendingly at the screen. Why would they have thrown the money away? That didn't make any sense.

"Another call from Inspector Harris," his secretary said.

Knight picked up his phone immediately. "Yes, inspector. What in the world is going on down there?"

"It didn't work, Mr. Knight. The extortionists went crazy when they found out that we sent them only $10,000. They threw it right back in our faces and gave us an ultimatum. We've got thirty minutes to deliver all the ransom; no more stalling. There apparently are injured hostages still in the tower. This is it. We have to have all the money immediately."

"Wait just a minute. Are you saying that you didn't tell them that I was sending only $10,000 instead of the full ransom amount? You just let them find out for themselves?"

"What choice did I have? You've—"

Knight cut him off, his voice rising angrily. "Are you telling me that you never even told them about my offer?"

Harris was growing angry now too. "Of course I didn't tell them. I'm trying to keep all those people alive up there."

Knight shook his head in disgust. "You've really blown it now. If you had told them about my offer and my position, none of this would have happened. My offer still stands, but it's $5,000 now. If you want to kick it back up to $10,000, then you'll to take it out of your own pocket. Now you tell those animals that they don't get another penny from me until they have accepted my offer."

Knight slammed the phone down. The FBI's bumbling had just cost him $10,000 of his own personal money. He cursed silently, but then an unexpected notion struck him. It might be worth it after all. He would come out looking like a martyr for suffering through the FBI's monumental foul-ups. Sure, this might not turn out to be too bad. It just served to make Colby Knight stand out like the Rock of Gibraltar while everyone else lost their heads and made the situation even worse.

Knight buzzed his secretary. "Yes, sir?"

"Linda, would you call down to the bank and have them take another $5,000 out of my personal account? Ask them to make it quick. I've got a feeling that we'll be needing it before too much longer."

"Right away, Mr. Knight."

Knight took a leisurely sip of his coffee. Things were falling rapidly into place exactly as he had predicted they would. It wouldn't be much longer now before the situation would be settled favorably, but on his terms.

"Mr. Knight," his secretary called.

"Yes."

"I can't get the bank on the phone; the lines are all tied up. The switchboard operator says that we're suddenly getting jammed with people calling in to demand that we save the hostages."

"That isn't surprising. I would have expected that sort of initial reaction in this situation. What are the operators telling them?"

"They're just saying that as far as they know there has been no change in the company's position on the matter."

"That's fine. The kooks will call for a while and then it'll die down. Send someone downstairs to pick up the money. I don't want you to go, though; I might need you up here."

"Yes, sir."

"Are we in Cleveland yet?" Frank jumped at the
unexpected voice right behind him and jerked around
to find a stooped little old lady standing before him.

"Are we in Cleveland yet?" she asked again.

"Cleveland?"

"I'm going to visit my son. He'll be worried if
we're late. Are we there yet?"

Amidst all the terror and turmoil he had created,
Frank was suddenly filled with remorse and guilt at
the plight of this poor woman who obviously had no
conception of what was going on around her or even
where she was.

"There's not anything wrong with the airplane is
there?" she asked hesitantly.

"Oh no ma'am," he assured her. "You'll be getting
off in just a minute. Here," he said as he guided her
to a chair in the waiting area. "You have a seat right
here for a few minutes and then you'll be getting off
the plane."

She smiled up at him. "Thank you so much, young
man."

Frank picked up his radio and summoned Harris
again. "We've got a little old lady up here who thinks
she's on an airplane to Cleveland. She hasn't got any
idea what's going on. She's probably going to get in
the way and get herself hurt, so I'm going to send
her down in the elevator."

"Okay, we'll take care of her," Harris said, surprised at this unexpected act of compassion.

Frank walked back to the lady and helped her into
the elevator. "Now ma'am, you hold onto the hand
rail right there and you'll be getting off in just a
minute."

"Oh I will," she replied. "Thank you again. I'm
going to write a nice letter to the airline telling them
how helpful you've been."

Frank couldn't hold back a smile. "Ma'am, I sure would appreciate that." He stepped back and allowed the doors to close.

When the car reached the bottom, Doug stepped inside and took the lady by the arm. "Welcome to Cleveland, ma'am. I'll take you to some real nice people now who will help you."

Doug jumped as she swung her cane at his arm. "Don't you speak condescendingly to me," she snapped. "I know where I am." Noting the surprised look on his face, she smiled. "Isn't it amazing what you can get away with when people think you're old and senile?"

Chapter Eleven

Frank and Carl stood nervously with their guns pointed at the elevator doors, waiting for the elevator to return after taking the little old lady downstairs. When the doors finally opened once again, revealing an empty car, Frank breathed a sigh of relief and once again reached inside to push the stop button. As they turned and started to walk back away from the elevator, however, Frank stopped abruptly. There had been a noise from the stairwell area; he was sure of it. It hadn't been loud or distinct, but he had definitely heard something.

Frank cautiously moved to the door and placed his ear against it, listening intently. Nothing. Frowning, he turned to Carl and whispered, "Get Angelo."

Carl walked quickly around the corner to Angelo's position and waved him over. Frank held a finger to his lips as Angelo joined them at the stairwell door. "I heard something out there," Frank whispered. "I'm going to stay here and listen. Go downstairs to the restaurant and listen at the stairwell doors, but don't make any noise."

Angelo nodded and quickly disappeared down the spiral staircase. "Carl, are you sure absolutely sure that the wires are set right on this door?" Frank asked.

Carl looked closely at the small explosive charge on the door. "It looks all right, but I don't guess it would hurt to double check it." He stuck the pin back into his grenade and stuffed it back into his pocket, then squatted down and laid his shotgun on the floor beside him. Frank leaned down and peered over Carl's shoulder, inspecting the wiring that had been placed on the charge. Frank didn't really know what he was looking at, but he figured that he probably should learn just in case something were to happen to Carl. The explosives worked both ways; not only could they keep the cops out, but they could end up keeping him in.

"Oh Charlie, I'm getting so tired of sitting. My bottom hurts and I've gotta go to the bathroom."

Laughlin stared at Tina without speaking for several moments in order to emphasize his reply. "It's Charles," he said firmly. "And I'm sure that everyone else up here is tired too. But for heaven's sake, don't do or say anything that might draw attention to us." Tina assumed a pouty expression, but declined further comment.

After sitting directly across the table from her for quite some time now, Laughlin had come to the conclusion that Tina wasn't nearly as young as she seemed at first glance. Until now, he had not spent enough time looking at her face to realize that she had some mileage on her. It became more apparent after you got past the peroxide and the big boobs and the heavy makeup.

Laughlin's eyes suddenly widened in shock and surprise as a movement behind Tina caught his attention. Just five tables away a man had unexpectedly slipped from his seat, dropped to one knee, and was now bracing a gun over the railing with both hands.

Jack Hilliard sighted carefully on the back of the

man on the left; the one still holding the shotgun. Both of the men now had their backs turned to him, but the one on the right had laid his weapon on the floor. The first shot was for the one with the gun and then the next two would go to the one who had laid his down. Hilliard then would direct his fire back to the first man for a fourth and final shot if it were necessary.

But Hilliard knew there would be no need for the additional shot. Not at this distance with the railing for support. He would put two bullets into the second man, since they would have to be squeezed off much faster. They wouldn't be as carefully and accurately positioned as would be the first. And too, if the second man were fast enough, he might be moving by the time the third shot went off. But Hilliard seriously doubted it. The third shot would be well on its way before the second man would have reacted to the sound of the first. It was almost too easy.

Once the first two men were taken out, Hilliard was in perfect position, with an unobstructed view of the spiral staircase, to hold off the third man indefinitely. The way Hilliard was crouched down between two tables, the man in the stairwell would have to look around for several seconds before he could find him. And if the third man exposed himself for that long, it would be too late for him; far too late.

It made no difference that the third man would have the superior weapon, the superior firepower. Hilliard had the position on him and that would far negate the advantage of the shotgun over his revolver.

With his sights resting steadily on the man with the gun, directly between his shoulder blades, Hilliard slowly and deliberately tightened the pressure on the trigger. The roar of the gunshot was deafening, the echo seeming to multiply the stunning effects of the blast as the sound careened off the glass walls. Before Jack Hilliard was even conscious of the sound, the hollow point bullet entered his shoulder and, as it was designed to do, exploded into numerous shrapnel-like fragments. The external reaction was identical to that of a sledgehammer striking him on the shoulder. Knocked completely off balance, he hit the floor hard face first.

The internal reaction was distinctly unlike the blow of a sledgehammer. The exploding bullet sent minute fragments all through his shoulder and into the left lung. The explosion disintegrated the shoulder joint, sending slivers of bone out into the surrounding muscle and flesh as if a second bullet had exploded alongside the first.

The force of the exploding bullet caused his own shot to go wildly off target, burying itself harmlessly into the ceiling. Lying on the floor in a growing pool of his own blood, it was only now that Hilliard dimly realized that he had been shot. Strangely enough, he felt much pain in his face, where he had hit the floor, but only a dull ache in his shoulder. Through a bloody red haze he could now see that the flashy buxom blonde who had been seated a few tables away was standing with a gun trained on him.

If he had been fully conscious and completely aware of what was going on around him, Hilliard wouldn't have moved. But that wasn't the case. Without realizing what he was doing, he simply reacted, groping for his gun which lay on the floor just a few inches from his outstretched hand. The second shot from Tina's gun struck him squarely in the chest, exploding through the sternum and into his heart. She hadn't been planning to kill the man; she just meant to stop him. But whatever it took.

She unemotionally watched him die. Eleven years of whoring in west Texas renders one quite immune to any feelings of remorse over the sight of blood or violence, or even death.

At the sound of the first shot, Frank and Carl had

rushed wildly from their positions at the stairwell door. They now stood looking out over the crowd, nervously waving their weapons back and forth, though the terrified hostages didn't need any warning to stay exactly where they were.

Tina turned back around and pointed her gun unwaveringly at Charles Laughlin's face. "You use people; you're garbage."

If Laughlin had been in a state of near shock when Tina had pulled the gun from her purse and shot the man, he was now actually quaking, white faced and terrified. He would have pleaded, begged, but when his mouth opened no sound would come out.

"You think you're so great. Every woman you meet oughta be thankful for the privilege of letting you have her. Take off your pants."

Laughlin by now was hunched over almost as if he were trying to hide behind the table. His face screwed into an expression of tearfulness as he finally managed to squeak out a pitiful plea. "Please, don't."

Tina regarded him contemptuously over her gun sights. "Don't worry, I'm not going to hurt you as long as you do exactly what I tell you to do. I oughta blow it off, but I won't. Get the pants off and throw them over here."

Laughlin was far too frightened to feel any sort of emotion as minor as embarrassment. He was much further down on the hierarchy of needs at the present moment. He unfastened his belt as quickly as he could with his hands shaking as much as they were, slid the zipper down, and then wriggled out of his pants without leaving his chair.

"The rest of them," Tina ordered.

Laughlin looked helplessly around as if hoping to find someone who would intercede on his behalf, but there was no one. He glanced back at the blood splattered form lying motionless on the floor and then, without another word, quickly pulled off his light blue bikini briefs with the bright red hearts.

"Now the rest of the clothes."

When Laughlin was finally reduced to his true whimpering self, sitting totally nude at the table, Tina scornfully turned her back to him and walked away. Frank placed his arm around her and gave her a squeeze as she stepped up to the reception area.

"I'd have to say that you just earned your share."

"Maybe yours too."

Frank smiled. "Your stuff's in the men's room in my briefcase."

Tina stepped into the rest room and laid her gun on the counter. She carefully wiped off the heavy makeup and mascara and pulled off the long false eyelashes. The bleached blonde wig came off last. She pulled on a ski mask, reloaded her gun, and then joined Frank and the others outside.

Harris had only five minutes left in which to do something, but he really had only one option still available. That was to tell the extortionists about Knight's offer and have the SWAT team standing by when he did so. He wearily glanced at Doug. "How long until the SWAT team could be ready to go in?"

"They're ready right now."

"What about the helicopters?"

"Both are standing by in position and ready."

"Good, we may need them all. I'll have to tell the extortionists that Millard Hotels refuses to give them any money no matter what they threaten to do."

"It's finally come down to that?"

Harris nodded glumly as he stuck two more ant-acid tablets into his mouth and chased them down with a gulp of cold coffee. No point in putting it off any longer. Resigned to his most undesirable, but only, course of action, he picked up the walkie-talkie

in front of him and pressed the transmit button.
"Tom, this is Inspector Harris. Are you there?"

"Yes I am, go ahead." The reply was immediate,
still angry.

"I'll give it to you straight, Tom. You were right
when you said that I've been stalling you on the
money. Now I'll tell you why. Millard Hotels refuses
to pay the ransom. They refuse to negotiate. They
don't even care if you start killing the hostages. They
do say, however, that they'll give you $5,000 and use
of their company plane to go wherever you wish.
That's it. We've spent all afternoon down here trying
to convince them to give us the money, but they
won't budge an inch."

Harris released the transmitter and waited. There
was no answer. Those around him strained to hear
any sounds from the bugging device. They didn't
know it, but there would be no more sounds since
Frank had flushed it down the toilet an hour before.

Fifty stories above them, Frank slowly laid down
the radio and looked around at his three companions who were all watching him anxiously. "They say
that the hotel won't pay the ransom. They won't
even negotiate with us."

The three looked at one another. Their planning
and execution had been meticulous. They had covered every contingency, considered every angle. But
not this one. They had never dreamed that the hotel
chain might refuse to pay the ransom. Big companies always paid ransoms; everybody knew that.

Carl spoke first. "We can't just start killing people."

"No, no we can't," Frank muttered in agreement.
Even if Frank had been willing to kill some of the
hostages, such an action would have been the one
sure way to have a SWAT team crawling all over
them.

"We don't need to start killing a lot of people,"
Angelo said.

"What do you mean?" Frank asked.

"There's a knocked up broad sitting over there."

"Knocked up?" Carl asked blankly.

"Knocked up—pregnant. Big as a cow."

"What about her?" Frank asked.

"The cops aren't taking us seriously; not really. They think we're just messing around up here. That means that we ain't going to get a penny until we show them that they can't screw with us anymore. She's worth $3 million to us. All we gotta do is kick her tail down the stairs."

Chapter Twelve

Frank and Carl exchanged glances of discomfort as Angelo spoke. "They ain't gonna come busting in here with all the explosives we've got on the doors. They're afraid to breathe on them."

Frank shook his head. "We've got to be extremely careful about doing anything like that. If we go too far, the authorities won't be concerned with the explosives on the doors. They would probably blow the doors in themselves."

"That's right," Carl said. "They wouldn't have any other choice."

Angelo shrugged sourly. "Yeah, well what do you suggest, then?"

Frank frowned, deep in thought. "Give me a minute."

"What you mean is that you hadn't got the slightest idea what to do. Ain't that right?" Angelo asked.

"Come on, get off his back for a minute, will you?" Carl snapped.

As Frank looked around, he caught sight of the small television they had found in the manager's office. They had been using it to keep abreast of the news reports on their situation. He stared at it for several moments.

"Hold on, I've got an idea." Frank then picked up the public address microphone at the hostess stand.

He cleared his throat and keyed the button on the microphone. "Listen up. I want everyone's attention. The hotel chain has refused to pay for your release. They don't care what happens to you. So everybody here is going to write a nice little letter to the hotel, begging them to give us the money so you won't get hurt. When you write this letter, make sure that you remind everybody about your darling little kids that you want to see again or your wife or your husband or whoever. You can tell them how dangerous we are and how we're not fooling around.

"We're going to make a little contest out of it. The five people who write the best letters will win the grand prize; they'll be allowed to leave. I'll be the judge and all decisions will be final. Void where prohibited by law." Frank smiled at his slight humor.

"Okay, go ahead and start writing. Use your napkins or any scratch paper you can find. If you don't have anything to write with, borrow something from the person sitting next to you. I want a note from every single one of you. Come on now, we haven't got all day. Let's get started."

The hostages immediately began scratching out notes and letters on anything they could find, spurred on by the possibility that it might be a quick ticket to freedom and safety.

"You really think this is gonna do any good?" Angelo asked skeptically.

"It's worth a try at least." Frank picked up the walkie-talkie again and called back downstairs. "Hey Harris, are you still there?"

"Sure, I'm not going anywhere."

"Some of the people up here have written letters. We're going to send them down. One stipulation, though—you give a copy of all the letters to the news people right away. If they're read on live television, I'll let five more people go."

Harris suddenly realized that this new demand was a godsend. He had been expecting the absolute

worst, but now, not only would he get five hostages
out of the deal, but it would put tremendous pressure on Colby Knight to come up with the ransom
money. Harris knew that he, too, could play the
media game. He hadn't yet informed the press that
the hotel had refused to pay the ransom; Colby
Knight wouldn't like it one bit when that news was
leaked out.

"Sure, Tom," Harris responded eagerly. "Send the
letters on down. We'll get copies of them to the press
just as quick as we can."

Harris laid the walkie-talkie back down and signaled to Doug who had just come back into the
office. "The extortionists are going to send down
some letters that they want read on live television. I
want you to make copies and keep the originals for
us. When you pass a copy on to the press, let them
know about the hotel chain's refusal to pay the ransom, emphasizing that they selfishly won't pay to
save the innocent victims. Do you have all that?"

"Yes, sir, but the hotel issued a statement to the
press just a few minutes ago; it's already been read
on television."

"On television? What did they say?"

"The vice president who's running things up there,
Colby Knight, did a good job of making himself
sound like a hero who is singlehandedly fighting off
the extortionists. He says he's going to save the hostages and put an end to this sort of thing once and
for all."

Harris cursed silently. He was fighting a two fronted
war and faring badly on both. Millard Hotels presented just as great a problem as did the extortionists. At least the extortionists would listen to reason
and were willing to negotiate a little.

Frank had instructed the people to pass their notes
and letters along and now accepted the thick stack of
papers and napkins. He quickly began leafing through

them. Whenever he ran across one that caught his eye, he removed it from the stack and stuffed it into his pocket. He was more than pleased with the type of response he had managed to elicit.

It took almost ten minutes to go through them all and to pull out the two dozen most effective ones. He wasn't all that concerned with who really had the best note; he primarily wanted to make sure that nothing slipped out which he didn't like. As it turned out, though, all the notes were acceptable. Selecting two of his favorite ones, he pulled out a pen with ink that matched the ink on the notes. On each of the two notes he wrote "P.S." and added another line.

Finished at last, he stepped back up to the public address microphone. "Let me have your attention again, folks," he announced. "Here are the winners of our little contest. April Johnson, Donna Harris, Shirley Ferguson, Bob Faulk, and Mrs. P. Carroll."

The women had turned out to be much better at producing the effect he had wanted than the men. Perhaps they were able to communicate their feelings more readily, or maybe their letters just sounded more pitiful.

"If the people I just named will come on up to the front, the elevator will take you downstairs." A rustle of movement preceded the five people who quickly lined up before him.

"Go right ahead," Frank said as he gestured toward the open, inviting elevator.

One lady hesitantly raised her hand for permission to speak. "Excuse me."

"Yes, ma'am?"

"I don't mean to cause trouble, but my husband is still here. Do I have to leave him?"

"Oh, all right, go get him."

Two more of the five hesitantly spoke up, a man and a woman who each expressed the same sentiment as the first woman. Frank once again gave in, until eight people had lined up to leave. He handed

the two dozen letters he had selected to the first
woman in line.

"There you go, ma'am. If you'd deliver these to
the FBI agents downstairs, I'd appreciate it."

"Yes, I'll be glad to."

The other letters Frank had simply thrown away.
He knew that the newscasters wouldn't read almost
two hundred letters over live television, so Frank
had taken it upon himself to make sure that the few
most befitting his cause would be the ones that were
read. Two dozen would be just about the right number. The television newscasters would have a field
day with them.

Feeling quite generous, Frank moved back out
into the lounge and looked over the remaining crowd.
He still had more than enough hostages, and to a
point, the fewer he had the less trouble it would be
to keep a close eye on them and keep them in line.
He walked over to a table where an elderly couple
was seated and nudged the man.

"Take off, the elevator's waiting for you." The
couple looked up in surprise and then hopped up
and headed for the elevator just as fast as they could
go.

Frank saw the elevator away and then called down
to Harris once again. "I'm sending you five extra
people just to show that I'm a nice guy and that I'm
willing to negotiate. That makes a total of ten people
I'm letting go. Make sure that the press gets that
message when you give them the letters. I want to
see it on the set here."

Harris perked up a little at this. It was the only
good news he had heard all day. "Okay, Tom. We'll
pass it on to the news people."

"Which television station are you planning to give
the letters to?" Frank asked.

"Ah, well, I really haven't thought about it. I guess
we'll just give a copy to all of them. If we don't, the
others will be all over us."

"Yeah, that's great. Just make sure that they're read on live television right away."

"Don't worry. We want those letters to be heard just as much as you do."

Two minutes later Harris was reading through the notes and letters with relish. They were exactly what he needed.

When Harris finished he handed them to Doug. "Here, get some copies of these and give them out to the press with the extortionists' stipulation that they must be read immediately over live television and radio. Be sure that you make it absolutely clear to the press that we don't approve of the hotel chain's selfish refusal to pay the ransom."

Harris picked up the walkie-talkie again. "Tom, the news people should have the notes in about five minutes."

"Good, we'll be watching for them."

Frank turned up the volume on the set. The station he had tuned was running an interview with some shrink who was giving his expert opinion of the psychological make-up of the extortionists. It was totally wrong. The picture abruptly changed a couple of minutes later as a reporter on the scene came back on the air, Reunion Tower looming behind him.

"Excuse us for cutting in on you, Barry, but we have just received word from the FBI here at Millard Tower that the extortionists have released ten hostages as part of an exchange deal. The extortionists told the hostages to write letters to Millard Hotels International asking that the ransom be paid for their release. A released hostage has informed us that although the extortionists initiated the idea of the letters they did not tell the hostages what they could or could not write. The hostages were completely free to say anything about the extortionists that they wished.

"The extortionists offered to release several hostages if the letters were read on live television. The hostages have been released as agreed, and we have just been handed copies of about two dozen notes and letters. I have had just a moment to glance at some of the letters, and I must tell you that it presents a sobering picture of what it is like in the tower for the remaining hostages. The FBI officials in charge at the scene have also informed us that they do not agree with Millard Hotels' policy of refusing to negotiate with the extortionists. The FBI spokesman has stated that they are now convinced that the only way to secure the safe release of the remaining hostages is to meet the ransom demand.

"I am now going to read you excerpts from the letters that have been handed to me from the FBI. I must warn you that what you are about to hear may be shocking."

Frank rolled his eyes upwards as he listened to the reporter hamming it up with his breathless report. The guy was a total jerk, but he was exactly what Frank needed at the moment. He then began to read through a pile of papers before him.

"Please give the men the money. I only have $300 in my savings account, but I will give it all to the hotel if they will help us."

"I am so scared. These men have hurt us and will kill us if you do not do what they say. I do not want to die."

"They will kill us if you do not pay. What will my wife tell my two year old little girl? She will not understand what dead means. Just tell her that Daddy will not be coming home anymore. P.S. If anyone wants to help us, please call Millard Hotels and cancel your reservations."

"My six year old daughter, Debbie, has leukemia. I want to see her again. I do not have long left with her as it is. Do not do this to her too. Help us. You have plenty of money."

"I love you Bob and Amy."

"These extortionists have bombs and guns and have already killed some people. They have nothing to lose by killing us all. You have a lot of money. Why not give a little of it to help us? You must have families too. Try to think how you would feel if it were them here instead of us. Wouldn't you pay the money for them? P.S. I want all my friends to call Millard Hotels and tell them that they will never stay with them again if they don't help us."

The reporter continued on with at least some portion of each of the two dozen letters, selecting the juiciest parts and laying it on thick. Several "in the street" interviews then followed, the reporter asking various people if they thought that the ransom should be paid. To a person, the answer was a resounding "yes," with the hotel chain pictured as a greedy corporation that didn't care about the hostages. The effect was better and more complete than Frank could have possibly hoped for.

Colby Knight had watched the performance of the newscaster with total disgust. The idiots were playing right into the extortionists' hands. Well, it didn't matter. When they realized that this ridiculous stunt would get them nowhere, the criminals would give in soon enough.

Knight tried to busy himself with a report from the accounting department for a while, though with all that was going on it was somewhat difficult to concentrate on something as dry and boring as accounting. His secretary buzzed him again an hour later.

"Mr. Knight, Mr. Powers is on the line." George Powers was in charge of the company's reservations system, a division that included several hundred reservationists along with a hundred million dollars worth of computers.

"Yes, George, what can I do for you?"

"Mr. Knight, I guess you're aware of the letters

that the extortionists sent out to be read over live television?"

"Yes I am. What about them?"

"They've apparently stirred up an awful lot of people. If it had been just a few calls or had started to peter out after a while I wouldn't have bothered you with it, but it's picking up steam."

"What do you mean?"

"The cancellations are unbelievable. Our switchboards are jammed with thousands of people calling in from all over the country cancelling their reservations. We normally get a small surge of cancellations whenever we get some sort of bad publicity, but I've been in this department for eighteen years and I've never seen anything like it. It's actually getting worse now instead of better. As the story about the letters is being delay-broadcast around the country, more and more people are calling in. And we haven't even heard from the west coast yet. So far we've had ten percent of our total reservations canceled, and that includes conventions as well."

Knight was stunned by the last figure. The lifeblood of a huge hotel chain is in its reservations. If they had to depend on people who just walked up and asked for a room at the last minute, they wouldn't have lasted over a week.

Powers continued. "At this point I can't even begin to guess how much lost revenue we're talking about, but it's well up into the millions."

"Okay, George, thanks for the report. Let me know if there's any change, will you?"

"Yes, sir, I sure will. But are we going to pay the ransom now? Should we tell that to the people who are calling to cancel their reservations?"

"No, no we aren't going to give in to a bunch of common criminals." Knight angrily hung up the phone. How could people be so stupid? It was too late to release another statement to the press attempting to support his position. The quickest way out of the mess was to end it once and for all. After the hostages were freed, the people who had cancelled their reservations would all come running back along with a lot of new business. The only business that they might actually lose was between now and when the extortionists gave up. The extortionists obviously were too dumb to realize it, but they had sealed their own fate with this stupid letter writing ploy. If he handed over the money now, both he and the company would receive plenty of bad publicity for refusing to pay up until they were forced to by public opinion. Knight knew that he was in the corner now. His only way out was to stand his ground.

"Linda," he shouted angrily. "Get Inspector Harris on the phone." A few minutes later Knight was shouting into the phone once again.

"Harris, who's side are you on? What's the idea of pulling the stunt with those letters on television?"

Harris feigned surprise. "I don't know what you're talking about. That was the extortionists' idea in exchange for releasing some of the hostages. We were able to get ten hostages out of the deal, so I'd have to that say it was a pretty good trade on our part. Don't you think now that it's time we got the rest of the hostages out of there?"

"You mean to tell me you fell for that cheap trick? Use your head. They're desperate and this is a last chance try for the money. They know it's over as well as we do. This will cap it when they realize that they're still not getting the money. Now I've had it. You tell the extortionists right now that there will be no money and no negotiations. I want this thing over immediately."

Harris didn't like what he was hearing. He had hoped that the letters, along with the accompanying public outcry, would change Knight's position. Without the money, things would soon be coming to a head in a manner he didn't look forward to.

Knight looked up from the phone to find Bill Post

standing in the hallway eavesdropping on him. 'You can't be serious," Post said in an accusing tone of voice. "Don't you understand what's going on out there? People are actually picketing out in front of the building now. If you continue with this insane course of action, you're going to ruin us. You've already done irreparable damage to the company's reputation. Give them the money; don't make it any worse than it already is."

Knight turned purple. Almost choking on the words, he almost screamed at Post. "Out! Get out! Stay out!"

Taken aback for the second time that day, Post beat a hasty retreat to his office where he carefully added the latest events to his thick file on Knight. Still on the other end of the line, Harris clearly heard what had happened. Firmly convinced now that further arguments would be a waste of his time, Harris hung up the phone and resigned himself to his only remaining course of action.

Kathy O'Leary suddenly gasped and bent over the table, her arms crossed over her stomach. "Kathy, what's wrong?" asked one of her companions.

"I'm having a contraction."

"Are you sure?"

"Of course she's sure; just look at her," snapped the third member of their party. "We've got to get her out of here."

"But how?"

"They've let a few other people go, so they should be reasonable about this. We'll just tell them the truth; she has to get to a hospital as quickly as possible."

"No, don't say anything," Kathy groaned. "They might do something to us. We can't do anything to draw attention to ourselves. I'll be okay in a few minutes."

"No you won't be okay," said the third lady firmly.

"And I'm not going to sit here while you have your baby in the middle of all this." So saying, she turned and waved her arm vigorously at the armed man who stood guard just a few tables away. "Excuse me," she announced in a loud voice. "We need some help over here."

"She's going into labor," she said as the man warily approached their table. "We need to get her to a hospital as soon as possible."

Kathy was obviously quite pregnant, and her face was slightly devoid of color and strained, her eyes closed as she bit her lip. "Hang on just a minute," the man said.

A few moments later he returned with another man, the one who seemed to be the leader. "She's in labor," the first man explained. "We still have a lot more hostages than we need, so I think we should send her down."

The leader nodded his agreement. "Yeah, you're probably right. A woman in labor would be more of a distraction than we need at this point. We would be better off without her."

The leader nodded and pointed his shotgun back in the direction of the elevators. "Okay, all three of you can leave now."

Kathy's two friends helped her up out of her chair and then walked her to the elevator. Unexpectedly, however, a third masked man stepped in front of them and blocked the doorway.

Chapter Thirteen

"I'm telling you for the last time, Frank. Kick her tail down the stairs. Don't let her just walk away. She's the best bargaining chip we've got."

Frank judged his reply carefully, lest he convey an image of dissension which would be relayed to the FBI below. That was the sort of thing which then could be turned around and used against them. "No, we don't need to do anything like that right now. We've got the public pressure going for us now that the television people are in on the deal."

."Well at least keep her up here and tell them that she's fixing to drop her load. You could tell that to the television people. That'll put plenty of pressure on the hotel to come across with the money."

Frank stopped for a moment to consider Angelo's last suggestion. That indeed would put pressure on the hotel chain; plenty of it. But then he looked at Kathy O'Leary's painfully drawn face again. This wasn't a game for her.

"Go ahead, you're free to go."

Within just a few moments of having spoken up, the three women were free and on their way to the ground. "I can't believe it," Kathy laughed through the pain of another contraction. "All we had to do was tell them we wanted to leave. And we even got a free lunch out of it. If it was so easy, why didn't we think of it six hours ago?"

Harris personally met the elevator when the doors opened. "Ma'am, are you all right? Do you need an ambulance? Or maybe a patrol car to take you to the hospital?"

Kathy shook her head, grimacing slightly as she held her stomach. "No, I'll be all right. I've been having some false labor pains for the last couple of days and this is probably just more of the same. Could I lie down and rest somewhere for a few minutes? It will probably pass quickly and then I'll be okay."

"Certainly. There's a couch in an office back there where you can rest in privacy. Feel free to take just as much time as you need. Doug, would you show the ladies where to go?"

"Yes sir." Doug escorted the three women to an office with a long couch, and then while Kathy lay down, he quietly questioned her two companions about the situation at the top of the tower. They could offer no new information, simply confirming that things had not changed much since the last people had been released. The picture the authorities now had was as complete as they were likely to get. The information they dearly wished they had concerned the type of explosives and fuses which were attached to the doors.

Harris's walkie-talkie crackled again. "Harris, did you get the pregnant lady all right?"

"We sure did, and she's being taken care of now. Thanks."

"What's the latest word from the hotel about the money?"

Harris had just been waiting, doing nothing since he had last heard from Colby Knight. He had nothing more to gain by stalling further. "I talked to them just a little while ago, and they still won't budge on the money."

Frank dropped his head in dismay. He was well aware that a SWAT team was probably sitting on ready, just waiting for his reaction, so he measured his reply carefully.

"Hang on, don't get excited. Let us think about it for a few minutes."

"I can't believe it," he exclaimed to Carl. "The hotel people have to be taking quite a hit from all the bad publicity they're getting. They must be pretty smart, or crazy, or both. Any ideas?"

Carl slowly shook his head. "I don't know. You think maybe we should just give it up and try to get out while we can?"

"Forget it! After all I've been through I'm not about to give up and come out of this thing empty handed. Let me think for a minute," Frank muttered as he wandered aimlessly back and forth in front of the elevators.

Carl carefully leaned his gun against the wall and pulled off his ski mask, the static electricity making his hair crackle and stand out in places. He ran his fingers through his hair and then rubbed his hands over his face where the rough material had been itching so badly. It felt so good to be free of it at last. He then turned his attention to the stairwell door and carefully removed the fuse from the explosive charge.

He didn't bother to look first to make sure that the stairwell area was clear, he just opened the door and stepped out onto the landing. He walked up the last flight of stairs and without hesitation began to climb the metal ladder which led up to the trap door in the roof of the tower.

The money wouldn't be coming. That was more than clear now. And even if it did things could no longer work out for him. He opened the trap door and crawled up onto the roof. The early evening air was fresh and brisk with a slight breeze that fanned his face as he walked to the edge. He felt good again; better than he had in several weeks. It was best this way. The insurance would take care of his wife; he had seen to that. There was no exclusion for suicide in the policy, though he certainly had not planned to end things this way. And now there would be no reason for them to hurt anyone because of him.

Carl closed his eyes and leaned forward. It was so comfortable, so quiet. So simple.

If Kathy O'Leary or her two friends had happened to look straight up as they walked away from the tower toward their car, they might have noticed something in the darkness above that seemed to be growing ever larger and closer. As the body slammed head first into Kathy, the force of the disintegrating bodies literally knocked her two companions off their feet as blood, along with bits of flesh and bone, was splattered for a hundred yards in all directions.

The couple seated in the first class section of the Boeing 747 might have appeared to be father and daughter except for the way they acted toward one another. Mr. Millard firmly believed that one of the symbols of corporate status, along with a big office and a company car, was an executive assistant with large breasts. And Patsy was certainly no exception to his rule. While his executive assistant may not have been the most efficient in the company when it came to typing and shorthand, she was by far the most attractive—and had the largest breasts. Judging her overall performance, one would have come to the conclusion that she was very, very good at what she did.

Mrs. Millard wasn't aware of all of Patsy's duties; thus Mr. Millard could get away with taking his executive assistant to Hawaii rather than his wife. Mrs. Millard considered her husband to be too old and undesirable to be suspicious of him, but just because such characteristics were true of herself, she shouldn't have been so ready to project such an image onto her husband. In any case, the arrangement worked well for all involved.

At first, Harris thought they must have thrown a hostage off the top of the tower. And then, when Frank realized that Carl was missing, he thought that the cops were just engineering the entire story to cover the fact that they somehow had taken him. But then Frank found the wires removed from the explosive charge on the door, and after the angry shouting and accusations over the radio were finished, the situation was defused for the moment and each was right back where he had started, neither man happy with his lot.

"The best thing we have going for us right now," Frank said to Tina, "is the live television coverage. We don't want to lose that. We have to keep using it to increase the pressure on the hotel."

Frank walked out toward the windows and signaled to Angelo who had been keeping watch on the far side of the tower. "The letters apparently didn't work. The hotel chain still won't give us a penny."

"Time to start kickin' some tail?"

"No, we can't go too far or we'll have a SWAT team swarming all over us. I tell you what, though. Go find me a good looking young lady with a nice figure."

Beneath the mask Angelo broke into a delighted smirk. "Oh I already spotted one. A real classy blonde bitch."

"Good, bring he on up front."

Angelo wheeled around and started off eagerly, but Frank stopped him momentarily. "Oh, hold it, Angelo. Better make it a brunette instead of a blonde."

Angelo shrugged. "Whatever."

Frank called downstairs once more. "Harris, I want a television camera with one of those super powerful long range lenses on top of the hotel right away."

'Well now, Tom, I don't know if the television crews will be willing to come out into the open like that after what happened to your uncle."

"Get smart, Harris. They'll jump at the chance to get a close-up shot. If they don't want to do it you can always stick your own boys on the camera. I don't care who's up there as long as I see a super close-up shot of the tower on the set here."

"What do you want it for?"

"Don't worry, you'll see. Nobody gets hurt, though, as long as we get the camera. Just remember that."

"How many hostages do I get in return for getting you the camera?"

"One."

"Make it ten."

"Two and that's it."

"All right, you've got your camera. Give us a few minutes to get it in place."

Harris hung up the phone with both relief and concern—relief because the extortionists apparently weren't going to start killing the hostages in a fit of rage; concern because he had no idea what they were now up to. Still, it was much better to play along than to bring things to the final conclusion that he still hoped to avoid.

"Doug, get in touch with a television crew. I want one of their cameras with a long range lens up on the roof of the hotel. Put several snipers up there with them, too. But tell the snipers not to fire, they're just out there for show."

"Okay."

"And one other thing. The extortionists have agreed to send us two hostages in return for us putting the camera on the roof. Let's hang onto the elevator for a little while this time; or at least as long as we can. I don't know exactly what to expect, with them wanting this television camera and all, but I sure don't like it. The shield with the firing slits is all ready to go now isn't it?"

"Yes, sir, it's out in the hall."

"Okay, keep it handy. We may be needing it before long."

Angelo had walked halfway around the lounge and stopped beside a shapely young woman in her late twenties. The attractive brunette was stylishly dressed with just the right amount of tastefully expensive jewelry. "The man wants to see you up front," Angelo said. "Let's go."

"What? But why?" came the startled reply.

"Just move it," Angelo ordered brusquely, grabbing her by the arm and hauling her up out of her seat.

The well dressed man seated across the table from her, apparently her husband, instantly jumped to his feet and attempted to pull Angelo's hand off her arm. "Wait just a minute," he demanded.

Angelo's right hand still grasped the shotgun; he had only to jerk the barrel up quickly so that it caught the man directly under the jaw. The man's head snapped back so far that he toppled over backwards, knocking over his chair and coming to rest prone on the floor. The girl shrieked and tried to pull away, but Angelo, now thoroughly angered, savagely twisted her arm and shoved her forward so that she went sprawling to the floor on all fours.

"Come on, get moving," Angelo shouted.

The sobbing girl staggered back to her feet with Angelo still shoving her from behind. The other hostages averted their eyes, no one daring come to her aid. She finally stumbled up to Frank, tears and mascara smeared down her cheeks.

Frank was pleased with Angelo's selection. The girl was strikingly pretty, and it was readily apparent that the figure was really all hers.

Frank had already selected a couple from a nearby table to leave via the elevator, thus fulfilling his part of the trade for the television camera. Frank first stepped into the men's room to retrieve his briefcase before entering the elevator behind the girl and the couple he had selected. He pressed the button for the observation deck level and then stepped out a few moments later, having to pull the girl along with him. The elevator was then allowed to continue on its way to the ground level. After the doors had closed, Frank pressed the up button so that the car would stop at the observation deck on the way back up.

Frank walked over to the edge of the platform and looked down. The railing was about four feet high and then there was a small ledge just a few inches wide on the other side of that. The ledge was just wide enough to stand on.

Frank turned to the girl. "I'm not going to hurt you. If as you do exactly as I say, then in a little while I'll send you down in the elevator. Do you have someone waiting for you upstairs?"

She nodded wordlessly.

"Okay, then he or she can go with you too. Does that sound okay?"

Another nod.

"Good, now take off your hose; I need them." She stared at him but didn't move.

"Do you want to take them off, or do you want me to?"

When the girl still didn't move, Frank reached out for the bottom of her skirt. She pulled away abruptly without saying a word, reached up under her dress, and angrily jerked her hose down. She then kicked off her shoes, pulled the hose off, and defiantly tossed them at him.

"Stick your hands out," Frank ordered.

She waited just long enough to show her defiance again before raising her arms in front of her, her fists clenched. Frank wrapped one end of the hose around her wrists a couple of times and then tightened it into a knot. He reached up above the railing

for a metal brace which stuck out about a foot farther than the edge of the platform. He hesitated for
a moment, though, suddenly realizing that as he
leaned out over the railing to tie the other end of the
hose to the brace he would be slightly off balance
and perfectly in position for her to push him right
over the side if she wished. And he had no doubt
that she would have done it if given half a chance.

He stepped back and steered her over against the
railing so that he was now standing safely behind
her, his weight against her as he leaned out over the
railing and looped the other end of the hose around
the brace. He pulled it in snugly before finishing the
knot so that her arms were lifted up over her head,
her hands almost touching the brace. She was now
up on her toes just a bit as she leaned out over the
railing.

Grabbing the zipper in the back of her dress, Frank
ran it all the way down with one quick motion. The
girl gasped and tried to jerk around and kick at him,
but Frank's response was quick and effective. He
grabbed a handful of her long dark hair and jerked
her head back so that she was looking up at him as
he stood behind her.

"Honey, I'm only going to explain this to you one
more time. I'm not going to hurt you, but if you give
me any more trouble, I'm going to throw you right
over the side. Do you understand me?" The last
question was accompanied by another attention getting jerk of her hair.

Held in a position where she could hardly breathe,
the girl barely managed to choke out a positive sounding grunt. Frank let go of her hair and unhooked
her dress only to realize that it wouldn't come off
with her arms tied above her head. He grabbed the
material and tried to rip it, but the expensive gar-
ment wasn't about to tear.

"This is like one of those crazy Chinese puzzles,"
Frank muttered to himself. Finally he grasped the

dress at the bottom, pulled it up over her head, and pushed it up her arms so that it was wrapped around her hands and the metal brace. As he unfastened her bra, the girl tensed, but she didn't try to move again. Frank stepped around beside her to take a look. The whiteness of her breasts stood out well against her dark tan, creating an effect which Frank knew would show up well for the television camera. He was going for the shock effect; a woman with a lighter complexion wouldn't have shown up as well for the cameras, thus his reason for choosing a brunette.

Frank knelt beside her, inserted his fingers under the band of her panties, and slid then down her legs. Once again, the whiteness of her exposed skin contrasted well with her tan.

As he slipped her panties off, his hands brushing against her skin, he was suddenly aware of how soft her legs were. Frank stared at her, suddenly aroused. His life had been in such disarray for the past month that he hadn't even thought about a woman. His fiance had left him three months before when all the problems associated with his gambling had begun to come to a head, driving an irreversible wedge between them.

Before he had driven her away the sex had been good; no complaints there. She had always been ready and willing to try anything. They had often played at sex games, pretending that he was raping her. He had even tied her up on occasion. She had enjoyed it as much as he had, but that was only a game. This was totally different. This was no game; it was real.

The thought of the girl being totally at his mercy made his breath come short. She would fight him. He knew that. But the thought made it even more exciting. Her wild thrashing resistance would make it just that much better.

Frank felt hot and flushed. He took a deep breath of air in an attempt to relieve the tightness in his chest and then looked around. They were all alone. No one would be interrupting them, that was certain, and a large support column blocked the view of the TV camera on the hotel roof. It was crazy, but there was no reason not to. No one would know. There was nothing to stop him.

The girl suddenly broke his thoughts. "I'll do anything you want if you'll just let me and my husband go. I'm afraid he's hurt badly enough to need medical attention. I'll go along with whatever you like. I won't fight you and I promise I'll make it good for you."

Suddenly the aura faded. It wasn't the same anymore. The attraction was gone. The excitement had come from the thought of her responding to him in wild ecstasy, unable to resist him. It had been but a fantasy, and now it was gone. She meant what she said; she was willing to go along with anything to help her husband. She wouldn't fight him.

Frank looked around guiltily, suddenly feeling as if someone might have been watching and reading his thoughts. What had he been thinking? He wasn't a rapist. He was involved in all this because he had no choice. He didn't want to cause anybody any more harm than he already had. What was coming over him? He suddenly felt frightened by his own emotions, sickened at the thought of what he had been fully prepared to do.

He took another deep breath and licked his dry lips. "Don't be ridiculous. Like I told you, I'm not going to hurt you. I'll check your husband when I go back upstairs. If he needs medical attention, then I'll send him on down in the elevator. How does that sound?"

The girl nodded. "Thanks."

Frank leaned out around the support pillar and looked across the space that separated them from the hotel roof so many stories below. There was just enough moonlight to see that there was a crew set up with a large camera trained in their direction. The lights which were mounted on the tower would provide more than enough illumination for the cameras to show the girl clearly.

"I want you to stand on the ledge on the other side of the railing. I've got you tied securely, and once you're in position I'll put my belt around your waist and the railing so that there's no way in the world you can fall. There's a television camera over there on the hotel roof, but they're so far away they won't be able to tell who you are. They'll only be able to see that there's a woman tied up out here with no clothes on, which is exactly what I want them to see."

Frank didn't tell her the truth, that with the long range lens they had on that camera they would be able to count the hairs on her eyebrows, or on whatever else the camera examined.

"Here, swing your legs over the railing. There's no way you can fall, so you're perfectly safe." Frank helped her into position so that she was standing on the ledge, facing out into thin air toward the hotel in full view of the camera.

Frank quickly removed his belt and placed it around her waist and the railing behind her, fastening it snugly. That would not only make her more secure as she tried to balance on the small ledge, but it would also keep her from climbing right back over the railing after he left.

Once he was satisfied that the girl was totally secure, Frank reached into his pocket and removed his grenade. He pulled the pin and reached over in front of her. "Spread your legs a little more."

The girl stiffened when she realized what he intended to do. "No, don't."

"Come on," he snapped, forcing his hand between her legs and pulling. Trembling, she allowed her legs to be spread apart. Frank slipped the grenade between her thighs.

"Okay, close them," he ordered with a nudge. She carefully did so and Frank slowly let go of the grenade so that it was now held securely between her legs.

"Now honey, you just be real still. If you wriggle, and this clip pops out, it'll blow you apart. If you jiggle enough for it to fall all the way out, then it'll kill a lot of people down below us."

Harris had been keeping a close eye on the TV screen since he knew that whatever was coming next would be on it. He almost choked when the camera, which had been focused on the upper level of the tower, suddenly dropped down and zoomed in close on the observation deck. There, for all the world to see, was a young woman hanging out into thin air, precariously tied to the ledge with no clothing on. And then the camera's long lens left no doubt about what had been placed between the girl's legs.

Harris grabbed the walkie-talkie and immediately signaled the tower. "Tom, are you there?" Harris snapped.

Angelo answered this time. "He had to step out for a minute."

"Listen, you're pushing too far now. When that happens we run out of options and a lot of people get hurt—including you. Tell Tom to take the girl off the platform. You've made your point."

"Just settle down, my man. Nobody's getting hurt."

"I'm warning you."

"No, I'm warning you," Angelo snapped. "Before you do anything you'll regret, you just keep watching your TV screen there."

About a minute later, Harris, the camera crew, and everyone with a television turned on watched in awe as a twenty foot long ball of fire sprayed from the observation deck, accompanied by a thunderous roar transmitted clearly by the camera.

Chapter Fourteen

Harris almost choked. "They've got a friggin' flame thrower up there." He slumped down into a chair mentally and emotionally defeated. Even a military unit with paratroopers and helicopter gunships couldn't have mounted an effective assault on the tower without it resulting in the deaths of many if not most of the hostages. Harris realized that he could do nothing now but stand idly by as the extortionists did as they pleased. There would be internal FBI investigations. There would be Congressional investigations. The press would dig up dirt and point the finger. He would be the whipping boy, the sacrificial lamb they needed. The hand holding the walkie-talkie shook noticeably, revealing a severe need for another drink. Only two more years to retirement. Two lousy years!

Back in the tower Frank busied himself with packing up his homemade flame thrower which consisted of little more than a fire extinguisher packed with a flammable cleaning fluid under high pressure. A cigarette lighter had served as an igniter. The only problem had been finding a spray nozzle that would keep the fire from coming back into the bottle and blowing it up. The device was only a one shot affair, but all they were after was the psychological effect, which Frank was sure they had achieved.

He now returned his attention to the girl. He was well aware that if she should move and allow the grenade to fall from between her legs, it would immediately be apparent that they were attempting a huge bluff, and their chances of getting any money would be greatly diminished.

"Honey, I don't want you to get hurt, so you just take it easy. I'm going back upstairs now to check on your husband, and I'll be back to check on you in a little while in case you get to feeling like that thing may be about to fall out."

Ten minutes later Harris was back in touch with the latest bad news—both for himself and for the extortionists. "Sorry, Tom. The latest word from the hotel is still no ransom."

Frank's face fell as he sagged back against the wall. He had played all his cards. He just wasn't prepared nor willing to start killing people even if he could have been assured that such an action wouldn't bring a SWAT team in on them. Tina had much the same reaction when told of the latest setback, but when Angelo was given the latest news, he reacted far differently.

"Stop screwin' with me!" he shouted, bashing his fist against the wall. "You had your chances—plenty of 'em!"

He ran directly across the lounge to the nearest windows, brought his shotgun up to waist level, and fired at point blank range. The people seated nearby made a desperate effort to hit the floor or scramble out of the way as thousands of fragments of glass exploded out into space.

Angelo pumped, fired again, and pumped again, continuing to blast at the glass until the gun was empty and a huge hole gaped in the side of the building. Then he threw the shotgun to the floor and vaulted over the railing, running back toward the kitchen area. Just inside the swinging doors he ripped a fire ax from the wall and started back toward the windows again.

He came to a halt before the body of Jack Hilliard, still lying exactly as he had fallen from Tina's shots. Placing one foot on the man's shoulder, Angelo swung the ax as high above his head as he could, then brought it down with all his might, striking an out-stretched arm halfway between the shoulder and the elbow. With most of his weight solidly behind the blow, the sharp blade sliced all the way through the arm, bone and all, completely severing the limb from the body.

With no hesitation, Angelo grabbed the limb around the wrist and strode determinedly toward the blasted out windows. "Wait a min-" Angelo roughly shoved Frank out of his way as Frank attempted to speak. Then Angelo drew back and flung the arm through the large hole, far out into space.

The limb turned slowly end over end as it sailed out and then downward. Half a dozen television cameras were immediately trained on the object when it hit the ground. It was then more than clear what had been thrown from the tower. The live television cameras showed a close-up color picture of the arm as the clutched fingers appeared to grip the ground for security.

Angelo grabbed the walkie-talkie and shouted into it. "You see that? You get another arm every thirty minutes until we get the money!"

Harris didn't fully comprehend the angry threat until he peered closer at his television monitor. He was now painfully aware that this was no idle threat. He had the head of the SWAT team on the phone within seconds.

"You've got fifteen minutes. Get yourself into po-sition and go in when ready."

"Yes, sir." The reply was crisp and ready.

Harris laid the phone down and gazed off into space. He was only an observer from this point on. He had finally run out of both time and options.

The flight attendant opened the door of the 747, allowing the first class passengers to file out first. Millard made his way out of the plane to the terminal with Patsy giggling and clinging to him much more than she actually needed to.

They continued on through the terminal with Patsy bouncing at every step and drawing quite a few looks. Her primary duties on this trip would be to lie around in a string bikini that couldn't even begin to cover her adequately. Besides enjoying the sight himself, Millard planned to have a couple of business associates over for drinks around the pool, and he looked forward to their envious stares.

"Whoa," Patsy said as they came to a stop before a rest room. "I've got to go potty. You stay right here."

Millard watched her disappear into the rest room and reflected that she was a little too frivolous and certainly too expensive, but she was worth every penny of it. She made him feel young again. When he was home with his wife he found himself doing nothing but concentrating on his aches and pains.

Patsy came bouncing back out of the rest room shortly and gave him a hug and a kiss. "Hi, I missed you."

"You did?"

"Uh-huh."

"Everything okay?"

She held up one finger, indicating the number one.

"Good," he replied. "Did you wipe good?"

She drew back in mock anger and slapped at him. "That's a disgusting thing to ask a lady." She started off down the terminal by herself, forcing him to catch up with her.

"Where are we going first?" she asked as he took her arm again.

"What do you mean where are we going first?" he replied with exaggerated surprise in his voice. "After flopping all over me for six thousand miles, you know exactly where we're going first."

Patsy giggled as Millard grasped her arm more firmly and hurried her along.

Harris watched almost with disinterest as the steel shield was moved into position behind the four officers who had entered the elevator. They would blow just one door on the second level since all the extortionists and hostages were believed to be on the third level. Then they would come up the spiral stairway into the lounge just as the elevator with the shield was reaching the lounge. If a sniper on the hotel roof had even a chance shot he was to take it.

The hostages were expendable from the standpoint of taking out the extortionists as quickly as possible. If the extortionists were able to set off any of the explosives, they might take most of the hostages out with them. Harris knew that they would have to sacrifice some to save most. He figured that if they lost only a quarter of the hostages and not more than half a dozen members of the assault team they would be lucky.

Millard assisted Patsy as she slipped into the cab, and then tipped the porter who was handling their bags. "Thank you."

"Thank you, sir."

Millard slid in beside his assistant and was just closing the door when a young man rushed up to them.

"Pardon me, sir," he blurted. "Are you Mr. Millard from Millard Hotels?"

"Yes I am."

"I'm glad I caught you. I must have missed you

when you got off the plane. You've got an urgent
message to call your office back in Dallas the second
you arrive."

"Okay, thanks a lot. I'll call them from my hotel."

"The caller asked that you phone directly from the
airport and not wait until getting to your hotel."

Millard looked both puzzled and annoyed. "I can't
believe that anything could be that important." He
reached over and touched the inside of Patsy's thigh.
"Would you mind waiting for a couple of minutes?"

"No," she said, squeezing his hand between her
legs. "You go right ahead."

Millard followed the messenger back into the terminal and into an office where he was offered the
use of a telephone.

"Thank you."

He tried the headquarters number three times,
but got a busy signal each time. "Well, it's busy for
some reason," he remarked to the messenger. "I
guess I'll have to wait until I get to the hotel after
all."

"Oh, I'm sorry," the young man groaned. "The
message said that you were to call on Mr. Post's
private extension. Hold on a minute and let me find
the number." He dug around in a pile of notes and
messages on his desk until producing the one he was
seeking.

"Here it is." Millard accepted the note and dialed
the new number.

"Mr. Post's office," the secretary answered.

"Hello, this is Mr. Millard. I just arrived in Honolulu and had an urgent message to call Mr. Post."

"Oh, Mr. Millard," the secretary gushed. "I'm so
glad that it's finally you. You just can't imagine what
a mess we have here. You just stay right there and
let me go find Mr. Post. Don't go anywhere now."

Millard was more puzzled than ever at the girl's
reaction to his call. He certainly wasn't about to go

anywhere now. Post picked up the phone about two minutes later.

"Hello, Mr. Millard?"

"Yes, Bill, what in the world is going on back there?"

"You're not going to believe it, sir."

"Well let's have it. Quit dancing around."

"Not long after you left this morning, three men armed with explosives took over the top of Millard Tower with almost 200 people in it. They've demanded a $3 million ransom for the hostages."

"Three million dollars! Have you given it to them?"

"No, sir. That's the problem. The FBI says that if we don't pay the ransom, the extortionists will kill the hostages, but Knight won't give them a penny. He won't even bargain with them. As a result, at least three or four people have already been killed and the extortionists just cut someone's arm off and threw it off the top of the tower. But the worst part is the public outcry against the company. The entire thing has been on live television, and we're being blamed for everything. We've got pickets outside now and people are calling in by the thousands cancelling their reservations in mass protest."

"What are the authorities doing?"

"Their hands are tied. The extortionists have guns, bombs, and even a flame thrower. There's no way to save the hostages without paying their ransom demand."

"Then why won't Knight pay it? Has he been waiting to hear from me all this time?"

"No, sir. He says that he won't bargain with the extortionists no matter what. He's got some idea about stopping anybody else from pulling this sort of thing by holding out. I can't even reason with him."

"So your advice is to give them the money."

"Yes, sir, definitely."

"Okay, then get it together as soon as you can."

"I've already got it. I saw to that without Knight knowing about it."

"Good. Then get it to the FBI."

"Okay, but I'll need you to talk to Knight for me. As I said, I can't reason with him anymore. In fact, I can't even talk to him."

"Okay, put him on the phone."

Millard could hear Post instructing his secretary to summon Knight to the phone immediately. Post then continued while he waited for Knight.

"Mr. Millard, I can't tell you how bad things are here. The hostages wrote letters which were read over live television. They were begging us to pay the ransom to save them. A few of them asked people to cancel their reservations if we wouldn't pay the ransom, and that's when the cancellations started pouring in from all over the country."

Millard grimaced. "You better start working on one heck of a public relations campaign right away. I'll be on the next flight back, but you need to go ahead and hold a news conference as soon as this thing is over so we can start trying to reverse our losses. I don't have all the details, so I'll let you decide what should be said and how."

"Yes, sir, I'll take care of it. Hold on, here comes Knight now."

Knight's voice came across the line. "Hello, Mr. Millard?"

"Yes, Colby. I want you to pay the ransom demand as soon as possible. Let Bill take care of it for you since he's already been working on it."

"But Mr. Millard, we can't pay the money now. Don't you see? We have to show that we can't be forced into dealing with criminals."

"This is not under discussion," Millard stated in a stern voice. "Pay the ransom. Immediately."

"Look," Knight pleaded, "At least let me have a little time to bargain with them. I'm certain that I can get the amount of the ransom reduced significantly."

"Forget it. We've got to get our house back in order as quickly as possible. Give them whatever they want immediately. Now let me talk to Bill again."

"Yes, sir," Post answered.

"Bill, I want you to take charge of things and run them as you see fit. I believe that our thinking is together on the matter."

"Yes, sir. I assure you that it is."

"Fine. I don't know when the next flight is, but you can check the schedules and get an idea of when I'll be back. I'll get with you when I arrive."

"Yes, sir, have a good trip back."

"Thanks, and good luck on your end."

The steel shield at the elevator door was given a final adjustment so that it completely sealed the opening except for an inch at the top. The firing slits were arranged so that two men would be kneeling, two standing. The button was pushed for the restaurant level and the doors silently closed, then the car began its ascent.

Doug called from across the room. "Telephone, inspector."

Harris just waved him away. He didn't have the energy or the stamina or the will, whatever you wanted to call it, to do anything else other than wait. It'd all be done and over with in a matter of seconds now, anyway.

"Inspector, I think you should take it. It's from Millard Hotels."

"I've talked to that character all I'm going to. Get rid of him."

"But it's not Knight. It's one of the other executives up there. Somebody named Post. He says he's in charge of things now."

Harris frowned a bit, but still didn't want to be

bothered. He wearily walked across the room and took the phone receiver that Doug passed to him.

"Yes, Inspector Harris here."

"Inspector Harris, this is Bill Post, vice president of financial planning for Millard Hotels. I have the ransom money for you."

Inside the elevator, the team commander had positioned himself and the three men with him, gun barrels inserted through the slits in the heavy metal shield. He repeated the final instructions from Harris once again.

"Remember, if a target is holding a hostage in front of him, use your judgement. The target may move or the hostage may move giving you a better shot. But if the target begins to move back away from us, so that he could move around the wall out of our range of fire, we have to take him out before he can do so. Fire at their legs first. That might cause the target or the hostage to fall, giving us a better shot.

"If that doesn't work, or if the target is trying to set off an explosive device of any sort, then any hostages are expendable. The target will have to be taken out immediately. It is our job to take out any target we can see, one way or another. The team coming through the door on the lower level is primarily a backup in case any of the targets aren't in sight when we reach the top."

The car darkened slightly as they left the moonlight and zoomed rapidly up into the bottom of the tower, moving past the observation deck. The walkie-talkie on the commander's belt crackled just then with a loud shout. "Stop the elevator, do you hear? Don't go in. Stop it right now."

The commander immediately snapped his hand out and hit the stop button, bringing the elevator to a sudden halt halfway between the restaurant and lounge levels, just five feet from their objective.

"We've stopped between floors," the commander reported.

"Good," Harris said. "Stay exactly where you are. Don't try to move. Now, I want the team inside the stairwell to withdraw."

"Sir, we've already got the charges in place on the door. Do I understand that you now want us to withdraw completely?"

"That's right. Get the charges off the door and get away from there. Clear everybody out." Harris felt like laughing and crying all at the same time.

"Do you want us to move just a few levels back down the stairs or should we come all the way back to the bottom?"

"Come all the way back down to the bottom. Keep it quiet, but move out just as fast as you can." Harris could have left the team in the stairwell, safely out of sight a few levels below the lounge, but he wanted no chance of some sort of mix-up occurring at this point. He had barely been saved at just the last moment as it was.

"Leave the elevator right where it is or it'll probably move on up to the lounge level and open. We'll get some people from engineering to override the automatic controls and bring you back to the bottom."

Harris laid down that walkie-talkie and picked up the one that connected him to the lounge. "Tom, we've got the money. The hotel finally came through with it."

Frank was understandably skeptical. "Is this another one of your tricks, Harris?"

"No, no tricks. We just got word that they'll have the money to us within half an hour."

Frank couldn't believe what he was hearing. They were handing over the entire amount without even trying to bargain with them. He had asked for three million in the hope that they could get one and a half out of them.

Angelo and Tina, standing right beside him, too, were skeptical. "I'll believe it when I see it," Tina said.

Frank had just keyed the transmit button on the walkie-talkie again when a spitting sort of sound was heard. Slivers of glass showered over a couple of tables near the windows as Tina pitched forward, a huge gaping hole suddenly appearing in the side of her neck.

Harris heard the shot from two sources, both over the walkie-talkie and over his television monitor. The sniper who had fired the shot had been right beside the camera crew on the hotel roof. No one had notified the snipers that the assault had been called off.

"Call them off, call off the snipers," Harris shouted angrily. Then he shouted desperately into the walkie-talkie. "Tom, listen to me. That was a mistake. There will be no more shooting. Everything's okay now. Do you hear me?"

Frank cautiously raised his head from the floor. The blood which had spurted forcefully from the hole in Tina's neck had ceased.

Chapter Fifteen

Now that emotions over the shooting had cooled, Frank was at last confident that Harris was being truthful about the money. Feeling certain that they would have it in just a few more minutes, he left Angelo to watch the lounge while he took the elevator back down to the observation deck. The girl was still positioned exactly as he had left her. Frank leaned out over the railing, though taking care to keep the girl between himself and the snipers on the hotel roof, and carefully removed the hand grenade from between her legs. Now that they were so close to their goal he didn't want to take any further chance that the girl might drop the grenade, thus giving away their bluff.

Frank helped her back over the railing and untied her hands. She rubbed her wrists for a moment, now quite tender and reddened where the hose had chafed the skin, and then bent down to retrieve her clothes. As she leaned over and pulled her panties back on, Frank couldn't help staring at her breasts again, feeling the stirrings that had hit him earlier.

She straightened up abruptly and looked him directly in the eye, making no attempt to cover herself or to turn away from his gaze. "What are you staring at?" she demanded sharply.

Surprised and taken aback, Frank suddenly felt his face reddening in embarrassment. He awkwardly turned his head and looked out over the railing while she finished dressing.

"Can I go now?" she asked a few moments later.

"Sure, go right ahead," Frank said as he gestured to the open elevator door. "I sent your husband on down a little while ago. I don't think he had anything more than a badly bruised jaw, but they probably took him to the hospital for x-rays just to make sure."

The girl stepped into the elevator without another word and pulled the run button, then turned and stared at Frank contemptuously until the doors finally closed between them. After she was gone Frank was left with a vague feeling of discomfort. He hadn't felt this way since the first time he had masturbated at the age of eleven.

When the elevator returned a few minutes later, four large briefcases were sitting on the floor. Frank stepped inside and pressed the button for the lounge level, still keeping his hand on the stop button in case the elevator should unexpectedly start to go back down instead of up. Angelo was waiting with his gun at the ready when the doors opened.

Frank laid one of the four cases on the hostess stand and quickly popped open the unlocked latches. When he raised the lid he found the case to be filled with neatly arranged stacks of $100 bills. He picked up a bundle and flipped through the new crisp notes. The serial numbers didn't seem to be in any particular order, though he realized that they could have taken bills that had been in sequential order and merely mixed them up. He certainly didn't intend to take the time to check out that possibility. He had only demanded that the bills not have sequential serial numbers in the hope that the authorities wouldn't then attempt to mix them up.

He rapidly fanned a stack back and forth beneath

his nose and sniffed. If there were any obvious chemical odors, he couldn't detect them. One by one he went through the other three briefcases with the same results while Angelo watched intently.

"Looks good," Frank announced at last with a thumbs up signal. A broad smile and a huge sigh of relief greeted his positive assessment.

"Aren't you going to count it?" Angelo asked.

"There's no need to. It takes thirty thousand $100 bills to make up $3 million, and thirty thousand bills should weigh sixty-three pounds. That's about sixteen pounds per case, and these feel pretty close."

Frank closed the lid on the last case and snapped the latches shut again. "Keep an eye on this," he said. "Don't let anyone steal it."

He then strode around the corner to the empty manager's office and picked up a telephone which would provide him with a clear outside line. He dialed a number and had to wait only one ring before it was answered. "We're ready," Frank said and then hung up the phone without waiting for a reply.

A short while later, Harris stepped outside again, hoping that the cool night air would make him feel better. It didn't. He leaned his head back and looked up again at the sphere, the perfect fortress that towered above him in more ways than one.

There were the usual noises from the late evening downtown traffic and the nearby freeways along with the sounds of the large crowd which had gathered throughout the evening and now milled around behind the barricades. But there was something else; another noise. Then he knew. He understood at last. The parachutes they had delivered to the extortionists had been nothing but a decoy.

"Get those searchlights on, all of them," he shouted. "There's a helicopter up on top of the tower."

Within a matter of seconds, four huge search-

lights, two on the ground and two on nearby buildings, lit up the tower as if it were broad daylight.
And there, caught in the glare as it perched atop the
sphere like a giant dragonfly on a flower, was a
helicopter.

"Inspector, do you want me to give the order to
fire?" Doug asked.

"No, we can't risk it. They said they would be
taking hostages with them. I thought that was just to
confuse us about the parachutes. This is what they
meant. No, reiterate that everyone is to hold their
fire, but get the full tactical squad started back up
the stairs. Tell them not to open any doors, though;
they're probably still rigged with explosives. Just tell
them to move back into position and be ready to go
in at any moment. And get our helicopters into the
air, but tell them to keep their lights off. I want them
to stay well back and give the other helicopter plenty
of room until it takes off. Then they should follow it,
but make it clear to them that there may be hostages
still involved."

Doug promptly conveyed Harris's orders to the
various groups. This time the six man detail that
moved quickly into the stairwell didn't bother to
remove their boots. Noise was no longer a factor for
them.

Harris squinted into the glare of the searchlights
as something else caught his eye. "No, please no," he
said through clenched teeth.

Fluttering down from the top of the tower, perfectly illuminated in the crisscrossing lights, were
hundreds, maybe even thousands of bills. This was
what the onlookers had been waiting for, why the
crowd had swelled from a few hundred in the early
afternoon to almost six thousand now. Not even the
increased manpower at the barricades could stop
them. Like the onrush of an enemy attack, they
surged forward. At first one place and then another

and another they broke through the police lines like water breaking through cracks in a dam.

Harris turned away, not wanting to watch. He knew exactly what would happen. It would be a mob scene. People would be trampled and injured and they'd blame him. But what could he have done to stop them? He'd have had to evacuate the entire downtown area and block off portions of two interstate highways. He would have had to place patrolmen in riot gear shoulder to shoulder around the entire area in order to have gained the slightest chance of keeping them out; there weren't that many officers in the entire county.

Like an army of ants advancing across a carpet, they came; sweeping down the streets and across the parking lots. And then they were grabbing and pushing and shoving in a money crazed frenzy. At that exact moment the stairwell door behind Harris unexpectedly burst open with a bang and the released hostages began pouring out. "Hold it, stop right there," Harris shouted. He signaled to Doug who was already directing several men to help cordon off the area in an attempt to keep the hostages together before they lost them in the mob.

Suddenly the sound of gunfire erupted from inside the stairwell and there were shouts and screams of panic. The people coming from the stairwell had been fairly calm, willing to do as directed, but now they panicked, scattering in all directions. The rest of the mob, until this point intent only on the money, now heard the gunshots along with the accompanying shouts and screams, felt the panic, and added to the total chaos as they, too, began running in all directions.

Harris pulled his service revolver as he ran toward the stairwell after Doug and half a dozen uniformed officers. He tried to shout at the people still running from the stairwell, to ask what was happening behind them, but the panic was total by now and they heard nothing. Like a pack of wild animals, they were intent only on their flight from danger.

All Harris and his group could do was stand back out of the way as the last of the hostages ran from the stairwell. Harris did a double take as one man ran by him wearing nothing but a tablecloth. He didn't know what was going on inside, but Harris realized that the best course of action at this point was to get all the hostages out of the stairwell as quickly as possible. The last thing he wanted was to block any of them inside. It took only a minute more and then the doorway was open and clear. Two people were lying halfway up the first flight of stairs where they had been knocked down and trampled in the panic, blood pouring from head and face wounds.

"Let's get an ambulance over here," someone shouted.

Harris peered cautiously up the stairs along with Doug and the other uniforms. "Who's in radio contact with the squad we sent upstairs?"

Everyone looked around blankly. "Well didn't the idiots bother to take a radio?" Harris shouted.

Doug looked down at his feet uncomfortably. "It all happened so fast," he managed weakly.

Harris gritted his teeth. "I want another squad with flak jackets and automatic weapons to clear this area on the double. All the way to the top. And get the explosives team up there with the dog again."

"Yes sir." Doug hurried off, thankful of an excuse to escape his superior's displeasure.

Harris stepped back outside, his stomach burning and his head pounding. With the panicked rush away from the sounds of the gunfire, the mob outside had thinned considerably. A few people still milled around in confusion, but now that all the money had been scooped up, most were making their way back to wherever they had come from, the action apparently over for the night. Most of the patrolmen had given up any pretense of keeping their barricades and lines in place and just stood watching the people, letting them do as they pleased.

Harris stepped back away from the tower a few paces and looked up. The helicopter was gone.

Several blocks away on the helicopter pad at Dallas City Hall, Lt. Bill Allsup and the three officers with him had been strapped into their police copter for almost ten hours. Occasionally one of the men would step outside to stretch, or to relieve himself behind the tail, but only for a moment. Then it was right back in to buckle up again.

Allsup had the chopper set up like they used to do it in Nam. Everything was ready. All he had to do was flip on the battery switch and hit the starter. A squad car parked nearby provided radio contact. If they had kept their own radios powered, they could have run down the craft's battery. Or they could have run out of fuel if they had tried to sit there with the engine running for a long period of time.

Allsup squirmed uncomfortably, his butt feeling as if it had gone to sleep hours ago. Sitting without moving was the worst part by far. When you were buckled in for a long flight it wasn't so bad; the motion and the vibration all tended to help the circulation.

Suddenly the uniformed officer in the patrol car just a few feet away jumped out and shouted. "There's a helicopter on top of the tower. They may be taking hostages with them, so leave your lights off, give them plenty of room, and then follow them."

Finally! Allsup flipped on the battery switch and was rewarded with the familiar glow from his instrument panel. He hit the starter and with a whine the huge rotor slowly began to turn. Ninety seconds later he was hovering a thousand feet higher than the top of the tower, laying off a half mile away.

The noise wasn't a concern no matter how close they were. The other pilot wouldn't be able to hear it over the noise of his own machine. The night was now partly cloudy, but they were high clouds which effectively blocked out most of the moonlight without making it dangerous to fly. It would be difficult to be spotted. But then, by the same token, it would be more difficult to follow their quarry.

Allsup's headphones crackled as a call came from the second police copter, in position a mile to the west of the tower, directly opposite Allsup's location. "Five Delta Papa (delta papa was the call sign for all Dallas police craft), this is three Delta Papa. Do you read?"

"That's affirmative, three Delta Papa. Go ahead."

"It looks like you've got it on your own. We've got a no go mechanical problem."

"Roger that, we're in position now," Allsup responded. The truth be known, Allsup was just as happy to be following the other helicopter by himself. Since they would be running with their lights off, he would have been forced to direct most of his attention to the other police copter to avoid hitting it. Now he was free to concentrate totally on the craft atop the tower.

"He's starting to move, Lieutenant," the officer beside him observed.

Allsup nodded as he adjusted his altitude a few feet, ever the perfectionist. The other copter had risen slightly and was now dipped forward at an angle as it began to move slowly away from the tower.

Allsup keyed his transmitter. "He's starting to move. He's coming right to a heading of 045 degrees." Allsup let the other machine begin its motion so that he could be sure of its course before beginning to follow. He didn't want to commit himself too soon and then unexpectedly have the other craft turn back toward him. He was careful to stay slightly above his quarry as it began to climb along its north-easterly course.

With the help of the searchlights on the ground, Allsup had been able to judge the make and model of the helicopter he was following; he knew that speed would be no problem. He could easily overtake the other craft and pull alongside if need be, but with a possible hostage situation such a maneuver would not have been wise.

The other pilot apparently hadn't seen them, because he took no evasive action. He just climbed up to an altitude of 3,000 feet, leveled off, and headed out to the northeast at an average cruise speed. Allsup kept up a continuously running update on their location as they followed about three quarters of a mile behind. The other copter wasn't running any lights either, so Allsup was hesitant to widen the distance between them any farther. On the other hand, he didn't dare get any closer since the other pilot might make a sudden unexpected turn and spot them.

They hadn't gone all that far, maybe fifty miles, when the other copter began a descent. "They're starting down," Allsup radioed, giving his exact position once again.

He kept his position on the chopper in front as the copter approached a small airport and then slowed, slowly settling to a stop on the deserted ramp below. The ramp was dimly lighted, but Allsup and his group could plainly see that there were no other signs of activity, no cars waiting to meet the other craft.

Allsup quickly transmitted the airport's location and called for backup ground units. "Look, his rotor's slowing," Allsup commented to the officer beside him. "It looks as if he's shutting it down."

"Should we go in?" asked the officer.

"I don't know. Let's give them just another minute or so and see what happens. You would think that if a car were planning on picking them up they would have been here waiting with the engine running. I don't see any signs of life around here at all."

"Maybe some sort of a trap? They realized we were following them and they figured that they couldn't shake us?"

"Maybe so," Allsup said. "But whatever's going on it looks like it's our move. I'll drop on down a little more, but I'll keep a good distance away. Get the spotlight on them."

The officer switched on the spotlight and directed the strong beam toward the grounded chopper as Allsup slowly dipped the ship toward the ground. "If you see any muzzle flashes coming out of the thing, kill the light and I'll get us out of here," he warned.

Finally they were within a hundred yards of the other machine, hovering just above the ground. Even with the bright spotlight, however, they couldn't tell what was going on inside the other craft. Allsup glanced to his left as the sight of flashing blue lights racing down the nearby road caught his eye. "Looks like the backups are here, so we might as well go on in now. What do you think?"

"Sure, the timing isn't going to get any better. Why don't you land behind them so we'll have a clear approach?"

"Good idea." Allsup maneuvered around behind the other copter and then carefully moved in as close as he dared before setting down. He quickly shut off the engine and peered out at the machine in front of them. There was still no sign of movement. "If this is some kind of trick where they plan to take off again real quick, they aren't pulling it off very well. Their rotor's almost stopped."

The officer beside him nodded his agreement. "Why don't we let the patrol cars pull up into position and then we'll move in?"

"That sounds good to me." Allsup and the three men with him watched as the two cars with their flashing blue strobe lights pulled to within forty feet of the helicopter and then stopped. Allsup jerked his .357 magnum from his shoulder holster and hit the ground running, his three heavily armed companions right behind him. Allsup waved at the officers stepping cautiously out of their patrol cars, signaling them to stay back in a covering position.

The group of four knelt behind the tail of the copter as Allsup quietly waved two of the officers around to the right side and indicated that he and the other man would take the left. On his signal they jumped from behind the tail and snapped their weapons into firing position at point blank range at the windows. Allsup reached up and jerked the door open, but was totally unprepared for what he found inside. The pilot, sitting quietly in his seat with his hands raised, was the sole occupant of the helicopter.

Allsup stepped back as two of the officers pulled the man from his seat, then frisked and cuffed him. "What happened to the people you picked up from the tower?" Allsup demanded.

"I didn't pick anybody up. I was forced into being a decoy for them. They said they'd kill my wife and kids if I didn't go to the top of the tower when they told me to and hover for two minutes. Then I was supposed to fly up here and land."

Allsup looked at the other officers blankly. The sound of more sirens was beginning to be heard in the distance, bearing down on the airport. "Well where in the world are they?"

Doug found Harris sitting in the stairwell on the steps, his head in his hands. "Sir, we just got the report from the chase copter. The helicopter landed at a small airport not too far outside Dallas."

"And it was empty. There was no one in it but the pilot."

Doug widened his eyes in surprise. "Yes, sir, that's right. But how did you know?"

Harris held up a few scraps of paper and a small,

unexploded firecracker. "There wasn't any firing in the stairwell. I didn't think the noise sounded exactly right, but I assumed it was just because of the unusual acoustics in here. They set off a string of firecrackers in order to stampede everyone into a panic. The extortionists simply walked down the stairs with all the hostages and then ran out in the middle of all the confusion. We stood there and literally held the door open for them."

Doug could only stare with his mouth open. "But how," he finally managed.

"It wouldn't have been too hard. W'll find the ski masks and some clothing upstairs somewhere. They could easily have taken off the masks, changed clothes, and then blended in with the rest of the hostages coming down the stairs. Nobody would have noticed a thing. After all, there were almost two hundred people up there, and with the restaurant being round like it is, none of the hostages would have known what was going on except right around them."

"What do we do now? Do you want us to cordon off a larger area and search everyone?"

Harris rose from the steps without bothering to reply. Doug watched him trudge wearily, unsteadily away. At times he didn't like working for the man, at times he even hated him, but he felt only pity for him now. The press and the self serving finger pointing politicians were going to crucify the poor old stooped figure.

Frank stopped at the door to Carl's apartment and set down the two briefcases he was carrying. It was only then that he realized he had another problem. Carl had, quite literally, taken the key with him. There weren't any lights on inside, but Frank went ahead and tried knocking anyway. The door was promptly opened by Angelo.

Frank stepped inside with his two cases and Angelo closed the door behind him.

"Any problems?" Frank asked.

"Piece of cake."

"You're sure you weren't followed?"

"I'm sure."

"Okay. Let's take a final good look around this place before we clear out."

"What are we looking for?"

"Anything that could possibly point back to either of us. And try to think of anything you may have touched and wipe it off. Since that woman recognized Carl, the cops are bound to be here before long, and they'll be dusting everything in sight."

Knowing that the FBI would be there shortly, Frank's first inclination was to run, but he knew that to do so carelessly would be disastrous. It took about fifteen minutes of fast paced searching and wiping before he was finally satisfied. One of Frank's main concerns was that Carl might have left any written evidence against them hidden anywhere, but nothing of that sort turned up.

"Well, that should be the end of it," Frank said.

He bent over and checked the latches on his two briefcases again, not bothering to look back at Angelo. "Take it easy on spending your money. If you start blowing it, it'll attract attention and they'll be on you in no time. If you're smart, you'll sit on it for a year except for occasional pocket change."

"You're through telling me what to do. You're through telling anybody what to do."

It wasn't the words so much as the tone that caused Frank to turn around. He found Angelo's .45 pointed at his chest.

"Wait a minute. This doesn't make any sense. You've already got more money than you can ever spend."

Frank didn't get an answer, but he hadn't really expected one. He watched as Angelo's finger tightened on the trigger. Even that small thing, the way he pulled the trigger, said much about him and about Frank and about their relationship—such that it was. Had it been but a simple quick killing for the money, the finger would have jerked the trigger and it would have been over. But this was different, far different. Angelo was enjoying, even savoring the moment.

Frank hadn't been stupid enough to think that he meant anything to Angelo, that they had actually developed any sort of feeling or respect for one another. Each had simply been using the other—and each knew it. As long as Carl had been along, there hadn't been a problem of one against one. But then, Frank hadn't planned on Carl not being there. Frank smiled wryly, humorlessly to himself. In a strange way, Angelo's actions were actually a verification of Frank's own judgment. After all, it was this sort of behavior that had led Frank to pick Angelo for the job.

Angelo's finger tightened a millimeter more and the hammer fell forward. The loud click the hammer made was surprising. Or at least it was surprising to Angelo. He quickly snapped the .45's slide back in an attempt to get a bullet into the chamber, but found that the gun was empty. He looked up to see Frank holding his .45.

"It's not loaded. I took the bullets out when you laid it down in the tower," Frank said.

A look of hatred, not fear, crossed Angelo's face. "You son of a—"

"Do you want me to act like you? Or do you want me to walk away and leave you half the money after you just tried to kill me?"

"I didn't try anything you hadn't already thought about."

"That's where you're wrong. You see, even with all of the death and horror I've caused, I'm still not like you. I did what I did because I had to. I didn't have any choice. But the bottom line between you and me is that I didn't like it."

Frank lowered his gun.

"That's garbage," Angelo snapped. "Don't give me that self-righteous act, talking like you're some kinda saint. You're no better than me."

"Oh? Do you honestly think so?" Frank raised the gun and pointed it at Angelo again. "Maybe you're right after all."

Angelo's breathing started coming in short nervous gasps as he stared not at the gun but at Frank's eyes. For there, he knew, he'd find the answer that would mean the difference between life and death for him.

Frank's eyes seemed to harden as his finger gradually increased the pressure on the trigger. Frank held it for a moment, then abruptly dropped the gun to his side.

"You're wrong."

Frank picked up his suitcases, stepped out the door and closed it behind him. Though it all seemed to be over at last, neither man, in his wildest dreams, could imagine the fate which would befall him. Suffice it to say, it was the last time either man would see the other alive.

Chapter Sixteen

Inspector Robert Harris rose with the early light of what promised to be a beautiful morning and vomited up the remains of the bottle of scotch he had downed a few hours earlier. He desperately wanted to crawl back into bed and not come out again, but he was more afraid to do that than to go out and face whatever the day after might bring.

After a shower, shave, and one more drink, he once again looked the part of a respectable law enforcement official. The facade securely in place, Harris had one stop to make before going to his office. He had spent a considerable amount of time the day before on the phone with Colby Knight, and he now had a few choice words he wanted to say to his face. It took him almost twenty minutes out of his way with the usual early morning rush hour traffic. Traffic was even more snarled in front of the Millard Hotels headquarters building where several police cars and an ambulance sat with flashing lights. Harris didn't bother to drive around looking for a parking place, a frustrating task at best in downtown Dallas. He just double parked behind one of the police cars.

A uniformed police officer met him as he entered the door. "Can I help you, sir?"

Harris flashed his badge. "What's going on? Who's in charge here?"

"Lieutenant Sparks, the man in the checked coat right over there."

Harris moved across the room and introduced himself to the police lieutenant who proved more than happy to tell him what he knew. "It's the craziest thing I ever heard of, inspector. The secretary says that these two vice presidents, a Mr. Knight and a Mr. Post, were arguing about a cigarette burn in the lobby carpet and who was going to pay for it. Then Knight pulls out a gun, pumps five shots into Post, and puts the last one into his own head. Went in the temple and came out through his mouth."

"Is he dead?"

"They rushed him over to the hospital; don't know if he'll make it or not."

"What about Post?"

"He was dead before he hit the floor from the first shot. Then Knight stood there and took his time with the next four shots, making sure he had finished him off. With the kind of bucks these high class executives types make, what difference could it make who fixed the stupid carpet?"

By the time Harris got to the office, the place already was bustling with activity. People were in the process of quickly and efficiently running down every lead, every hunch, and every tip they could find. It had to be done, though Harris already knew that in this case almost all of it would turn out to be a complete waste of time.

Doug met him at the front door. "What have you got?" Harris asked.

"We've mainly been interviewing all the hostages—at least the ones we can find."

"Why can't you find them all?"

"The way they scattered last night, a lot just walked away and don't want to get involved any further."

"That figures," Harris said sourly. "What about the ones you have talked to? Have you gotten anything other than a lot of wildly varying descriptions?"

"We've interviewed sixty people so far, and we've already got sixty-one different descriptions. We did have several people tell us one thing, though."

"What's that?"

"They heard the leader of the group called Frank several times."

"So it definitely wasn't Tom Agnew."

"Right. But other than that, this line of attack doesn't look very promising. Half a dozen hostages have named other people who they think might be one of the hijackers—you know, like a neighbor. One guy claimed that his mother-in-law was in on it, and one of the women said that the leader was her dog reincarnated."

Harris shook his head. "With all the nuts we've got running around loose, it's a wonder we don't have more incidents than we already do."

"Yeah, that's right. Oh, but there's something else that may be worthwhile."

"What's that?"

"The assistant manager at the restaurant hasn't shown up for work in two days now. He's just disappeared and they haven't been able to get in touch with him."

Harris frowned. "That sounds a little fishy. Why weren't we told about it sooner?"

"I don't know. I guess that it was one of those things that nobody really thought about."

"This sounds almost too good to be true. Let's take a ride over to this guy's place. Do you know his address?"

"No, but I'll get it. I'll be right back."

Harris suddenly felt better than he had since this thing had started. He almost felt as if he were back in control of the situation once again, rather than vice versa.

Thirty minutes later Harris and Doug pulled into the underground parking garage at the missing man's condo building. A talk with the manager produced a key easily enough, and they soon were knocking on the door to apartment 4E. As expected, there was no answer, so they used the passkey.

"He's got good taste," Doug observed as he admired a large oil painting.

"Do you hear water running?" Harris asked.

"Yes I do. Sounds like it's coming from in there," Doug replied, indicating a half opened door to an adjoining room. Doug led the way into the bedroom, finding nothing out of the ordinary. He cautiously peered into the bathroom and then let out a long whistle. "It looks like we hit pay dirt this time. Take a look at this."

He stood back to give Harris room to squeeze past. Harris stepped in to find a girl's body draped over the side of the bathtub, water still running, with her head immersed. Her hands were tied behind her back with a pair of stockings, and she was nude except for a pair of panties around her knees. A trail of dried blood snaked down her legs. Harris stepped over her gingerly and shut off the water.

"Did you notice the closet?" Harris asked as he dried off his hand.

"No, what about it?"

"The clothes are strewn around pretty good. Looks like somebody left in a hurry."

"Yeah. Well, I can't believe that this guy killed the girl, packed a few clothes, and then on a whim decided to take over the tower with three other people."

"Maybe she threatened to expose his plans, so he killed her," Harris suggested.

"Who knows. Seems like we've just got more questions now."

Having checked the apartment thoroughly, but finding nothing more, they returned the key to the manager with strict instructions to let no one in until their lab people arrived. They were just driving out of the garage when Harris stopped the car.

"What is it?" Doug asked.

"That's the guy's space. Four E."

The green Cutlass was still sitting in the parking space. Harris and Doug walked over to the car for a closer look.

"You wouldn't think that the guy would have walked away after killing the girl and then packing his things," Doug said.

"No, unless somebody picked him up."

Everything seemed normal with the car, but then Harris wrinkled up his nose. "You smell something?"

"Yeah, I sure do."

"Get something to open up this trunk."

Doug quickly got a tire iron out of their car and inserted it into the crack of the trunk. It took only a little work to pop open the lid, then both men involuntarily stepped back—both from the almost gagging smell and from the almost gagging sight.

Having been locked in the small, almost airtight compartment, the gases given off by the decomposing body had done their work, swelling the head and face to almost twice their normal size.

The rest of the morning wasn't much more productive for Harris than the first part had been. He ran down a few leads, checked a few things out, but he knew he was wasting his time. His actions were designed to avoid his telephone as much as anything else. Having put it off as long as possible, he went back to the office. "Where's Doug?" Harris inquired as he passed by his secretary's desk.

"I don't know. He was here a little while ago, but he got a phone call and then took off like he had been fired out of a cannon. He almost broke the glass out of the door when he knocked it open."

"Any idea who the call was from?" Harris asked.

"No, sir. I answered it, but the man wouldn't give

his name. He just insisted on speaking with an FBI agent who was working on the Millard Tower case. Doug happened to be the first person I saw at the time, so I passed it along to him."

"Maybe somebody offered him a job with the CIA," Harris remarked sarcastically before stomping off down the hall. He sat down to think, trying to decide how best to get organized and where he should be going from here, but he just couldn't get started. This was the part he hated most—the aftermath. He usually found himself forced to become a desk bound administrative coordinator in such situations. He would have much preferred to be out doing something constructive instead of just sitting around with his ulcers eating away at him.

His secretary buzzed his intercom a few minutes later. "Call for you, inspector."

"Please hold all my calls, Tracy. Either take a message or give it to someone else."

"It's Inspector Broughton long distance from Washington."

Broughton was one of the top bureau men in Washington. He was Harris's superior's superior. "Okay, I'll take this one, but hold all the rest."

"Good morning, Inspector Broughton, how are you?"

"Fine, Robert. How's the investigation going?"

"It's beginning to come along quite well now. We weren't able to get too much done last night, but things are really coming together this morning."

"Do you have any solid leads on who did it and where the money is?"

Harris began to feel slightly uncomfortable. "No, that's what we're working on right now. We have a number of leads that are heading in that direction at the moment, but I don't know if you would exactly call any of them solid. I should know something more by this evening."

"Well Robert, I'll throw it right on the table. We're

taking a considerable amount of heat from everybody on this thing; the press, the hotel, even Congress. Certain people are saying that your outfit blew it, and we're getting a lot of pressure to replace you. Some people around here are of the opinion that you're over the hill, burned out. You and I both know that you've done some excellent work for us in the past, but, of course, none of that matters now. Let's face it, Robert, this thing is more than just an investigation now. It's political. They want someone to dump on, and you're first in line. I've gone to bat for you, but all I can do is buy you a little time. The rest is up to you. Keep me posted now, will you?"

"Yes, sir, I'll do that. I appreciate the warning."

When Harris hung up the phone, he wasn't alarmed, he wasn't subdued or hurt. That wasn't his style. He was angry. It just wasn't fair. You work your rear off trying to do a good job and what do you get? You get it kicked. That extortionist, the leader of the group, had done this to him; it was all his fault. The more he rolled that thought around in his mind the madder he became. Finally, after stewing as long as he could take it, Harris leapt from his chair and swept everything off the top of his desk in one enraged motion. Books, papers, the telephone— all went flying across the room to bang up against the wall.

"He's not going to get me! I swear I'll get him if it's the last thing I ever do!"

The entire office came to a halt. People in various cubbyholes up and down the halls were used to Harris's occasional outbursts, but no one had ever heard anything exactly like this. They could hear him still stomping around in his office, throwing things back onto the desk and muttering to himself. The hallway remained deserted for some time, as nobody dared walk by his open door.

A half hour later Doug sauntered in and casually seated himself in one of Harris's chairs. Then he made a big show of propping his feet up on the adjacent chair.

Harris leapt to the bait instantly. "What do you think you're doing? Get your feet out of that chair."

Doug ignored him completely. "I'm about to save your rear end from the wolves."

"Have you lost your mind?"

"I know where the missing extortionists are."

Harris's mouth dropped open and for once he was at a total loss for words. "Where?" was the best he could finally come up with.

"Well, let me qualify that. I know where one of them is going to be."

"Where?" Harris demanded, leaning forward over his desk.

"Well, let me qualify that. I will know where he's going to be if we set it up right and cancel a big drug investigation by the FBI, the U.S. Coast Guard, the U.S. Navy, and half a dozen police departments." Harris looked as if he were going to strangle his assistant. Wondering if he had indeed overdone things, Doug took his feet off the chair and started doing some fast talking.

"I got a call from a Mr. Red Kelly, a local literary agent. He said that he had been in contact with the extortionist, and that I should come to his office for the story and the proof. So, naturally, I hotfooted it right over. He showed me a copy of a letter that he just received. Somebody slipped it through his mail slot before he got to his office this morning."

Doug pulled a folded piece of paper from his coat pocket and passed it to Harris. He unfolded it to find a copy of a neatly typed letter.

Dear Mr. Kelly:

Enclosed please find ten one hundred dollar bills. This is to serve as an initial retainer should you elect to accept my request for your services. I would like you to market the literary rights to the Millard Tower takeover. The rights should go to the highest bidder, with $1 million to be the minimum acceptable price. Your commission, should you decide to accept my offer, will be 10%.

Should you elect not to accept my offer, the $1,000 is yours to keep with no strings attached, and you will not hear from me again. Of course, if you go to the authorities, they will have to confiscate the money as evidence.

If you are interested in my offer, you will find further instructions. . .

"Where's the rest of it?" Harris asked as he turned the paper over.

"That's all the guy would give me. He won't tell us where he's supposed to go for further instructions until we make a deal with him. But he says that he has to be somewhere by four-thirty this afternoon to get the next information."

"Let me get this straight. This guy, this extortionist, wants to sell the story of the takeover? For $1 million?" Harris shook his head in disbelief. "I don't buy it. Nobody would try to pull something like this after what he's done. This is obviously a scam of some sort to milk some money out of a publishing company. I can't believe that you really fell for this thing."

Doug smiled broadly. "All the serial numbers match exactly."

"What?"

"The ten one hundred dollar bills that were enclosed in the letter are part of the ransom money. I checked the serial numbers."

Harris stared at the letter in absolute amazement. "I've never heard of anything like this in my entire life. Doesn't this guy ever stop? Isn't $3 million enough? He's gotta have the biggest set of balls on record. He terrorizes almost two hundred people, kills some of them, and then expects to be paid to tell about it? He's got to be crazy!"

"Think about it for a minute," Doug replied. "Do you have any idea how many copies a book like that would sell—with them still running around loose with the $3 million? A publisher would jump at the chance to get a story like that. They'll probably even make a movie out of it."

"You said that this Red Kelly wants to make a deal?"

"That's right. He wouldn't come right out and admit it, of course, but he's apparently involved in some kind of drug ring. There's a big coordinated undercover operation called 'apple cart' that's about to close in on them. He implies, of course, that his part in the thing is very minor. He's just handled some of the money for them."

"And the navy is in on the investigation?"

"Exactly. This ring supplies drugs to naval personnel, so the navy originally started the whole investigation. I suspect that this guy is a lot more involved and in a lot more trouble than he's admitting. If it weren't for that, I have no doubt that we would have never heard from him."

Harris picked up the letter and scanned it again. "How did our extortionist come to pick this Red Kelly? There must be a lot of literary agents in Dallas."

"From what I can tell, Kelly is very successful and has quite a few contacts. But the clincher is that he's handled books for several people in prison—even one on death row."

"But our extortionist had no way of knowing that Kelly was in some sort of trouble and would use him to make a deal with us. What does Kelly want? Immunity I would guess?"

Doug shook his head. "It's not all that simple. He wants the entire drug investigation stopped. He makes a valid point. If this investigation comes to a head and he's the only one left untouched, it's going to look like he turned the others in. If that happens he figures that he's dead. So if we don't stop the entire thing, he'll be better off just going to prison for a while."

"He says that he's got to pick up more instructions by four-thirty this afternoon?"

"That's what he says."

"And if he doesn't keep the four-thirty appointment, he never hears from the extortionist again?"

"That's what he says."

"Do you really think this thing is for real?"

"It has to be. The bills match up."

"Okay, I better call Washington. You and I sure don't have the authority to stop that investigation by ourselves."

Harris looked through a small address book and located the bureau number. "Inspector Broughton please," he told the operator.

"I'm sorry, Inspector Broughton is out to lunch right now."

"In that case I'd like to leave a message. Tell him to call Inspector Robert Harris in Dallas as soon as possible. It's extremely urgent."

"Yes, sir, I'll give him the message as soon as he comes in."

"Do you have a phone number for Red Kelly?" Harris asked as he hung up.

Doug pushed a slip of paper across the desk. Encountering another receptionist at Red Kelly's office, Harris went through the usual song and dance routine of identifying himself and assuring the girl that it was indeed important. Kelly was on the line within seconds.

"Hello, this is Red Kelly."

"Good morning, Mr. Kelly. This is Inspector Robert Harris with the Dallas office of the FBI. My assistant, Doug Baus, has just filled me in on your meeting this morning." Harris's voice and manner had now shifted into the smooth, diplomatic tones that he was so practiced at using when necessary.

Red Kelly wasted no time in getting down to business. "So what's the word? Do we have a deal or don't we?"

"Mr. Kelly, all I can say at this point is that I'm certainly interested in discussing your offer. However, as you can imagine, I don't have the authority to cancel the investigation you've mentioned. That decision would have to come from Washington. I've already contacted my superiors and expect to hear from them shortly. In the meantime, though, it's vitally important that you keep your four-thirty meeting with the extortionist. Where was it you said you'd be meeting with him?"

"I didn't say, and I'm not meeting him. I'm only picking up further instructions. But I'm not going anywhere until I've got it in writing that the investigation—apple cart—will be halted."

"How is it that you know so much about this investigation?"

"I've got a few friends here and there. They let me know what's going on."

"All right, fine. The only problem I can see at this point is that we won't be able to get you the guarantee in writing by four-thirty this afternoon since it will have to come out of Washington."

"Okay, then you give it to me in writing yourself. I'll then keep my appointment and expect to get the written guarantee from Washington via the next flight."

"That sounds fair enough. I'll be more than happy to give you my personal guarantee that the investigation will be stopped."

"Okay, I'll be waiting right here to hear from you."

Doug gave Harris a disapproving look as he hung up the phone. "You can't guarantee that this investigation will be stopped."

"You know it, and I know it, but Kelly doesn't know it." Harris leaned back and rubbed his temples. "Why can't we just go charging into this creep's office and take the letter? Then we could show up at his four-thirty appointment in his place."

"He's already covered himself on that. He told me that the letter isn't in his possession, not even a copy of it, and an associate has orders to destroy it if he's arrested or if anything happens to him."

"Well personally, I don't think that anyone in Washington is going to agree to call off a drug investigation of that size, so when Kelly goes to his meeting we're going along with him. In the meantime, have you checked out the helicopter pilot's story?"

"We sure did, and he seems to be telling the truth. His wife was told to take the kids to a motel and check in for two days. She was told that if she tried to contact her husband he would be killed, and then later they would come after her children."

"So the pilot thought someone had kidnapped his family when really they had just been told to drop out of sight for a while."

"Right. The guy has a good record. He has been flying helicopters for the same oil company for eleven years now. It was the oil company's copter that he used. His employers are certainly backing him up all the way. They've even said that they'll pay any legal expenses he faces."

Harris raised an eyebrow. "That's awful nice of them. He's probably going to need the legal help."

"Why? Do you really think that they'll try to prosecute him?"

"Sure, as an accomplice or for obstructing justice or some such thing. Though if he has a defense attorney who's any good they'll have his victimized wife and kids up there telling their story, and there won't be a dry eye in the house. The most he'll get is a light suspended sentence."

Doug grimaced. "That was a bad situation for the

guy. It's hard to say what you'd do when your family is threatened like that."

"Yeah, tough call."

With nothing to do but wait, the two returned to the routine reports that had been piling up for several days. As Harris often pointed out, "Paperwork waits for no man."

Harris looked at his watch for the umpteenth time that afternoon. It was three o'clock. "If we don't do something pretty soon, we're going to end up sitting here until we run out of time."

A quick search through the pile of papers before him turned up Red Kelly's number once again. With a grimace of frustration, Harris dialed it and asked for Mr. Kelly.

"Yes, inspector, this is Red Kelly."

"I'm sorry it took so long to get back to you, Mr. Kelly, but you know how fast anything having to do with the government moves." The voice was once again smooth and reassuring.

"Have we got a deal?"

"Yes we do," Harris replied. "Of course, I don't have it in writing yet, but I'll have it for you by tomorrow."

"Then you'll put it in writing yourself in the meantime?"

"Yes I will," Harris said, not missing a beat. "I'll send it over to your office right away."

Harris hung up the phone once again. "I've got to stay here and wait for Broughton to call. You head on over to Kelly's with the letter of guarantee."

Rolling a piece of paper into his typewriter, Harris began pounding away furiously with two fingers. After a couple of minutes he jerked the paper from the machine and handed it to Doug. He accepted it and read.

Dear Mr. Kelly:
    This is to inform you that in return for your

complete cooperation in the Millard Tower extortion investigation, all investigations currently being carried on under the code name 'apple cart' will be terminated at once.

Sincerely yours,

Robert L. Harris,
Inspector, Federal Bureau of Investigation.

"What happens if Washington won't approve this thing?" Doug asked as he rose to leave.

"If they don't approve it, I can't be any worse off than I already am. If they do approve it, then I'll come out smelling like a rose. What have I got to lose?"

Doug shrugged and nodded in agreement. "Take someone with you," Harris advised.

"Right." Doug headed down the hall and signaled to Buzz Thompson, one of his fellow agents, to follow him. He filled Buzz in as they drove across town to Red Kelly's office. Kelly greeted them twenty minutes later.

"Did you bring the guarantee?"

Doug handed him the letter and watched as Kelly scanned it. "This'll do for now. The one from Washington will be here in the morning?"

"That's what Inspector Harris tells me."

"Fair enough. Now, if you gentlemen will excuse me, I have an appointment to keep, and I had much rather be early than late."

Doug quickly spoke up. "Well, ah, we were planning on coming with you just in case anything were to go wrong. He has killed a few people, you know."

"Oh no. I'm not stupid. I'm not about to give you any more information until I get the official word from Washington. Now if I think that I'm being followed, I'll just walk around until I'm not being followed. And if that takes us right through the meeting, then so be it." With that as his final word, Kelly pushed past the two agents and left them standing awkwardly in his office.

Doug waited for a few seconds and then reached for the door. "Come on, let's go."

"Go where? What are you planning to do?"

"We're going to follow him. What do you think we're going to do?"

"But he told us not to."

Doug fixed Buzz with a disgusted look. "Do you want to go back and tell Harris that we didn't tail this guy because he told us not to?"

Buzz nodded. "Let's go."

The elevator doors were just closing as the two entered the hallway. They quickly located the stairs and ran down the five flights just in time to catch sight of Kelly passing through the revolving doors onto the downtown street. They waited a few seconds longer and then followed. Fortunately, Kelly was going to his meeting on foot. That made it simple to keep up with him while remaining hidden in the crowd.

Kelly moved along leisurely, pausing occasionally to window shop. Eventually, he crossed the street and entered a small park. His two escorts were forced to stretch out the distance between them now, as the crowds were a bit thinner. Kelly stopped to buy a soft drink, then resumed his walk. Finally, he stopped at a park bench and seated himself. Doug and Buzz managed to stay well out of sight behind a row of bushes.

Buzz moved a branch and peered closely at their quarry. "Think he spotted us and now he's just stalling? Or do you think this is where he's supposed to wait for the extortionist?"

"I don't know," Doug muttered. "All we can do is wait and see."

They watched as Kelly casually reached down beside the bench and picked up what appeared to be a crumpled up paper cup. He opened the end, pulled out a piece of paper, and began to read.

"That's it," Doug announced. "Let's go."

Making no further effort to conceal themselves, they started promptly in Kelly's direction. The man on the bench looked up and spotted the two agents when they were about thirty yards away. With no hesitation, he popped the note into his mouth and began chewing vigorously.

"Look, he's eating it! Hurry!" Buzz shouted, breaking into a run.

Just as they reached the bench, Kelly made an exaggerated swallowing motion and then licked his lips. Buzz danced around shouting and gesturing. "Get it, quick. Stop him."

Equally flustered, Doug grabbed Kelly by the collar. "Very funny. Now what was on the note?"

Kelly smiled, opened his mouth, and loudly belched.

Chapter Seventeen

The courtroom was filled with the usual mix of people who didn't seem to match; from whores to white collar businessmen. It had always struck Frank as being somewhat like a melting pot.

Frank came back from his thoughts as the judge spoke to him. "Mr. Mosley, do you have any further evidence for this afternoon?"

"No sir, that's all I have for today."

"Very well, court is dismissed and we'll reconvene at ten o'clock tomorrow morning."

The judge slammed down his gavel and all stood to leave. Frank was simply going with the flow; going through the motions. He planned to stick it out for three months and then take a long leave of absence because of family problems. Taking the leave or simply quitting immediately might have seemed to be a bit of a coincidence so soon after the takeover. Three more months would be about right. He didn't have to beat his head against the wall as he usually did, he simply went through the motions, took it easy, and enjoyed his new debt-free status.

Frank pulled into his parking space in the underground garage. He noted that the green Cutlass was now gone, but there were no police around. It didn't disturb him that they had found it so quickly. The smell of rotted, decaying flesh alone would probably have led them to it sooner or later.

As Frank got out of the car, he saw them. It was the same two. The leader, with the sharp toed cowboy boots, grinned at him.

"You do good work, Frank."

Frank felt a sinking feeling in his stomach. He didn't know what they wanted, but he knew it wasn't good for him. "Hey, our deal's over. I'm not saying what I did and what I didn't do, but I don't owe you guys anymore."

"We didn't say you did."

"So—what do you want?"

"We thought we could take a little ride."

"Where?"

"To wherever you've got that three million dollars stashed. It's safe to say that you hadn't got it up in your fancy condo there."

"Hey, whatever I've got, it's none of your business. You tell Louis that I held up my end of things and I expect him to hold up his. There's no way any of this can come back on me, and that means that there's no way it can come back on him. I'm clean and he's clean."

The one with the boots grinned again. "Frank, this hadn't got anything to do with anybody but you and us. Plain and simple."

Frank realized that he had been a bit slow. He now understood. This was indeed just between the three of them. They knew that he must have the extortion money, or a large chunk of it, and they simply intended to take it. What could he do—call a cop?

"Ah, look, I don't have the money. You're right, I'm not keeping it around where somebody might run across it."

"So let's go."

"It's not in town. I've got it in a Swiss bank account. It'll take me about three days to get my hands on it."

The leader pulled a .357 magnum out from under his coat and pointed it at Frank's stomach. "Uh-uh. I know you better than you think. You'd have it close enough to get your hands on it quick if you needed it."

The second man pointed to a nearby car. "Let's go. I'll drive."

The bank was simply a small, nondescript branch in one of the northern suburbs. Almost every shopping center seemed to have at least one. Frank and the leader entered, while the second man waited around the side of the bank in the car. Frank made his way down the stairs and over to a lady who sat behind a desk in the safety deposit box department.

She looked up and smiled. "Yes, sir, may I help you?"

"I need to get my safety deposit box."

The lady handed him a piece of paper. "Sure, just sign this form."

As Frank took the form, the lady was distracted by another customer in the next room.

"I'll be right back to check the signatures," she said as she stepped out of the room.

Frank patted his pocket but found that all he had was a felt tip pen. "Have you got a ball point?" he asked his guard.

The man wordlessly handed him a standard ball point pen. Frank clicked the point out on the pen as his guard watched from behind him. It's often fascinating to note how just one seemingly insignificant gesture or move can affect one's life immeasurably. The guard leaned forward just a bit to make sure that Frank was indeed signing his name rather than leaving a warning message. While the move was certainly reasonable and cautious enough, it had a profound affect upon the man's life.

Frank held the pen with one hand and clicked the point out with his thumb. With the pen thus held like a dagger momentarily, it took but a quick flick of his wrist for Frank to snap it back at the man's face. It struck precisely where Frank had intended, plunging deeply into the man's right eye.

As the man froze for an instant, in virtual shock, it gave Frank all the time he needed to jerk around and slam his palm against the pen, driving its point through the optic nerve and four inches into the man's brain. There wasn't a scream, or even an out-cry. It was more of a final, terrible gasping intake of breath.

The man's hands clutched desperately, claw-like at his face as his nails ripped furrows across his skin, trying desperately to pull out the piercing shaft. His hands then shook, his body convulsed, and he dropped to his knees and pitched forward onto his face.

Having the lady as a witness didn't bother Frank in the least. It wouldn't be a problem. Knowing, as he did, the gross inaccuracies of eyewitness testi-mony, the woman wouldn't be able to give but a general description of him at best; mainly because he had attracted no attention, had not appeared to be anything out of the ordinary.

Frank quickly reached under the man's coat and removed the .357 magnum. He stuck it up under his left arm, covered by his coat, and held his arm tightly, though not noticeably so, against his side. Fighting his mind's internal scream to run, run as fast as he could, Frank sauntered casually out of the room, across the lobby and out of the bank.

The second man was relaxing in his car without a care in the world. Life must certainly have seemed pretty good at that exact moment. He looked around and his face registered the surprise, the shock, and the fear, all in a part of a second, of seeing Frank pointing the gun at his face.

The explosion of noise, the shock of the impact and the initial searing pain were all fused together as one.

A couple of witnesses would later report seeing a man walk quickly away from the car, but none had a good look at his face. Thus, as far as the police would officially report, the killer walked away and was never seen or heard from again.

Harris's intercom finally buzzed with his secretary's message that Inspector Broughton was on the line. "Good afternoon, sir. This is Robert Harris."

"Yes, Robert. I had a message here that I should call you at once. I just got back to the office."

"Yes, sir. To make a long story short, one of the extortionists has contacted a local literary agent in an attempt to peddle his story for at least $1 million. The literary agent, a Mr. Red Kelly, wants to make a deal. He's willing to cooperate with us fully, but only if we give him a written guarantee that a drug investigation code named 'apple cart' will be terminated immediately. This Kelly is afraid that he'll be implicated for a small part in the drug ring. He refuses to consider a deal simply granting him immunity, though, because he's afraid that he then would be killed."

"How can you be sure that this isn't a con of some sort?"

"Kelly received a letter from the extortionist with ten one hundred dollar bills in it. The serial numbers match those given to the extortionists."

"This guy might as well be asking us to close down the FBI. Do you have any idea what all 'apple cart' entails?"

"No, not really, but I understand that it's pretty big."

"Pretty big doesn't begin to describe it. On the other hand, as I told you this morning, with the live national television coverage that the takeover got, there's a lot of pressure from up above to do something about this case. If we don't do something, and soon, the entire Justice Department's going to end

up with a black eye. You stay right where you are.
Don't move. I'll do some checking and get right back
to you. I assume that you need to move quickly on
this?"

"I can't tell you how quickly we need to be moving
on it."

"Okay, just sit tight."

Harris was now tied to the phone on two accounts.
Not only would Broughton be calling back, but Doug
should be checking in as well. Shortly after five o'clock,
Doug and Buzz appeared at the door. "About time,"
Harris growled. "What did you find out?"

Doug began his tale of woe in obvious discomfort.
"Well, Red Kelly wouldn't let us go to the meeting
with him since he didn't have the final guarantee
from Washington, so we had to follow him."

"And you lost him?" Harris asked accusingly.

"Oh no," Buzz assured him. "We didn't lose the
guy. We stuck right with him."

Doug gave Buzz a withering look and continued.
"He went to a park and picked a note up from
under a bench. By the time we could get to him he
had read it and eaten it. Then he wouldn't tell us
what it said."

They waited for the explosion, but it didn't come.
Harris leaned forward and placed his face in his
hands. "You must have misunderstood me. I guess
that I didn't make myself clear. When I told you to
take someone with you, I didn't mean for you to take
another stupid incompetent idiot. You see, two stupid incompetent idiots are no better than one stupid
incompetent idiots. I'm going to count to three now
and then move my hands. When I look up, I want to
see no stupid incompetent idiots at all. One, two,
three."

When he looked up Harris found himself alone
again. He shuffled papers around until he relocated
Kelly's number. The phone rang several times before Kelly finally picked it up.

"This is Inspector Harris."

"Yeah, inspector, I expected you to be calling. Did you talk to your two stooges?"

"Yes I did. I need to know a little about the new instructions. You don't have to tell me where if you don't want to, but I do need to know when you're supposed to meet again. I assume that you'll be meeting or at least picking up another message."

"You know, you better be glad that I want to deal as much as you do, or I would've told you to stick it by now. I've got to take this guy $100,000 day after tomorrow as a down payment. In return, I get the wallet that belonged to the off duty cop who was killed as well as the murder weapon. He wants me to bring the money to a certain place in a briefcase, and then I'm supposed to open the case and hold it for a minute. I'm only guessing, but either he's going to have someone walk by or he'll be sitting somewhere with a telescope so he can tell if the money's really in there."

"I'm not a bit surprised," Harris grunted. "This guy thinks of everything."

"Let's make sure that you've got one thing straight, though. I don't budge again until I get that written guarantee from Washington. I don't care if we miss the next meeting or not. No guarantee, no meeting."

"Don't worry, we'll have it for you tomorrow without fail."

At eight o'clock Harris sent out for a sandwich. By nine o'clock he wished he could send out for a bottle. When the phone rang two hours later, he was sprawled out on his couch asleep. He jerked up to a sitting position, not sure what was happening for a moment. After another ring he reached across the desk and fumbled with the phone before getting a firm grip on it.

"Hello, this is Harris. Inspector Harris."

"This is Inspector Broughton. Are you still awake down there?"

"Oh yes, sir. It'll be quite a while before any of us gets home at a decent hour."

"Good, I'm glad to hear that you're still plugging along. The attorney general has approved your deal with Red Kelly, but there are a couple of reservations."

"The attorney general?" Harris didn't even attempt to hide the surprise in his voice.

"That's right. I told you that the entire Justice Department is taking a lot of heat on this thing."

"Oh."

"It turns out that your Mr. Kelly isn't exactly what you would call a minor figure in the drug investigation. In fact, he's one of the main ones involved. As a result, the attorney general does have a couple of stipulations."

"Such as?"

"First, 'apple cart' will be terminated, but only the top people including Mr. kelly will be exempt from arrest and prosecution. The suppliers as well as the local distributors will all be picked up right away. That way Kelly won't seem to have turned state's evidence. He can't be singled out by anyone. It's doing things backwards to concentrate on the little guys and let the big ones go, but the attorney general considers it to be a necessary compromise. Secondly, Mr. Kelly isn't exempt from any other investigations in the future. And thirdly, if there is ever any evidence that Kelly is involved in drug smuggling again, the agreement will be nullified."

Harris allowed himself a deep sigh of relief. "That's certainly more than I could have hoped for. I just hope that Kelly feels the same way."

"He will. He's facing a long time in prison if he doesn't."

"There's a new development, though," Harris added. "Kelly received another message from the extortionist. He has to give him a $100,000 cash payment by Saturday, but Kelly won't go to the meeting until he has your written guarantee in his hands."

"That's no problem. I'll send it down tomorrow."

"But there's one catch, kind of. Kelly has to open e briefcase full of money at one point, so that the tortionist can tell if it's really there. That means at we've either got to get some real money or some unterfeit for Kelly to take with him."

"What is this, a down payment of some kind?"

"Exactly."

There was silence on the line for a few moments fore Broughton spoke again. "If we blow it and e extortionist realizes that we're onto him, we'll ver hear from him again. On the other hand, even he should get away with the $100,000, we would t another shot at him when he came back for the xt payment. Tell you what. If we send counterfeit oney, we take a chance on blowing it and losing m for good, so I'm going to send you the letter of arantee and the real money via courier first thing morrow morning. I should be able to round it up om what's left of the 'apple cart' cash since they on't be needing all of it now. But all I've got to say that you better take good care of the money. After erything that's happened so far, if something were happen to that money . . ." Broughton's voice ailed off, but there was no mistaking his meaning.

"Don't you worry about that. I've never lost any oney before. Ah, I mean, besides the uh, the $3 illion from the other day, but I'm going to get that ack."

Broughton declined further comment. "The cou- er will be there on the 10:00 A.M. flight. Meet him rsonally."

The next morning at eleven o'clock Harris was ated in Red Kelly's office. "This is your written arantee," he said as he passed Kelly an envelope.

Kelly opened it, read carefully, and then handed it his secretary with instructions to make several pies. "That will do just fine."

"Now it's your turn," Harris said. "Exactly what

was in the note the extortionist left for you in th
park?"

"Not enough salt, I can assure you of that." Kel
looked at Doug and Buzz and grinned broadly. "Tha
the problem with you feds. You have no sense
humor. The note said that at eight o'clock tomorro
morning I'm to take the case of money back to th
park. I go to the concession stand, turn right, and ç
down the trail to the first stone waste basket. I'
supposed to open the case and hold it up in th
direction of the apartment buildings on my right f
at least thirty seconds. Then I look under the bus
next to me for further instructions. It'll be just li
the last time; a note in a crumpled up paper cup."

Buzz snickered. "Heck, we've got the guy. We dor
even have to use the money. All we have to do is s
if the note's there yet. If it isn't we just watch th
bushes. Then when he plants the note we grab him

Harris shook his head. "What if he saw you di
ging around in the bushes? We'd never hear fro
him again. This guy doesn't miss a trick. That's prol
ably the entire point of the second message—to fir
out if anyone is onto him or if Mr. Kelly is playing
straight. No, I think it's best if we go along with h
instructions, but we'll have Mr. Kelly wired so he ca
tell us right away what the new note says."

"There's one other thing," Kelly added. "I'm a
lowed to bring a representative from the publishir
company with me when I pick up the instructions.
guess he figured that a publisher might not be tc
willing to hand me $100,000 in cash and then ju
watch me walk away with it."

"That's beautiful," Harris commented. "He's n
so perfect after all. Doug here will be the representa
tive from the publisher."

"You're going to send this stooge with me? Yo
have to be kidding."

"Mr. Kelly, I'll have you know that these two me
are among the top agents in the entire bureau. I'

ut them up against anybody in any kind of situa-
on. You should consider yourself fortunate to be
vorking with them."

Doug and Buzz weren't sure if they had just re-
eived an authentic compliment, or if it was just
10re of Harris' diplomatic B.S. They each tended to
elieve the later.

"Do you mind if we take a look at the first letter
hat the extortionist sent you?" Harris asked. "You
nly showed us part of it."

Kelly obligingly reached into his top drawer and
ulled out a folded piece of standard white typing
aper. "Is this the original?" Harris inquired.

"That's it."

"I thought you had it hidden somewhere."

"I did hide it—right here in my desk drawer. I just
ave that line to your boy here to keep you from
etting any fancy ideas about grabbing it and cutting
ne out of the deal."

Harris unfolded the note and scanned down to the
niddle of the page. He started reading aloud at the
art that he had not yet seen. "Leave your office on
oot and enter the nearest entrance. Walk past the
irst concession stand, then take the first footpath to
he right. Stop at the first bench and sit down. Di-
ectly underneath the bench you will find a wadded
p paper cup with a note inside containing further
nstructions. Be there at exactly 4:30. No earlier, no
ater."

"Mind if I keep this?" Harris asked.

"Go right ahead, but what good is it now?"

"We'll have our lab people take a crack at it. Maybe
he typewriter can be traced. I doubt it, though. This
uy hasn't slipped up yet."

"So what do we do tomorrow?" Kelly pulled out a
ack of cigarettes as he spoke and offered them
round. Though Buzz smoked, and would have liked
ne, he didn't dare do so in front of Harris. Smok-
ng wasn't allowed.

"We'll meet you here at seven o'clock tomorrow morning," explained Harris. "Once we're set up I' be in a communications van just outside the park It'll be painted up like a repair truck, so there's n chance of our man spotting us. All our people will b wired with transmitter receivers, including you an Doug. You'll be able to both talk to me and hear me When you pick up the new set of instructions, I wan you to read them out loud as if you're reading it t Doug. That will enable us to know right away wher you're going next. He'll probably have you go some where else to make the exchange. Do exactly wha the instructions say unless I tell you otherwise. Sinc Doug will be right there with you, whatever he say takes precedence over what I say. If he tells you t jump, do it and don't ask any questions. If there' any shooting, you just hit the ground and stay out o our way. Any questions?"

"Nah, nothing to it. I've seen Efrem Zimbalist J do this kind of thing a hundred times."

The large rock formed a graceful arc as it saile up and then in toward the building, bouncing of the brick wall and then falling back to the sidewalk A second rock, close behind the first, found its tar get, smashing through the third floor window. small wrinkled face soon peered cautiously out th window at the street below.

"Hey you old hag, cat woman. I'm coming afte you. Are you so stupid you thought I was just gonn sit back and let you put me away?"

If Angelo had been worried about being seen o heard, either by the old woman or by any of he neighbors, he would simply have kicked her door in But he wasn't worried about either; not in this neigh borhood. Most people had enough sense to min their own business. You'd have thought that afte what happened to the old man who was going t testify that she would have learned too, but she hadn'

Well, it would be simple to fix that. Once and for all, he was going to make sure that she and everyone else around there knew what happened to anybody who tried to mess with him. He wanted them all to know he was there and what was happening. Then he wouldn't have to leave town. No reason to.

Angelo bounded up the stairs two at a time and stopped at the last door on the third floor. He knew which one was hers. He wouldn't even bother hollering at her to open it. He'd just kick it in to start off with. He jerked on the knob first, planning to rattle it and make plenty of noise so that she, and everyone else, would hear it clearly.

To his surprise, the handle turned easily. She at least had enough sense not to try locking it. She knew he was coming in anyway. Angelo shoved the door open hard, sending it slamming back against the wall with a loud bang. She was standing across the room beside a rickety old table, a dilapidated old refrigerator and a hot plate beside the sink comprising the small room's kitchen.

He didn't bother to close the door behind him. No need to. Nobody was going to do anything; risk seeing something they shouldn't. He moved slowly, threateningly across the room toward her.

There was an empty glass on the table and a pie tin with a couple of pieces cut out of it. "I thought you ate cat food," he sneered. "What's that?"

"Mrs. Thompson's granddaughter brought her some apples. I made some pies out of them."

"Yeah? Well you ain't gonna be needin' it, that's for sure."

The pie looked pretty good. It looked very good. Angelo dug three fingers into the middle and scooped out a large mouthful. "Ain't too bad," he mumbled with juice running down his chin. Three more scoops followed the first in quick succession.

Having had his fill, he abruptly hurled what was left of the pie across the room, sending it right by

her head. She flinched and stepped back fearfully as
the plate smashed into the wall, the pie leaving a
gooey trail as it oozed down the wall onto the floor.

"You got any beer?" he growled, wiping one sleeve
across his mouth.

"No, just water. I can't afford to buy anything like
that."

"Knock off the sympathy bit. I didn't come from
any better, so save the sob line for somebody else.
Except now it's different with me. I got more money
than you ever dreamed of."

Angelo jerked around at the sound of something
out in the hallway. At least he thought he had heard
something. He moved back to the door and looked
out. The dim hallway was deserted. It must have
been somebody on the next floor slamming a door.
Just to be sure, he walked down to the end of the
hall and peered up and down the stairs. No one in
sight, but he could hear a little noise upstairs. That's
all it had been. He was just getting jumpy over
nothing.

Angelo walked back into her room and plopped
down heavily on the ragged, torn old couch beside
him. He was beginning to feel a little tired. The
ordeal of the previous day must have taken more out
of him than he realized.

"Get me something to drink," he ordered.

The old lady wordlessly filled a glass from the
faucet. When she brought it to him, he grabbed it
away roughly and downed half, then tossed the glass
across the other side of the room to shatter against
the wall alongside the remains of the pie. Her quiet
response was to pick up an old tattered cloth and
kneel to dab patiently at the puddle of water on the
floor.

"I don't have apple pie much anymore," she said
as she turned her attention to the pie splattered wall.
"I usually don't have enough money for things like
that, but this was different. This was a special occa-

sion. Apple was my husband's favorite. He was an exterminator, you know. That's why we don't have any rats in our building. He left me a lot of his chemicals."

Working slowly and cautiously, she picked up the largest pieces of broken glass from the floor and placed them in a small trash can before laying the pie tin in the sink. Very carefully, almost meticulously, she washed and dried the tin, then put it back in its proper place beneath the sink. The large frying pan, under the sink beside the pie tin, she removed and laid on top of the hot plate. A precisely measured spoonful of cooking oil was placed inside the pan and then the hot plate was turned to high.

Angelo watched her without comment as she bustled about, still talking as much to herself as to him. "The stuff for the rats doesn't kill them, at least right away. It just paralyzes their muscles so they can't move. Then the other rats eat them alive while they are helpless."

The old lady opened a drawer and removed an old fashioned folding straight razor. "This was my husband's, too." She paused for a moment to run her hand gently over the white pearl handle, allowing it to bring back the memories it held. "I guess he was a little old fashioned. He shaved with the same razor for thirty years."

She hobbled back to the couch and stopped for a moment. "Fried liver was my husband's favorite. Mine too, but I can't afford it nowadays. The liver flavored cat food really isn't very good, but it's better than most of the others." Angelo watched expressionlessly, unmoving as she carefully unfolded the razor's finely honed blade from the handle and then bent down to pull up his shirt.

Chapter Eighteen

For Harris, having to get up earlier than usual was a difficult task indeed. The only thing that got him up and going was the desperation that was driving him to finish this abortion before it finished him. He knew he was quickly running out of time. Bleary eyed and nauseous, he arrived at Kelly's office a few minutes past seven. Technicians were already there, busily hiding wires and microphones on the participants. Harris slumped down in a chair and thankfully accepted a cup of coffee from Buzz.

A technician stopped at his side. "Inspector, we're ready for you in the truck."

"Okay," he groaned as he lifted himself out of the chair and followed the technician out of the office. They exited the building into an alley where a disguised van was parked. Harris and the technician climbed in and joined two more technicians already inside. The interior was a maze of radio equipment and tape recorders, leaving just enough room for the four of them to squeeze in. The head technician flipped a few switches and was rewarded with a faint humming sound. Several lights flickered, indicating the readiness of the systems.

"This is standard test alpha. Base one to station one."

The reply was immediate. "Station one, loud and clear."

"Base one to station two."

"Station two, loud and clear."

This same scenario was repeated through a total of eight stations, indicating that there were a total of six agents on the communications system in addition to Doug and Kelly.

"Working like a charm," the technician proudly announced.

Harris checked the digital clock in the console. 0736. He then examined a diagram showing the stations and locations. "This is base one. Stations one through five move into position."

"Station one."

"Station two."

"Station three."

"Station four."

"Station five."

"This is base one. Stations six, seven, and eight stand by to move out in five minutes."

"Station six."

"Station seven."

"Station eight."

"Base one is moving now," Harris said.

Hearing the last transmission, one of the technicians clambered over into the driver's seat and started the van. They backed slowly out of the alley, then moved out into the street and headed for their post.

As they pulled to a stop a few minutes later, Harris again noted the time. 0744. "Close enough," he commented. Then he keyed his transmitter again. "This is base one. Stations six, seven, and eight move out."

"Station six."

"Station seven."

"Station eight."

The small group in the truck settled back to wait as the last three stations, representing Kelly, Doug, and Buzz, headed for the park. Buzz was positioned behind Doug and Kelly by about a hundred yards. He was to follow in that position wherever they went.

"There they are," remarked the technician in the driver's seat after what seemed an eternity. "They're just going in. Hey, wait a minute. They're talking to someone."

Harris could just make out another voice but was unable to tell what it was saying. After several seconds, Doug's voice came over the van's speakers. "Go three blocks down, then two blocks to the right, and it's on the corner."

"Must have been someone asking directions," Harris observed. "Are they moving again?"

"Yes, sir. The man they were talking to is moving off in the direction they told him."

"This is base one. Station four, if anyone takes a look at the money when Mr. Kelly opens the case, you follow them, but don't let yourself be seen unless you're about to lose them."

"Station four, roger."

Harris's insides knotted again as Doug signaled their approach to the meeting place. "There's the first trail to the right, Mr. Kelly."

"Whadaya think, I'm blind or something?"

"Just play along," Doug muttered in return.

Two minutes later Doug's voice again came through the van's speakers. "That must be the stone trash can he mentioned in the instructions."

Kelly and Doug stopped by the waste can and looked around. They found themselves completely alone with the half empty can. "Go ahead," Doug urged. "Open the case."

Kelly obliged and popped open the two locks on the briefcase he was carrying. Then he carefully opened the lid and held the case out in the direction of the apartment buildings a block away. It was readily apparent that there could have been a telescope or a pair of binoculars watching them from any one of a hundred windows. Kelly continued to hold the case out. "My darned arms are about to kill me," he complained.

"So suffer a little," Doug said. "You might as well do something to earn your deal. Okay, that should be long enough."

Kelly lowered the case and snapped the locks shut again. No one had walked by while they stood with the money exposed. Doug now waded into the patch of shrubbery by the waste can. Almost at once he spotted a crumpled up paper cup and picked it up.

"There's nothing in it," he declared as he opened it.

Harris's ulcer immediately went into overdrive. "What do you mean? Are you sure?"

"You forgot to say base one and station seven," whispered the technician.

"Oh cut the garbage," Harris snapped. "This ain't a moon shot."

"Doug, are you sure there's nothing written on the cup itself?"

"No, sir, it's empty. What now? Should we wait?"

Kelly fixed Doug with a disgusted look. "You've got the wrong cup, stooge. Look over there." Doug looked down at the edge of the bushes and spotted another cup tucked up under the branches, just barely in sight.

"Oh, hold on." He dropped the first cup and retrieved the second. This time he was rewarded with a precisely folded piece of paper, neatly typed, as the first two messages had been.

Dear Mr. Kelly:
You will find the deceased policeman's wallet and the murder weapon wrapped in newspaper in the waste can beside you. Remove the package, place the briefcase in the can, and cover it with the newspaper from the package. Then go back the way you came. You will be contacted later with further instructions.

"It's in the trash can," Doug announced.

"What?" Harris asked over the radio.

"It says it's in the trash can."

"Read the note, stupid!"

"Oh, yeah," Doug stammered as he unfolded the note again. This time he acted as if he were reading it aloud to Kelly.

"Okay, do what it says," Harris ordered.

The can consisted of a heavy stone cylinder with a smaller, removable can inside. Doug reached down into the can and came up with a heavy package wrapped in newspaper. He quickly unwrapped it to find a .38 revolver and a man's wallet. "Throw the case in," Doug ordered.

Kelly dropped the case into the basket, then covered it with the newspaper.

"We got them, inspector," said Doug. "We're coming out now."

"You're not putting on the act," Kelly observed.

"Why bother? We're the only people within ten blocks of here."

Doug and Kelly had just started walking away from the can when, unexpectedly, they heard a strange swooshing sound behind them. Turning, they couldn't believe what they saw. The can now had flames leaping from it a full eight feet into the air.

"It's, it's on fire," Doug gasped.

"What?" Harris shouted. "What did you say? What's on fire?"

"The money, the trash can, it's all on fire. Quick, get some water. Put it out," Doug shouted as he danced around the can. Because of the way that the small waste can rested inside the stone holder, Doug would have had to reach into the flames to remove the inner can. He tried giving the heavy stone case a kick, but it remained firmly in place.

"Everybody move in," Harris ordered, and then he himself threw open the van's door and set out on the run for the meeting place. He rounded a corner in the path about forty-five seconds later to find

Doug still dancing around the can, yelling at Buzz who was unsuccessfully trying to beat out the fire with his jacket. The flames had died down considerably by now, but the jacket had no effect at all. In fact, it almost seemed that the fanning action was maintaining the flames.

Harris immediately joined Doug in shouting instructions at Buzz, who still flailed away gamely with his coat. By now the rest of the agents, along with the technicians and several curious passersby, had gathered around the performance being staged by Buzz and the fire. The flames had died down to a height of about two feet with clouds of thick black smoke billowing from the can. Finally, a full five minutes after the fire had started, someone arrived with a fire extinguisher requisitioned from a nearby building and thoroughly soaked what few ashes remained in the can.

Harris paced rapidly back and forth beside the can, muttering various unintelligible obscenities.

A technician returned to the truck and brought back a pair of work gloves. With these he was able to reach in and lift the hot metal can out of the stone holder. He dropped it on its side, allowing the contents to scatter out onto the grass. Nothing recognizable remained. Everything in the can that hadn't burned had been fused into a black shapeless blob coated with ashes.

Harris was still pacing back and forth muttering to himself. At last he dropped down on a nearby bench and rested his face in his hands. Kelly walked over and stood beside him. "Inspector, I'd just like to tell you what a pleasure it's been working with some of the top agents in the entire bureau."

A short while later a lab crew arrived and took control of the scene. Four men in white lab coats began crawling around on all fours picking unidentifiable specks out of the grass.

"Inspector, is this your bugging device?"

Harris looked up at the head of the lab crew.

"I don't know. Where was it?"

"It was stuck down inside the wallet you found in the can."

"And I thought that the guy had slipped up when he told Kelly to bring someone from the publishing company with him. With this bug, he was able to tell right away if Kelly was talking to a representative from a publishing company or to us. We never had a chance."

"It sure looks like the guy knew what he was doing," the lab technician agreed.

"Anything left of the money?" Harris asked hopefully.

"A couple of blobs of metal that used to be the latches on the briefcase is all. We found another piece of metal that was probably a radio controlled detonator. It must have been attached to a fire bomb in the bottom of the can. The material in the bomb was a type of napalm. That's why the fire was so wild and hot. We found one other thing, though; a small fireproof safe. We haven't gotten it open yet, but it seems to be intact, so whatever's in it, if anything, should be in good shape."

Harris eagerly jumped to his feet at this unexpected news. "Where is it?" The lab technician pointed to two other men who were working on a small charred box.

"They've just finished removing the lock, so it shouldn't take too much longer."

Harris watched with baited breath as a technician inserted a thin tool into an almost invisible crack and tapped it gently with a small hammer. They were immediately rewarded by the door popping open about an inch. A large screwdriver soon had the door fully open. The worker reached in and carefully extracted a folded piece of paper. It was browned slightly from the heat and cracked as he unfolded it.

He read it and silently passed it to Harris. In the same neat type as the other notes, it simply read:

You blew it, Harris—again.

Harris knew that he would have to answer to Washington sooner or later, but he intended to put it off just as long as he could. He had even taken his phone off the hook so Broughton couldn't get him. In Harris's business, when you had no options left you stalled. And that was exactly what he was doing now—stalling. He wanted to give up, to quit, but deep down, beneath all else, he was a fighter, not a quitter. If he had been a quitter he would have never gotten to where he was in the first place. If only he had more time. But that was just what he no longer had. Not after today's fiasco, anyway. If only he had a smoke screen; a diversion of some sort that would buy him a little more time. Something would have to turn up eventually if only he had enough time to wait for it.

It was ten o'clock when the late evening news came on. Their headline story, of course, concerned the happenings at Millard Tower the day before. The reporter didn't actually come right out and say it, but he let it clearly be known that at least one man was dead because of the personal incompetence of Inspector Robert Harris of the FBI. The reporter went on to describe how Harris had sent the poor doomed man up to the top of the tower without first making it clear to the extortionist that the man was his uncle.

Harris sent a half empty bottle of scotch crashing through the television screen. "Shut up, you hear me! Shut your lying mouth!" he shouted.

They were out to get him; they all were. There hadn't been any mistake on his part, no miscalculation. Nor had there been any sort of mix-up at the top of the tower. D. J. Agnew hadn't been killed by mistake, by some failure to communicate. It had been a hit from the very beginning. Harris was fully aware of that, even if others had yet to realize it.

With his mind beginning to clear somewhat due to the adrenalin pumping heavily, Harris suddenly knew exactly what he was going to do. He had a lot of IOUs out. You often needed them in this business, so you cultivated and then used them with great care.

Harris picked up his coat off the floor and made a slightly wobbly beeline for his car. The cool night air revived him to some extent, though he still wished he had one of his underlings to drive him. If it had been a more routine mission, he wouldn't have hesitated to drag Doug out, even at that late hour, but this was different.

Forty-five minutes later he pulled to a stop in an unpaved parking lot ouside a bar on the southwest side of Ft. Worth. He pushed through the battered door and looked around, giving his eyes a few moments to adjust to the smoke and the dim light. It took him only a few moments to find what he wanted.

He walked across the room, avoiding a couple of ragged old pool tables with torn beer stained felt and passing by a bathroom that reeked of urine and vomit even with the door closed. Harris took a seat at the far end of the bar. The man beside him drinking beer from a longneck bottle was thin as a knife, his face pockmarked with old acne scars. A dirty bandage over one side of his neck was evidence of a recent disagreement; most likely over drugs or a whore.

The beer drinker signaled the bartender with a slight nod of his head. "Give him a scotch; double."

Harris watched the bartender pick up a glass with disinterest, add two shots of scotch, and then plop it down before him. Scotch, neat, one might call it in an expensive north Dallas nightspot. Not here, though. This wasn't some sort of high class social bar where anybody cared about appearances; it was a place for drinking and whoring and fighting. It was scotch in a dirty glass without any ice.

Harris turned it up and took a quick gulp.

"They got you this time," his companion observed.

"Yeah."

The other man continued to hold his beer up to his mouth at an angle so that every few seconds he had but to turn it up a little more to take another drink.

"Who did D. J. Agnew?" Harris asked.

"Who do you think? Who was he about to testify against?"

"I know all that. I want to know who did it; who was actually up in the tower running things."

Harris's companion turned the longneck up and drained the last few drops, signaling the bartender as he laid it back down on the bar. "You know, that's kinda funny. There's no talk at all about who it was. It wasn't anybody who makes a habit of pulling that kind of thing, or it would have been around by now. All those sort of people are known by somebody."

"I know it wasn't any full time professional hit man. Nobody who knew what he was doing would ever have gone to such lengths. A pro would simply have blown up the entire court house first. This wasn't a regular gun for hire. Whoever it was, he was after the ransom money too. Killing Agnew was just a part of it."

The man with the scarred face turned up a new lukewarm beer and downed a third of it. He lowered it slightly, still holding it to his mouth, and shrugged. "If it was somebody who isn't known, a one timer, you probably won't ever hear anything about him. Nobody will."

"So that's it?"

"You know those two guys they found at the bank yesterday?"

"Yeah. What's that got to do with this?"

"You know who they were—who they worked for?"

"Yeah, for Louis Parker. The same guy D. J. Agnew was going to testify against."

"That's right."

"So?"

"So word is that they weren't on the clock when they got whacked."

"Meaning?"

"They were on their own. They were freelancing. Now what could they have known that would have gotten them killed at that bank? The way I figure it, that's where the ransom is; or at least it's where they thought it was. And that means that the guy you're looking for is a local; and he's still around."

Harris had finished the scotch. He slid back off his stool and stood unsteadily.

"One other thing," the scar faced man said.

"What?"

"That chopper pilot that give 'em the diversion that let 'em get away?"

"Yeah, Fred Griffin."

"You know who he worked for?"

"Some oil company."

"You know who owns the oil company?"

"No, who?"

"Louis Parker."

Even through the haze and the headache, Harris suddenly realized that this information opened up quite a few fascinating possibilities. And while most weren't exactly legal or according to procedure, at this point, he didn't care.

"We square?" asked the man, actually more of a statement than a question.

"Yeah."

Chapter Nineteen

Harris was sitting in a soundproof interrogation room first thing the next morning when Doug escorted Fred Griffin, the helicopter pilot, into the room.

"I don't understand all this. I gave you my statement and told you everything I knew before," Griffin said.

"Guess what we found at a certain bank this morning?" Harris was shooting blind, but he figured that the odds were heavily in his favor. Griffin looked at him uncomfortably without saying anything.

Harris waited a suitable length of time, letting Griffin get even more uncomfortable before he continued. "A new bank account in your name with a substantial sum of money which was recently deposited."

Harris could tell from what he saw in Griffin's eyes that he had hit pay dirt. And Harris now knew exactly what he was going to do—every step of the way. From now on, he was no longer just a participant; he was in charge once again, and everyone else involved would have to react to his moves.

"Ah, well, that's just a coincidence," Griffin stammered weakly.

"The company you fly for is owned by Louis Parker, is that right?"

"Yeah, so?"

"So why didn't you mention that before?"

"It didn't have anything to do with what happened."

"Who paid you the money? Frank or Louis Parker?"

Griffin began to squirm slightly in his seat. "I can't say anything more about any of this without a lawyer."

Doug jumped in with a question. "A lawyer? I thought you said you were an innocent bystander just forced into this by a death threat on your family. Are you changing your story now?"

"Look, all I'll say is that Mr. Parker had no part in any of this."

"You ever been raped?" Harris asked suddenly.

Griffin looked frightened and shocked at this unexpected question. Harris continued without waiting for a reply. "You're a nice looking guy. That's what's going to happen when you get to prison. And you're going to be there for a long time."

"Hey, now wait just a minute here."

Harris started in again with that soothing, diplomatic voice. "Now Fred, we're not really interested in you. We want the people who pulled this thing off— the ones who are really responsible for the killings. We don't want you to be the fall guy for them. Come on, tell us what really happened."

Griffin needed no further encouragement. "Yeah, okay. It was like you said. I did get paid for it. But I had to or else, like I told you. That was all true. But I was just supposed to create a diversion. I didn't know anything about any killings."

"How did you get the money?"

"That Frank guy left half of it at a park and I was supposed to get the rest afterwards, but I've never heard anything else from him. I never even saw him. It was all done over the phone."

"That figures," Harris grumbled.

Griffin cleared his throat nervously. "Look, since

I'm going along with you, can I make a deal of some sort? You said that you were after the people who really did this. I've told you all I know."

Harris shook his head. "No, you haven't told us how Parker figures into this thing. Frank was working for him, right?"

"No, no I told you. Mr. Parker didn't know a thing about any of this."

Harris stood and began pacing back and forth with his hands clasped behind his back as if in deep thought. After several moments he began to speak again. "Fred, do you know what your boss does?"

"What do you mean?"

"Where does his money come from?"

"I don't know. He never tells me anything and I don't ask. It's none of my business."

"Oh come on. Surely you must have heard some rumors; put two and two together; did a little guessing?"

Griffin shrugged. "No, not really."

Harris stopped pacing and fixed Griffin with a stern look. "Do I need to bring a polygraph machine in here?"

Head down, Griffin mumbled. "No."

"You'd have to agree then that your boss probably deserves to be in prison for any number of things, but he's never been caught. He has high priced lawyers and covers himself very well. And while you don't think he was involved in this, you don't know for sure that he wasn't."

Griffin declined comment, so Harris continued. "I'm going to make you a deal. You'll testify in court that Parker was behind the takeover. That's why you created the diversion. Not for any monetary payment, but because it was your boss's order. You do that, and you can keep the money you already got from Frank. In addition, we'll grant you immunity under our witness protection program and give you a completely new identity and a new start far away from Louis Parker."

Griffin's eyes widened, as did Doug's. "I can't do that. It would never work, and they'd find me no matter where I went."

"It will work," Harris replied crisply. "All it would take is a little circumstantial evidence to convict Parker. We've got two things going for us. First, the entire country is up in arms over this thing. It's turned into a political football, and a jury would be dying to put somebody away. Secondly, with Parker's reputation—which the prosecution would manage to enlarge—the jury would figure that he deserved to be in prison anyway, so why not for this? As for your being found, our relocation program has a perfect record. You'll get a new identity with everything documented and enough money for a new start. Say $50,000?"

"What if I don't?" Griffin asked cautiously, almost afraid to hear the answer.

"Then you'll be the one who takes full blame for the hijacking since the jury won't be able to get its hands on anybody else. Also, we'll spread the word that you're trying to implicate your boss to save your own hide. And to make it look good, we'll even haul him in for questioning a couple of times. You might not live long enough to get raped after all."

"You've got to let me talk to a lawyer before you can do anything like that," Griffin whined.

"Sure, you can talk to your lawyer," Harris replied. "But once you do the deal's off. You deal with me here and now, or we don't deal at all."

Doug had held back as long as he could. "What in the world are you trying to do? You're talking about framing somebody."

Harris looked at him with disgust. "Don't stand there like some holier than thou idiot and tell me that Louis Parker is an innocent victim."

Doug jumped to his feet. "Sure, he probably deserves to be in prison for other things, but not for this. What you're trying to pull is completely illegal, and I won't have anything to do with it."

"There's only one way to end this thing, and I'm going to do it," Harris snarled. "If you haven't got the stomach for it, then get out. But if you ever so much as breathe a word of this, I'll deny it, and so will he. You won't be able to prove a thing."

Doug whirled around and stormed out the door, slamming it behind him. Harris allowed himself a slight tug at the corners of his mouth, giving just a hint of the smile he was holding back. He had expected and even planned to extort such a reaction from Doug. And the reaction had indeed been real; it wasn't any sort of act on Doug's part

Harris knew that he could trust his aide completely. One of Harris's strengths was that he had a second sense of when and how far to trust someone. And in Doug's case, Harris knew that he could trust him to do exactly what he would now do.

Griffin gave Harris a look of concern. "Will he screw up the deal?" Now that he felt that the offer might be taken away, Griffin suddenly wanted it desperately.

"No, no way."

Griffin shook his head with a pained expression. "I just wish there were another way out of this. Mr. Parker's always been good to me. I don't want to do this to him."

"You want to spend the rest of your life in prison? With Parker thinking that you tried to sell him out anyway?"

Griffin hung his head. "What do I do?"

"Just tell the story like it happened, except you're now to say that Parker was giving all the orders."

"But how do I keep away from Mr. Parker? You know he'll send people after me."

"I'll turn you over to our witness protection unit. You're lucky in that it won't be months before the

case comes to trial. This thing is so hot it'll go right
to the top of the list. You'll be through with everything and out of here for good within six weeks."

"Okay," Griffin sighed.

The deal concluded, Harris personally deposited
his valuable commodity in one of the FBI's safe
houses. From there Griffin would be shuttled around
until the trial, so that even Harris wouldn't be able to
find him again. Any more communications would
have to go through an intermediary.

Doug took a deep breath before speaking into the
phone. He had never called that number from his
own home, but he was even more nervous about
someone seeing him in a phone booth. "Harris is
setting up a frame."

"What kinda frame?" the other voice asked.

"He's got Fred Griffin cowed into testifying that
you were behind the takeover. He's probably already
in the witness protection program. And you know
how hard it was to get to D. J. Agnew once he got
that far."

"So take care of it."

"What can I do?"

"Go over his head. Go right up the ladder and
spill your guts about the frame. This couldn't have
worked out any better. He's sure stepped on it this
time."

"Okay, I'll see what I can do."

The voice was now sharp and pointedly threatening. "No, don't just see what you can do. Do it!"

Doug hung up the phone and consulted a pocket
phone list, then dialed another number. He had to
wait while a secretary put him through.

"Inspector Broughton, this is Special Agent Doug
Rogers. I'm one of Inspector Harris's assistants."

"Yes, Doug, what can I do for you?"

"I apologize for bothering you at home on a Sun-
day afternoon, but it's very important."

"Don't worry about that. I'm glad you called. I had expected to hear from Inspector Harris by now about the money we sent for the planned pick-up. Do you know anything about that?"

"Yes sir, I do. I was there, and it didn't go well at all. The extortionist figured out that we were onto him and set off a fire bomb that burned up the money."

The voice on the line was shocked. "Burned it up? All of it?"

"Yes, sir."

The voice was stern now. "Where is Harris? Why hasn't he called me?"

"Well, that's what I'm calling you about. Inspector Harris found out that the helicopter pilot who created the diversion at the tower was paid for it. He originally said that he was forced into it."

"Well, that sounds like a promising lead."

"That's the good part. I called to tell you about the bad part."

"He got away?"

"I wish he had. The pilot works for Louis Parker, an alleged mob figure."

"Yeah, I know the name."

"Harris has bulldozed the pilot into framing Parker for the takeover. Harris said that if the pilot didn't go along with him, not only would he end up in prison, but Harris would put out the word that the pilot had tried to implicate his boss to save his own skin. The guy knows that he's as good as dead if Harris does that, so his only way out is to go along with the frame."

"You heard this?"

"I was right there in the room with them. When I finally spoke up and told Harris that he couldn't do it, he told me to get out. He said that if I told anyone, he would deny the whole story."

"Did anyone else hear this?"

"No sir, it was just the three of us there."

"Doug, you did exactly as you should have, letting me know. Where are you now?"

"I'm at home."

"Give me your number."

Doug read off the number and assured Broughton that he would await his return call, however long it might take.

"Oh, and don't mention this to anyone else," Broughton cautioned. "You haven't yet, have you?"

"No, sir, you're the only one."

"Good. Just wait to hear from me."

Doug hung up the phone with a sigh of relief. He hadn't known what kind of reaction he would get. Fortunately, though, Broughton had seemed very receptive and genuinely concerned over the revelations.

At nine o'clock sharp the next morning, Harris presented himself along with half a dozen agents at Louis Parker's front door. Doug was noticeably absent from the group. The door was answered by a man who seemed to be a combination butler and guard.

"Inspector Harris, FBI," he stated with a flash of his badge. "I'm here to see Louis Parker."

"He ain't here."

"Yes he is. Now you can go get him, or we will."

"Stay put, I'll tell him you're here," the man replied grudgingly.

"What's going on here?"

Harris found himself confronted by an agitated Louis Parker. "I'm Inspector Harris. I have a warrant for your arrest on charges of murder and extortion. You're being charged with plotting the takeover of Millard Tower."

"You've gotta be outa your stupid tree. Clear out, the bunch of you."

"You'll have to come along with us now," Harris said firmly.

"Listen, jerk, I ain't going anywhere until I call my

lawyer. He'll have me out before you idiots even get me downtown."

Harris calmly shook his head. "No, there's no time for that now. You may call from our office if you like, but we have to go now." Harris nodded. Two of the agents stepped forward and handcuffed Parker's hands behind his back. The butler looked as if he were considering a move to stop them, but two more agents moved forward and changed his mind.

Forty-five minutes later Louis Parker was unceremoniously deposited in the same room that had held his pilot. Harris seated himself with a tape recorder and two agents for witnesses.

"Would you like to tell us about it?" Harris inquired.

"About what?"

"The takeover."

"You're crazy, you know that?"

"How about Frank? Want to tell us who Frank is? Or where he is?"

"I know a lot of Franks. I don't know which one you're talking about. What makes you think that I've got anything to do with this, anyway?"

"The chopper pilot who helped create the diversion flies for one of your companies."

"So what? I didn't have anything to do with him. Whatever he did he did on his own."

"Really? Well you might be surprised to hear that your pilot's going to testify that you and your friend Frank set up the whole thing."

"Fred said that?"

"That's right."

"Where is he? I want to hear him say it to my face."

Harris shook his head in his practiced, maddeningly calm manner. "We've got him under wraps. You'll hear what he has to say at the trial, and then you'll never see him again. He'll have a new identity and a new start somewhere far away from you."

"You're wasting your time. This ain't gonna stick. Just wait 'till my lawyer gets down here."

"Oh it's going to stick. I spoke to the D.A. this morning, and he can't wait. He comes up for reelection in six months, and you're personally going to put him right back into office."

Parker began to look a little uncomfortable for the first time. "Get them out and turn off the machine," he demanded. "I want to talk."

Harris nodded to the two agents and switched off the recorder. Parker waited until the two had left and closed the door before he leaned across the table and spoke. "Listen, you got enough sense to know that this ain't my style. I don't need to go around pulling stuff like this. This is a frame from the word go."

Harris merely smiled. Parker continued. "So what if maybe I did call the hit on Agnew? He was scum, trash. He got what he deserved, and you don't think any different. But I didn't have anything to do with this takeover stuff. This clown, he pulled that on his own."

"That doesn't matter. Everybody's out for a warm body on this one. They want someone to hang for it, and you're the best thing they've got. Hey, what can I tell you? You fit the ticket, and nobody cares if you really did it or not, because you probably deserve what you're going to get, just like Agnew did."

"You asked me about this Frank. Well I know who you're talking about, and he did pull this thing off. You let me out of the frame-up, and I give you the real guy who did it all."

"Will you go to court and testify that you hired him to hit Agnew?"

"Of course not. Are you nuts?"

"Then just giving me Frank's name and address does me no good. Nobody in the tower saw his face; there aren't any fingerprints. I can't touch him without your testimony."

Parker was beginning to look quite worried. "Listen, I'm willing to tell you who this guy is, and you ain't gonna believe it. You're gonna fall right off your chair. In fact, I bet that you give me a lie detector test just because you won't be able to believe it. So, do we deal?"

Harris was indeed curious as to who it was, but he wasn't setting this entire thing up just to satisfy his curiosity. He was after far more than just that. He smiled pleasantly at Parker. "Now why in the world would I want to trade a big fish for a little one, when I can't even fry the little one?"

"Because I didn't do it," Parker replied urgently.

Harris leaned across the table and whispered. "I know it, and Frank knows it, but nobody else knows it."

Chapter Twenty

Doug had waited by the phone until well after midnight before giving up and going to bed. He had then spent the entire morning in the same spot, so when the phone finally rang, he was almost too nervous to answer it.

"Hello?"

"Good morning, Doug, this is Inspector Broughton."

"Yes, Inspector, good morning."

"I'm sorry it took so long to get back to you."

"Oh, that's quite all right."

"Doug, I want you to forget everything you told me last night. What you heard with Harris never happened, and you never talked with me about it. Do you understand?"

Doug sat stunned. "No, no, sir. I don't understand. What did Harris tell you? Did he cover everything up?"

"I haven't talked to Harris about the matter, and I'm not going to. When he calls me to tell me about arresting Louis Parker, I'll pretend that I never talked with you. That's a favor to you. I would advise you now to mend your bridges."

Flabbergasted and not knowing quite what to say, Doug blurted out his immediate reaction. "Sir, I'm sorry, but I just can't go along with this thing. I mean no disrespect, but if you can't, or won't, do anything about this situation, then I'll just be forced to go over your head."

Broughton's voice was understanding and reassuring. "Doug, stop and think for a moment. I didn't make this decision. It came from over my head. I'll deny it if you repeat what I'm saying now, but the Attorney General personally told me to leave things be. You have to understand what a liability this case has become for the entire Justice Department. We've been offered a clean, quick, and ironically fair solution to the problem, and we're not about to turn it down. So my final advice to you is to leave it be."

Harris looked up to find Buzz standing in the door of his office. "Inspector, Mr. Parker's attorney is here, and he's so mad he can't see straight."

Harris leaned back in his chair and smiled. "Good, send him on back."

Within a few moments Harris could hear what sounded like a one-sided shouting match coming down the hall. A large man who looked like a crooked used car salesman entered the office. A pencil thin moustache accompanied a baggy, three piece suit. "Where is my client?" he shouted indignantly. "I demand that you release him immediately."

"Part of him is right here in my drawer," Harris replied calmly.

"What the devil are you talking about?"

"His balls; I have his balls right here. Now, shyster, we can sit down and talk about this thing in a civilized manner, or I can kick your tail back out the door. You've disrupted this office all that you're going to. Nobody is impressed with your little show."

The attorney was speechless. He had never been spoken to like that before. Normally, his shouting and legal threats left people off guard if not downright intimidated.

"I don't like your tone of voice—" he began, but Harris cut him off.

"Shut up and sit down or get out!"

Trying to make the best of a bad situation, the lawyer sat down and shut up. Well pleased with his own performance, Harris continued. "Here it is quick and dirty. We're charging Parker with conspiracy and accessory to murder. If that isn't enough, then we'll throw in a couple of other things later."

The attorney was subdued but still glowered. "I want to see my client."

"Buzz, show the shyster here to his boy."

The attorney paused at the door for a final retort. "I'll have him out of here so fast your head will spin."

Harris smiled that irritating smile once again. "And the D.A.'ll have him back in court so fast that your head will spin."

The lawyer greeted Parker warmly as he entered the detention room, but Parker was in no mood for greetings and small talk. "When am I getting out of here?"

"Settle down now," the attorney urged with a wave of his hand. "I've already arranged for bail and—"

Parker exploded. "Bail! I don't pay you to arrange bail. I pay you to take care of things so that I don't get bothered. What do I need bail for? You don't mean to tell me that this penny ante frame is gonna stick, do you?"

The attorney held up his hand again. "Settle down, settle down. First things first here. It's not like usual. This is politics. The D.A. is personally trying this one. This is his reelection. When's the last time you think that the D.A. showed up in person for a bail hearing?"

"He was there?"

The attorney nodded. "And he asked for the moon."

"And?"

"And what? The judge gave it to him. Five million."

"Five million! You gotta be kidding."

"Do I look like I'm kidding? Actually, that's what I said to the judge, and I thought for a while that you were going to have to bail me out."

"What happens once I'm out?"

The attorney sighed. "It doesn't look good. I haven't read your pilot's statement yet, but the D.A. seems to think that it's in the bag."

"So what do we do? Stall 'em as long as we can?"

"That would be our best route if this were a normal situation, but it's not. There won't be any stalling at all on this one. It'll be shoved right through with no delays. Everybody wants it over with as soon as possible. Like I told you, this is politics."

"What if something happened to the pilot before the trial?"

"Well, it would have to happen before Thursday. Once his testimony is on record before the grand jury, it probably won't matter if something happens to him before the trial or not."

Parker scratched his head. "Can't you demand to see the witness before the grand jury hears him? Aren't we entitled to see all the evidence?"

The lawyer shook his head. "All we get is a copy of his statement. We can't actually talk to him. I already tried that, and it didn't get off the ground."

Parker jumped to his feet. "Come on, let's get outa here. I got some ideas of my own about how to handle this setup."

Harris spent the rest of the day wallowing in the congratulations that flooded in. When he called Broughton to report his success and the unfortunate loss of the money, he received only praise. Broughton wasn't in the least concerned about the money. "It's a cheap price to pay," he remarked.

Harris held off, however, on letting any word of the

situation leak to the press. It was just about time t
head home for the day when Harris received the ca
he expected. This one came from an agent with th
witness protection unit.

"Yes, Dave, what can I do for you?"

"It's about this urgent meeting that you requeste
with your witness."

"What urgent meeting? I didn't request any meet
ing."

"That's what I was afraid of. We got a call fror
someone using your name, saying that it was urgen
that he meet with the witness as soon as possible.
thought I better check it out with you personally."

"Do you think Griffin's in any danger?"

"No, not at all. They may know how to get
message to us, but they still don't know where Grif
fin is."

"Good, just hang onto him. I don't think we'
need him much longer."

The timing was right. Louis Parker was now totall
convinced that Harris was willing and, most impor
tantly, able to set up a frame which would put hir
into prison. Harris dialed Louis Parker's home num
ber. Parker was on the line quickly after Harris iden
tified himself.

"What are you doing calling here?"

"Just wanted to let you know, we'll be releasin
Fred Griffin. He won't testify against you. Frank
though, has contacted us about testifying. He's wil
ing to blame it all on you for immunity for himsel
He says that you set up the whole deal."

Harris hung up the phone. Frank whoever-he-wa
was dead. But that wasn't enough. Harris wante
one thing more. He wanted Frank to know tha
Harris had beaten him.

Harris dialed another number. "Good evening, Da
las Morning Herald," answered the operator.

"Yeah, give me the city desk."

"Just a moment, sir. I'll connect you."

It rang for a long time before anybody got around to answering it. "City Desk."

"Is Jim Bone in?"

"No, he's already gone for the evening."

"Thanks." Harris hung up, then tried another number.

"Hello."

"Is this Bone?"

"Yes it is."

"Robert Harris. I've got something for you on Millard Tower. Will it make the morning edition?"

"You bet. What have you got?"

It didn't take long; maybe a minute at the most.

Frank stretched and yawned lazily. When he opened his eyes, he wasn't quite sure what he was looking at. He moved his head back a few inches so he could focus a little better on the thing in front of his face. Then he remembered. It was an ass; a $400 ass. Correction: It was a derriere. Fifty dollars gets you an ass; $400 gets you a derriere.

She stirred slightly as Frank rolled quickly out of bed and pulled on a robe. He took only enough time to hit the brew switch on the coffee pot before heading directly for the front door. The stock market was much more befitting someone of his stature now, and it was just as effective as the race track when it came to fulfilling his gambling impulses. He had missed the closing prices the afternoon before, and he was eager to find out how the latest tip from his broker had turned out. The new guy he was using was really a hustler, a go-getter. He could tell already that they were going to make a good team.

He picked up the paper lying just outside the door and stepped back inside, impatiently flipping to the business section. He moved back into the kitchen and sat down at the table, scanning rapidly down the page. AMR, the holding company for Dallas based American Airlines was in the first column. The broker had received a tip that American was about to announce a huge new aircraft purchase, the largest in commercial aviation history, and the stock would be rising on speculation if nothing else. He was right It was up a full point and a half just since mid morning the day before.

Frank quickly doubled the amount and added a few zeroes. That was $3,000 profit in a single day, and he was only dabbling compared to what he eventually would be able to do. He would have to start out slowly and build up, though. He couldn't just invest over a million dollars all at once or, sooner or later, he'd be faced with some pointed questions from the IRS.

He was aware of her bare feet on the carpet behind him just a moment before soft creamy breasts slid into place on each side of his head. He tossed the paper back onto the table as he turned his attention to the one on his left. That was the one with the two small beauty marks just beneath it. His investment planning could wait just a little while longer; certainly until the market opened anyway.

His heart suddenly pounding in his chest, his stomach in a hard sickened knot, Frank jerked back around, the large headline on the front page at last having caught his eye. MILLARD TOWER TAKEOVER: COVER FOR MOB HIT

Frank's breath caught in his throat, coming in erratic gasps as he scanned the front page article. The gist of it was exactly what the headline indicated. The article said that the FBI had been informed by reliable sources that the Millard Tower takeover had been just a cover for the mob ordered hit of D. J. Agnew who was scheduled to testify in an upcoming drug case. It went on to say that the FBI had planned to conceal the information to make it look as if Agnew's death had been only a freak mistake, not a successfully ordered killing. That would prevent the public from realizing that the witness protection unit had blown things as badly as they had.

Frank slowly lowered the paper. He didn't notice when it slid from his hand to the floor. He was back to square one. They couldn't possibly leave him around to talk now. Not after he had been tied directly to them. They wouldn't take any chance on being linked to the takeover. The pressure from the killing of a two-bit criminal like D. J. Agnew would have been nothing compared to what they would feel from all the public attention and outcry over the takeover. He was right back where he had started, but at least this time he had the money to run on and to get the sort of start he would need—if only it weren't too late already.

Harris couldn't have been more pleased with the front page article. He had just thrown in the part about a cover-up as an enticement. All the media needed was the slightest hint of a cover-up, no matter what it concerned or how little evidence there really was, and they'd be all over it like flies. If he hadn't thrown it in, the story probably would have been buried somewhere back on page twenty-three and no one would have bothered to pay much if any attention to it. But now all the rest of the media, print as well as television, would be jumping on the bandwagon, trying to dig up all the dirt they could.

Now that the story was assured of plenty of publicity and attention, the finger pointing would be spread around more equally. For the most part, they would leave him alone now. He'd still be sitting in hearings until he had sores on his butt, but he had enough points saved up to come out of it all right. That part didn't bother him. With the attention removed from him personally, the political need for him to serve as a dumping ground would quickly fade away.

Harris retrieved a glass from the coffee table, added two ice cubes, and filled it with scotch. He knew he was unlikely ever to have any sort of concrete proof

that he had hit what he was after, but then that
didn't really matter. He downed half the drink as a
sort of mute celebration, then poured the rest in the
sink. The contents of the bottle followed that, along
with the half case on top of the refrigerator. He
didn't need it anymore. He knew damn well he had
hit what he was after.

Chapter Twenty-One

Two white garbed orderlies stepped from the elevator onto the third floor of the state hospital for the mentally impaired. "Boy, this place gives me the shakes," said the first.

"That's normal. Everybody feels that way their first few days up here. You'll get over it after a couple of weeks, and then it won't bother you a bit."

"I hope so. Maybe it wouldn't seem so creepy if we weren't up here in the middle of the night."

"Well really, the midnight shift isn't so bad once you get used to it. There's not a whole lot to do except keep an eye on things, so you can catch a nap about anytime you want, or you can just sit around and read. On the midnight shift, it's not the patients you have to worry about."

"What do you mean by that?"

"It's Mrs. Hawkins."

"You mean the fat nurse down on the first floor?"

"That's right. I swear, that woman must lift weights in her spare time. You wouldn't believe how strong her legs are. The last time she got hold of me back in the linen room, she wrapped her legs around me so tight that I think I ended up with internal injuries. I was sore for a whole week."

He pushed open the door to room 315 and flipped

on the overhead light. "Come on, I'll introduce you to the guys."

"Doesn't the light bother them?"

"Nah, not these guys. They can't tell the difference."

The man in the first bed had a massive scar along with a large depression in the left side of his head. "What in the world happened to him?"

"He tried to blow his brains out, but he didn't do a very good job of it. He blew his brains out okay, but he didn't kill himself. You remember that big take-over they had back a few years ago at Millard Tower?"

"No, I guess that must have been before I moved here."

"Well, several guys took a bunch of people hostage up at the top of the tower. They ended up getting $3 million and then got clean away. This guy was an executive with the hotel chain that owned the tower and had to cough up all the money. He went nuts right after the takeover. Ended up shooting another VIP up there and then tried to kill himself."

"And he's just been lying here ever since?"

"That's right. Hasn't moved a muscle since he pulled the trigger."

"That's horrible."

"Not to him it's not; he doesn't know the differ-ence. If you want to see something horrible, take a look at this guy over here."

The man in the next bed, sleeping peacefully, seemed to be perfectly normal. "What's wrong with him?"

"Somebody fixed him up real good. They broke his neck, so he's completely paralyzed from the neck down, and gouged out his ears and both eyes with an ice pick. Then they tore out his tongue. He was an assistant district attorney, so everybody figures that it must have been somebody who he had prosecuted at some time. Can you imagine what it must be like to lie there, never able to tell anybody when you hurt or when you're hungry or thirsty? Just lying there in a black void praying that you could die?"

"Do you think he even knows that we're here?"

"There's no telling. They say that he probably went crazy after a while, but then, how could you tell?"